PHILIP K. DICK
NOW WAIT FOR LAST YEAR

Philip K. Dick was born in Chicago in 1928 and lived most of his life in California. He briefly attended the University of California, but dropped out before completing any classes. In 1952, he began writing professionally and proceeded to write thirty-six novels and five short-story collections. He won the Hugo Award for best novel in 1962 for *The Man in the High Castle* and the John W. Campbell Memorial Award for best novel of the year in 1974 for *Flow My Tears, the Policeman Said*. Philip K. Dick died on March 2, 1982, in Santa Ana, California, of heart failure following a stroke.

Also by Philip K. Dick
Available from Vintage Books

Confessions of a Crap Artist
The Divine Invasion
Flow My Tears, the Policeman Said
The Game-Players of Titan
The Man in the High Castle
A Scanner Darkly
The Three Stigmata of Palmer Eldritch
The Transmigration of Timothy Archer
Ubik
The World Jones Made
VALIS

NOW WAIT FOR LAST YEAR

PHILIP K. DICK

NOW WAIT FOR LAST YEAR

VINTAGE BOOKS

A Division of Random House, Inc.

New York

First Vintage Books Edition, July 1993

Library of Congress Cataloging-in-Publication Data
Dick, Philip K.
Now wait for last year / Philip K. Dick.—1st Vintage Books ed.
p.   cm.
ISBN 0-679-74220-4
I. Title.
PS3554.I3N6   1993
813'.54—dc20   92-50645
CIP

Manufactured in the United States of America
10   9   8   7   6

To Don Wollheim—
Who has done more for science fiction
than any other single person.
Thank you, Don, for your faith in us over the years.
And God bless you.

NOW WAIT FOR LAST YEAR

1

The apteryx-shaped building, so familiar to him, gave off its usual smoky gray light as Eric Sweetscent collapsed his wheel and managed to park in the tiny stall allocated him. Eight o'clock in the morning, he thought drearily. And already his employer, Mr. Virgil L. Ackerman, had opened TF&D Corporation's offices for business. Imagine a man whose mind is most sharp at eight a.m., Dr. Sweetscent mused. It runs against God's clear command. A fine world they're doling out to us; the war excuses any human aberration, even the old man's.

Nonetheless he started toward the in-track—only to be halted by the calling of his name. "Say, Mr. Sweetscent! Just a moment, sir!" The twangy—and highly repellent—voice of a robant; Eric stopped reluctantly, and now the thing coasted up to him, all arms and legs flapping energetically. "Mr. Sweetscent of Tijuana Fur & Dye Corporation?"

The slight got across to him. "Dr. Sweetscent. Please."

"I have a bill, doctor." It whipped a folded white slip from its metal pouch. "Your wife, Mrs. Katherine Sweetscent, charged this three months ago on her Dreamland Happy Times For All account. Sixty-five dollars plus sixteen per cent charges. And the law, now; you understand. I regret delaying you, but it is, ahem, illegal." It eyed him alertly as he, with massive reluctance, fished out his checkbook.

"What's the purchase?" he asked gloomily as he wrote the check.

"It was a Lucky Strike package, doctor. With the authentic ancient green. Circa 1940, before World War Two when the package changed. 'Lucky Strike green has gone to war,' you know." It giggled.

He couldn't believe it; something was wrong. "But surely," he protested, "that was supposed to be put on the company account."

"No, doctor," the robant declared. "Honest injun. Mrs. Sweetscent made it absolutely clear that this purchase was for her private use." It managed to add, then, an explanation which he knew at once to be spurious. But whether it originated in the robant or with Kathy—that he could not tell, at least not immediately. "Mrs. Sweetscent," the robant stated piously, "is building a Pitts-39."

"The hell she is." He tossed the made-out check at the robant; as it strove to catch the fluttering bit of paper he continued on, toward the in-track.

A Lucky Strike package. Well, he reflected grimly, Kathy is off again. The creative urge, which can only find an outlet in spending. And always above and beyond her own salary— which, he had to admit to himself, was a bit greater than his own, alas. But in any case, why hadn't she told him? A major purchase of that sort . . .

The answer, of course, was obvious. The bill itself pointed out the problem in all its depressing sobriety. He thought, Fifteen years ago I would have said—did say—that the combined incomes of Kathy and me would be enough and certainly *ought* to be enough to maintain any two semireasonable adults at any level of opulence. Even taking into account the wartime inflation.

However, it had not quite worked out that way. And he felt a deep, abiding intuition that it just never quite would.

Within the TF&D Building he dialed the hall leading to his own office, squelching the impulse to drop by Kathy's office upstairs for an immediate confrontation. Later, he decided.

After work, perhaps at dinner. Lord, and he had such a full schedule ahead of him; he had no energy—and never had had in the past—for this endless squabbling.

"Morning, doctor."

"Hi," Eric said, nodding to fuzzy Miss Perth, his secretary; this time she had sprayed herself a shiny blue, inlaid with sparkling fragments that reflected the outer office's overhead lighting. "Where's Himmel?" No sign of the final-stage quality-control inspector, and already he perceived reps from subsidiary outfits pulling up at the parking lot.

"Bruce Himmel phoned to say that the San Diego public library is suing him and he may have to go to court and so he'll probably be late." Miss Perth smiled at him engagingly, showing spotless synthetic ebony teeth, a chilling affectation which had migrated with her from Amarillo, Texas, a year ago. "The library cops broke into his conapt yesterday and found over twenty of their books that he'd stolen—you know Bruce, he has that phobia about checking things out . . . how is it put in Greek?"

He passed on into the inner office which was his alone; Virgil Ackerman had insisted on it as a suitable mark of prestige—in lieu of a raise in salary.

And there, in his office, at his window, smoking a sweet-smelling Mexican cigarette and gazing out at the austere brown hills of Baja California south of the city, stood his wife Kathy. This was the first time he had met up with her this morning; she had risen an hour ahead of him, had dressed and eaten alone and gone on in her own wheel.

"What's up?" Eric said to her tightly.

"Come on in and shut the door." Kathy turned but did not look toward him; the expression on her exquisitely sharp face was meditative.

He closed the door. "Thanks for welcoming me into my own office."

"I knew that damn bill collector would intercept you this morning," Kathy said in a faraway voice.

"Almost eighty greens," he said. "With the fines."

"Did you pay it?" Now for the first time she glanced at

him; the flutter of her artificially dark lashes quickened, revealing her concern.

"No," he said sardonically. "I let the robant gun me down where I stood, there in the parking lot." He hung his coat in his closet. "Of course I paid it. It's mandatory, ever since the Mole obliterated the entire class of credit-system purchasing. I realize you're not interested in this, but if you don't pay within—"

"Please," Kathy said. "Don't lecture me. What did it say? That I'm building a Pitts-39? It lied; I got the Lucky Strike green package as a gift. I wouldn't build a babyland without telling you; after all, it would be yours, too."

"Not Pitts-39," Eric said. "I never lived there, in '39 or any other time." He seated himself at his desk and punched the viscombox. "I'm here, Mrs. Sharp," he informed Virgil's secretary. "How are you today, Mrs. Sharp? Get home all right from that war-bond rally last night? No warmongering pickets hit you on the head?" He shut off the box. To Kathy he explained, "Lucile Sharp is an ardent appeaser. I think it's nice for a corporation to permit its employees to engage in political agitation, don't you? And even nicer than that is the fact that it doesn't cost you a cent; political meetings are free."

Kathy said, "But you have to pray and sing. And they do get you to buy those bonds."

"Who was the cigarette package for?"

"Virgil Ackerman, of course." She exhaled cigarette smoke in twin gray trails. "You suppose I want to work elsewhere?"

"Sure, if you could do better."

Kathy said thoughtfully, "It's not the high salary that keeps me here, Eric, despite what you think. I believe we're helping the war effort."

"Here? *How?*"

The office door opened; Miss Perth stood outlined, her luminous, fuzzy, horizontally inclined breasts brushing the frame as she turned toward him and said, "Oh, doctor, sorry to bother you but Mr. Jonas Ackerman is here to see you—Mr. Virgil's great-grandnephew from the Baths."

"How are the Baths, Jonas?" Eric said, holding out his hand; the great-grandnephew of the firm's owner came toward him and they shook in greeting. "Anything bubble out during the night shift?"

"If it did," Jonas said, "it imitated a workman and left by the front gate." He noticed Kathy then. "Morning, Mrs. Sweetscent. Say, I saw that new config you acquired for our Wash-35, that bug-shaped car. What is that, a Volkswagen? Is that what they were called?"

"An air-flow Chrysler," Kathy said. "It was a good car but it had too much unsprung metal in it. An engineering error that ruined it on the market."

"God," Jonas said, with feeling. "To know something really thoroughly; how that must feel. Down with the fliegemer Renaissance—I say specialize in one area until—" He broke off, seeing that both the Sweetscents had a grim, taciturn cast about them. "I interrupted?"

"Company business takes priority," Eric said, "over the creature pleasures." He was glad of the intervention by even this junior member of the organization's convoluted blood hierarchy. "Please scram out of here, Kathy," he said to his wife, and did not trouble himself to make his tone jovial. "We'll talk at dinner. I've got too much to do to spend my time haggling over whether a robant bill collector is mechanically capable of telling lies or not." He escorted his wife to the office door; she moved passively, without resistance. Softly, Eric said, "Like everyone else in the world it's busy deriding you, isn't it? They're all talking." He shut the door after her.

Presently Jonas Ackerman shrugged and said, "Well, that's marriage these days. Legalized hate."

"Why do you say that?"

"Oh, the overtones came through in that exchange; you could feel it in the air like the chill of death. There ought to be an ordinance that a man can't work for the same outfit as his wife; hell, even in the same city." He smiled, his thin, youthful face all at once free of seriousness. "But she really is good, you know; Virgil gradually let go all his other antique collectors after Kathy started here . . . but of course she's mentioned that to you."

"Many times." Almost every day, he reflected caustically.

"Why don't you two get divorced?"

Eric shrugged, a gesture designed to show a deep philosophical nature. He hoped it truly did so.

The gesture evidently fell short, because Jonas said, "Meaning that you like it?"

"I mean," he said resignedly, "that I've married before and it was no better, and if I divorce Kathy I'll marry again— because as my brainbasher puts it I can't find my identity outside the role of husband and daddy and big butter-and-egg-man wage earner—and the next damn one will be the same because that's the kind I select. It's rooted in my temperament." He raised his head and eyed Jonas with as good a show of masochistic defiance as he could manage. "What did you want, Jonas?"

"Trip," Jonas Ackerman said brightly. "To Mars, for all of us, including you. Conference! You and I can nab seats a good long way from old Virgil so we won't have to discuss company business and the war effort and Gino Molinari. And since we're taking the big boat it'll be six hours each way. And for God's sake, let's not find ourselves standing up all the way to Mars and back—let's make sure we do get seats."

"How long will we be there?" He frankly did not look forward to the trip; it would separate him from his work too long.

"We'll undoubtedly be back tomorrow or the day after. Listen; it'll get you out of your wife's path; Kathy's staying here. It's an irony, but I've noticed that when the old fellow's actually at Wash-35 he never likes to have his antique experts around him . . . he likes to slide into the, ahem, magic of the place . . . more so all the time as he gets older. When you're one hundred and thirty you'll begin to understand— so will I, maybe. Meanwhile we have to put up with him."

He added, somberly, "You probably know this, Eric, because you are his doctor. He never will die; he'll never make the hard decision—as it's called—no matter what fails and has to be replaced inside him. Sometimes I envy him for being—optimistic. For liking life that much; for thinking it's so important. Now, we puny mortals; at our age—" He eyed Eric. "At a miserable thirty or thirty-three—"

"I've got plenty of vitality," Eric said. "I'm good for a long time. And life isn't going to get the best of me." From his coat pocket he brought forth the bill which the robant collector had presented to him. "Think back. Did a package of Lucky Strike *with the green* show up at Wash-35 about three months ago? A contribution from Kathy?"

After a long pause Jonas Ackerman said, "You poor suspicious stupid creak. That's all you can manage to brood about. Listen, doctor; if you can't get your mind on your job, you're finished; there're twenty artiforg surgeons with applications in our personnel files just waiting to go to work for a man like Virgil, a man of his importance in the economy and war effort. You're really just plain not all that good." His expression was both compassionate and disapproving, a strange mixture which had the effect of waking Eric Sweetscent abruptly. "Personally, if my heart gave out—which it no doubt will do one of these days—I wouldn't particularly care to go to you. You're too tangled in your own personal affairs. You live for yourself, not the planetary cause. My God, don't you remember? We're fighting a life-and-death war. And we're losing. We're being pulverized every goddam day!"

True, Eric realized. And we've got a sick, hypochondriacal, dispirited leader. And Tijuana Fur & Dye Corporation is one of those vast industrial props that maintain that sick leader, that manage just barely to keep the Mole in office. Without such warm, high-placed, personal friendships as that of Virgil Ackerman, Gino Molinari would be out or dead or in an old folks' rest home. I know it. And yet—individual life must go on. After all, he reflected, I didn't choose to get entangled in my domestic life, my boxer's clinch with

Kathy. And if you think I did or do, it's because you're morbidly young. You've failed to pass from adolescent freedom into the land which I inhabit: married to a woman who is economically, intellectually, and even this, too, even erotically my superior.

Before leaving the building Dr. Eric Sweetscent dropped by the Baths, wondering if Bruce Himmel had shown up. He had; there he stood, beside the huge reject-basket full of defective Lazy Brown Dogs.

"Turn them back into groonk," Jonas said to Himmel, who grinned in his empty, disjointed fashion as the youngest of the Ackermans tossed him one of the defective spheres which rolled off TF&D's assembly lines along with those suitable for wiring into the command guidance structure of interplanetary spacecraft. "You know," he said to Eric, "if you took a dozen of these control syndromes—and not the defective ones but the ones going into shipping cartons for the Army— you'd find that compared with a year ago or even six months ago their reaction time has slowed by several microseconds."

"By that you mean," Eric said, "our quality standards have dropped?"

It seemed impossible. TF&D's product was too vital. The entire network of military operations depended on these head-sized spheres.

"Exactly." It did not appear to bother Jonas. "Because we were rejecting too many units. We couldn't show a profit."

Himmel stammered, "S-sometimes I wish we were back in the Martian bat guano business."

Once the corporation had collected the dung of the Martian flap bat, had made its first returns that way and so had been in position to underwrite the greater economic aspects of another nonterrestrial creature, the Martian print amoeba. This august unicellular organism survived by its ability to mimic other life forms—those of its own size, specifically—and although this ability had amused Terran astronauts and UN officials, no one had seen an industrial usage until Virgil Ackerman of bat guano fame had come upon the scene. Within a matter of hours he had presented a print amoeba with one of his current mistresses's expensive furs; the print amoeba had faithfully mimicked it, whereupon, for all intents and purposes, between Virgil and the girl two mink stoles existed. However, the amoeba had at last grown tired of being a fur and had resumed its own form. This conclusion left something to be desired.

The answer, developed over a period of many months, consisted of killing the amoeba during its interval of mimicry and then subjecting the cadaver to a bath of fixing-chemicals which had the capacity to lock the amoeba in that final form; the amoeba did not decay and hence could not later on be distinguished from the original. It was not long before Virgil Ackerman had set up a receiving plant at Tijuana, Mexico, and was accepting shipments of ersatz furs of every variety from his industrial installations on Mars. And almost at once he had broken the natural fur market on Earth.

The war, however, had changed all that.

But, then, what hadn't the war changed? And who had ever thought, when the Pact of Peace was signed with the ally, Lilistar, that things would go so badly? Because according to Lilistar and its Minister Freneksy, this was the dominant military power in the galaxy; its enemy, the reegs, was inferior militarily and in every other way and the war would undoubtedly be a short one.

War itself was bad enough, Eric ruminated, but there was nothing quite like a losing war to make one stop and think, to try—futilely—to second-guess one's past decisions—such as the Pact of Peace, to name one example, and an example which currently might have occurred to quite a number of Terrans, had they been asked. But these days their opinions were not being solicited by the Mole or by the government of Lilistar itself. In fact it was universally believed—openly noised about at bars as well as in the privacy of living rooms—that even the Mole's opinion was not being asked.

As soon as hostilities with the reegs had begun, Tijuana Fur & Dye had converted from the luxury trade of ersatz fur production to war work, as, of course, had all other industrial enterprises. Supernaturally accurate duplication of rocket-ship master syndromes, the ruling monoad Lazy Brown Dog, was fatalistically natural for the type of operation which TF&D represented; conversion had been painless and rapid. So here now, meditatively, Eric Sweetscent faced this basket of rejects, wondering—as had everyone at one time or another in the corporation—how these substandard and yet still quite complex units could be put to some economic advantage. He picked one up and handled it; in terms of weight it resembled a baseball, in terms of size a grapefruit. Evidently nothing could be done with these failures which Himmel had rejected, and he turned to toss the sphere into the maw of the hopper, which would return the fixed plastic into its original organic cellular form.

"Wait," Himmel croaked.

Eric and Jonas glanced at him.

"Don't melt it down," Himmel said. His unsightly body twisted with embarrassment; his arms wound themselves about, the long, knobby fingers writhing. Idiotically, his mouth gaped as he mumbled, "I—don't do that any more. Anyhow, in terms of raw material that unit's worth only a quarter of a cent. That whole bin's worth only about a dollar."

"So?" Jonas said. "They still have to go back to—"

Himmel mumbled, "I'll buy it." He dug into his trouser pocket, straining to find his wallet; it was a long and arduous struggle but at last he produced it.

"Buy it for what?" Jonas demanded.

"I have a schedule arranged," Himmel said, after an agonized pause. "I pay a half cent apiece for Lazy Brown Dog rejects, twice what they're worth, so the company's making a profit. So why should anyone object?" His voice rose to a squeak.

Pondering him, Jonas said, "No one's objecting. I'm just curious as to what you want it for." He glanced sideways at Eric as if to ask, What do you say about this?

Himmel said, "Um, I use them." With gloom he turned

and shambled toward a nearby door. "But they're all mine because I paid for them in advance out of my salary," he said over his shoulder as he opened the door. Defensively, his face dark with resentment and with the corrosive traces of deeply etched phobic anxiety, he stood aside.

Within the room—a storeroom, evidently—small carts rolled about on silver-dollar-sized wheels; twenty or more of them, astutely avoiding one another in their zealous activity.

On board each cart Eric saw a Lazy Brown Dog, wired in place and controlling the movements of the cart.

Presently Jonas rubbed the side of his nose, grunted, said, "What powers them?" Stooping, he managed to snare a cart as it wheeled by his foot; he lifted it up, its wheels still spinning futilely.

"Just a little cheap ten-year A-battery," Himmel said. "Costs another half cent."

"And *you* built these carts?"

"Yes, Mr. Ackerman." Himmel took the cart from him and set it back on the floor; once more it wheeled industriously off. "These are the ones too new to let go," he explained. "They have to practice."

"And then," Jonas said, "you give them their freedom."

"That's right." Himmel bobbed his large-domed, almost bald head, his horn-rimmed glasses sliding forward on his nose.

"Why?" Eric asked.

Now the crux of the matter had been broached; Himmel turned red, twitched miserably, and yet displayed an obscure, defensive pride. "Because," he blurted, "they deserve it."

Jonas said, "But the protoplasm's not alive; it died when the chemical fixing-spray was applied. You know that. From then on it—all of these—is nothing but an electronic circuit, as dead as—well, as a robant."

With dignity Himmel answered, "But I consider them alive, Mr. Ackerman. And just because they're inferior and incapable of guiding a rocketship in deep space, that doesn't mean they have no right to live out their meager lives. I release them and they wheel around for, I expect, six years or possibly longer; that's enough. That gives them what they're entitled to."

Turning to Eric, Jonas said, "If the old man knew about this—"

"Mr. Virgil Ackerman knows about this," Himmel said at once. "He approves of it." He amended, "Or rather, he lets me do it; he knows I'm reimbursing the company. And I build the carts at night, on my own time; I have an assembly line—naturally very primitive, but effective—in my conapt where I live." He added, "I work till around one o'clock every night."

"What do they do after they're released?" Eric asked. "Just roam the city?"

"God knows," Himmel said. Obviously that part was not his concern; he had done his job by building the carts and wiring the Lazy Brown Dogs in functioning position. And perhaps he was right; he could hardly accompany each cart, defend it against the hazards of the city.

"You're an artist," Eric pointed out, not sure if he was amused or revolted or just what. He was not impressed; that much he was sure of: the entire enterprise had a bizarre, zany quality—it was absurd. Himmel ceaselessly at work both here and at his conapt, seeing to it that the factory rejects got their place in the sun . . . what next? And this, while everyone else sweated out the folly, the greater, collective absurdity, of a bad war.

Against that backdrop Himmel did not look so ludicrous. It was the times. Madness haunted the atmosphere itself, from the Mole on down to this quality control functionary who was clearly disturbed in the clinical, psychiatric sense.

Walking off down the hall with Jonas Ackerman, Eric said, "He's a poog." That was the most powerful term for aberrance in currency.

"Obviously," Jonas said, with a gesture of dismissal. "But this gives me a new insight into old Virgil, the fact that he'd tolerate this and certainly not because it gives him a profit— that's not it. Frankly I'm glad. I thought Virgil was more hard-boiled; I'd have expected him to bounce this poor nurt right out of here, into a slave-labor gang on its way to Lilistar. God, what a fate that would be. Himmel is lucky."

"How do you think it'll end?" Eric asked. "You think the Mole will sign a separate treaty with the reegs and bail us out of this and leave the 'Starmen to fight it alone—which is what they deserve?"

"He can't," Jonas said flatly. "Freneksy's secret police would swoop down on us here on Terra and make mincemeat out of him. Kick him out of office and replace him overnight with someone more militant. Someone who *likes* the job of prosecuting the war."

"But they can't do that," Eric said. "He's our elected leader, not theirs." He knew, however, that despite these legal considerations Jonas was right. Jonas was merely appraising their ally realistically, facing the facts.

"Our best bet," Jonas said, "is simply to lose. Slowly, inevitably, as we're doing." He lowered his voice to a rasping whisper. "I hate to talk defeatist talk—"

"Feel free."

Jonas said, "Eric, it's the only way out, even if we have to look forward to a century of occupation by the reegs as our punishment for picking the wrong ally in the wrong war at the wrong time. Our very virtuous first venture into interplanetary militarism, and *how* we picked it—how the Mole picked it." He grimaced.

"And we picked the Mole," Eric reminded him. So the responsibility, ultimately, came back to them.

Ahead, a slight, leaflike figure, dry and weightless, drifted all at once toward them, calling in a thin, shrill, voice, "Jonas! And you, too, Sweetscent—time to get started for the trip to Wash-35." Virgil Ackerman's tone was faintly peevish, that of a mother bird at her task; in his advanced age Virgil had become almost hermaphroditic, a blend of man and woman into one sexless, juiceless, and yet vital entity.

2

Opening the ancient, empty Camel cigarettes package, Virgil Ackerman said as he flattened its surfaces, "Hits, cracks, taps, or pops. Which do you take, Sweetscent?"

"Taps," Eric said.

The old man peered at the marking stamped on the inside glued bottom fold of the now two-dimensional package. "It's cracks. I get to cork you on the arm—thirty-two times." He ritualistically tapped Eric on the shoulder, smiling gleefully, his natural-style ivory teeth pale and full of animated luster. "Far be it from me to injure you, doctor; after all, I might need a new liver any moment now . . . I had a bad few hours last night after I went to bed and I think—but check me on this—it was due to toxemia once again. I felt loggy."

In the seat beside Virgil Ackerman, Dr. Eric Sweetscent said, "How late were you up and what did you do?"

"Well, doctor, there was this girl." Virgil grinned mischievously at Harvey, Jonas, Ralf and Phyllis Ackerman, those members of the family who sat around him in his thin, tapered interplan ship as it sped from Terra toward Wash-35 on Mars. "Need I say more?"

His great-grandniece, Phyllis, said severely, "Oh Christ, you're too old. Your heart'll give out again right in the middle. And then what'll she—whoever she is—think? It's undignifed to die during you know what." She eyed Virgil reprovingly.

Virgil screeched, "Then the dead man's control in my right fist, carried for such emergencies, would summon Dr. Sweetscent here, and he'd dash in and right there on the spot, without removing me, he'd take out that bad, collapsed old heart and stick in a brand new one, and I'd—" He giggled, then patted away the saliva from his lower lip and chin with a folded linen handkerchief from his breast coat pocket. "I'd continue." His paper-thin flesh glowed and beneath it his bones, the outline of his skull, fine and clearly distinguishable, quivered with delight and the joy of tantalizing them; they had no entree into this world of his, the private life which he, because of his privileged position, enjoyed even now during the days of privation which the war had brought on.

" 'Mille tre,' " Harvey said sourly, quoting Da Ponte's libretto. "But with you, you old craknit, it's—however you say a billion and three in Italian. I hope when I'm your age—"

"You won't ever be my age," Virgil chortled, his eyes dancing and flaming up with the vitality of enjoyment. "Forget it, Harv. Forget it and go back to your fiscal records, you walking, droning-on abacus. They won't find you dead in bed with a woman; they'll find you dead with a—" Virgil searched his mind. "With an, ahem, inkwell."

"Please," Phyllis said drily, turning to look out at the stars and the black sky of 'tween space.

Eric said to Virgil, "I'd like to ask you something. About a pack of Lucky Strike green. About three months ago—"

"Your wife loves me," Virgil said. "Yes, it was for me, doctor; a gift without strings. So ease your feverish mind; Kathy's not interested. Anyhow, it would cause trouble. Women, I can get; artiforg surgeons—well . . ." He reflected. "Yes. When you think about it I can get that, too."

"Just as I told Eric earlier today," Jonas said. He winked at Eric, who stoically did not show any response.

"But I like Eric," Virgil continued. "He's a calm type.

Look at him right now. Sublimely reasonable, always the cerebral type, cool in every crisis; I've watched him work many times, Jonas; I ought to know. And willing to get up at any hour of the night . . . and that sort you don't see much."

"You pay him," Phyllis said shortly. She was, as always, taciturn and withdrawn; Virgil's attractive great-grandniece, who sat on the corporation's board of directors, had a piercing, raptorlike quality—much like the old man's, but without his sly sense of the peculiar. To Phyllis, everything was business or dross. Eric reflected that had she come onto Himmel there would be no more little carts wheeling about; in Phyllis' world there was no room for the harmless. She reminded him a little of Kathy. And, like Kathy, she was reasonably sexy; she wore her hair in one long braided pigtail dyed a fashionable ultramarine, set off by autonomic rotating earrings and (this he did not especially enjoy) a nose ring, sign of nubility with the higher bourgeois circles.

"What's the purpose of this conference?" Eric asked Virgil Ackerman. "Can we start discussing it now to save time?" He felt irritable.

"A pleasure trip," Virgil said. "Chance to get away from the gloomy biz we're in. We have a guest meeting us at Wash-35; he may already be there . . . he's got a Blank Check; I've opened my babyland to him, the first time I've let anybody but myself experience it freely."

"Who?" Harv demanded. "After all, technically Wash-35 is the property of the corporation, and we're on the board."

Jonas said acidly, "Virgil probably lost all his authentic Horrors of War flipcards to this person. So what else could he do but throw open the gates of the place to him?"

"I never flip with my Horrors of War cards or my FBI cards," Virgil said. "And by the way I have a duplicate of the Sinking of the Panay. Eton Hambro—you know, the fathead who's board chairman of Manfrex Enterprises—gave it to me on my birthday. I thought everyone knew I had a complete file but evidently not Hambro. No wonder Freneksy's boys are running his six factories for him these days."

"Tell us about Shirley Temple in *The Littlest Rebel,*" Phyllis said in a bored tone, still looking out at the panorama of stars beyond the ship. "Tell us how she—"

"You've seen that." Virgil sounded testy.

"Yes, but I never get tired of it," Phyllis said. "No matter how hard I try I still can't find it anything but engrossing, right down to the last miserable inch of film." She turned to Harv. "Your lighter."

Rising from his seat, Eric walked to the lounge of the small ship, seated himself at the table, and picked up the drink list. His throat felt dry; the bickering that went on within the Ackerman clan always made him dully thirsty, as if he were in need of some reassuring fluid . . . perhaps, he thought, a substitute for the primordial milk: the *Urmilch* of life. I deserve my own babyland, too, he thought half in jest. But only half.

To everyone but Virgil Ackerman, the Washington, D.C., of 1935 was a waste of time, since only Virgil remembered the authentic city, the authentic time and place, the environment now so long passed away. In every detail, therefore, Wash-35 consisted of a painstakingly elaborate reconstruction of the specific limited universe of childhood which Virgil had known, constantly refined and improved in matters of authenticity by his antique procurer—Kathy Sweetscent— without really ever being in a genuine sense changed: it had coagulated, cleaved to the dead past . . . at least as far as the rest of the clan were concerned. But to Virgil it of course sprouted life. There, he blossomed. He restored his flagging biochemical energy and then returned to the present, to the shared, current world which he eminently understood and manipulated but of which he did not psychologically feel himself a native.

And his vast regressive babyland had caught on: become a fad. On lesser scales other top industrialists and money-boys—to speak in a brutal and frank way, war profiteers— had made life-size models of their childhood worlds, too; Virgil's now had ceased to be unique. None, of course, matched Virgil's in complexity and sheer authenticity; fakes of antique items, not the actual surviving articles, had been strewn about in vulgar approximations of what had been the authentic reality. But in all fairness, it had to be realized, Eric reflected, no one possessed the money and economic know-how to underwrite this admittedly uniquely expensive and beyond all others—imitations all—utterly impractical venture. This—in the midst of the dreadful war.

But still it was, after all, harmless, in its quaint sort of way. A bit, he reflected, like Bruce Himmel's peculiar activity with his many clanky little carts. It slaughtered no one. And this could hardly be said for the national effort . . . the jihad against the creatures from Proxima.

On thinking of this, an unpleasant recollection entered his mind.

On Terra at the UN capital city, Cheyenne, Wyoming, in addition to those in POW camps, there existed a herd of captured, defanged reegs, maintained on public exhibition by the Terran military establishment. Citizens could file past and gawk and ponder at length the meaning of these exoskeletoned beings with six extremities in all, capable of progressing linearly at a great rate on either two or four legs. The reegs had no audible vocal apparatus; they communicated beewise by elaborate, dancelike weavings of their sensory stalks. With Terrans and 'Starmen they employed a mechanical translation box, and through this the gawkers had an opportunity to question their humbled captives.

Questions, until recently, had run to a monotonous, baiting uniformity. But now a new interrogation had begun by subtle stages to put in its very ominous appearance—ominous at least from the standpoint of the Establishment. In view of this inquiry the exhibit had abruptly terminated, and for an indefinite time. *How can we come to a rapprochement?* The reegs, oddly, had an answer. It amounted to: live and let live. Expansion by Terrans into the Proxima System would cease; the reegs would not—and actually had not in the past—invest the Sol System.

But as to Lilistar: The reegs had no answer there because they had developed none for themselves; the 'Starmen had

been their enemies for centuries and it was too late for anyone
to give or take any advice on this subject. And anyhow 'Star
"advisers" had already managed to take up residence on
Terra for the performance of security functions . . . as if a
four-armed, antlike organism six feet high could pass un-
noticed on a New York street.

The presence of 'Star advisers, however, easily passed un-
noticed; the 'Starmen were phycomycetous mentally, but
morphologically they could not be distinguished from Terrans. There was a good reason for this. In Mousterian times
a flotilla from Lilistar's Alpha Centaurus Empire had migrated to the Sol System, had colonized Earth and to some
extent Mars. A fracas with deadly overtones had broken out
between settlers of the two worlds and a long, degenerating
war had followed, the upshot of which had been the decline
of both subcultures to acute and dreary barbarism. Due to
climatic faults the Mars colony had at last died out entirely;
the Terran, however, had groped its way up through historical
ages and at last back to civilization. Cut off from Alpha by
the Lilistar-reeg conflict, the Terran colony had again become
planet-wide, elaborated, bountiful, had advanced to the stage
of launching first an orbiting satellite, and then an unmanned
ship to Luna, and at last a manned ship . . . and was, as a
chef-d'oeuvre, able once more to contact its system of origin.
The surprise, of course, had been vast on both sides.

"Cat got your tongue?" Phyllis Ackerman said to Eric,
seating herself beside him in the cramped lounge. She smiled,
an effort which transfigured her thin, delicately cut face; she
looked, for a moment, appealingly pretty. "Order me a drink,
too. So I can face the world of bolo bats and Jean Harlow
and Baron von Richtofen and Joe Louis and—what the hell
is it?" She searched her memory, eyes squeezed shut. "I've
blocked it out of my mind. Oh yes. Tom Mix. And his Ralston
Straightshooters. With the Wrangler. That wretched Wrangler. And that cereal! And those eternal goddam box tops.
You know what we're in for, don't you? Another session with
Orphan Annie and her li'l decoder badge . . . we'll have to
listen to ads for Ovaltine and then those numbers read out

for us to take down and decode—to find out what Annie does on Monday. God." She bent to reach for her drink, and he could not resist peering with near-professional interest as the top of her dress gave way to show the natural line of her small, articulated pale breasts.

Put by this spectacle in a reasonably good mood, Eric said playfully but cautiously, "One day we'll jot down the numbers the fake announcer gives over the fake radio, decode them with the Orphan Annie decoder badge, and—" The message will say, he thought glumly, *Make a separate peace with the reegs. At once.*

"I know," Phyllis said, and thereupon finished for him. " 'It's hopeless, Earthmen. Give up now. This is the Monarch of the reegs speaking; looky heah, y'all: I've infiltrated radio station WMAL in Washington, D.C., and I'm going to *de*stroy you.' " She somberly drank from her tall stemmed glass. "And in *addition* the Ovaltine you've been drinking—"

"I wasn't going to say precisely that." But she had come awfully darn close. Nettled, Eric said, "Like the rest of your family you've got a gene that requires you to interrupt before a nonblooder—"

"A *what*?"

"That is what we call you," he said grimly. "You Ackermen."

"Go ahead, then, doctor." Her gray eyes lit with amusement. "Say your tiny say."

Eric said, "Never mind. Who's the guest?"

The great pale eyes of the woman had never seemed so large, so composed; they dominated and commanded with their utter inner universe of certitude. Of tranquility created by absolute, unchanging knowledge of all that deserved to be known. "Suppose we wait and see." And then, not yet affecting the changelessness of her eyes, her lips began to dance with a wicked, teasing playfulness; a moment later a new and different spark ignited within her eyes and thereupon the expression of her entire face underwent a total change. "The door," she said wickedly, her eyes gleaming and intense, her mouth twitching in a mirth-ridden giggle almost that of an adolescent girl, "flies open and there stands a silent delegate from Proxima. Ah, what a sight. A bloated greasy enemy reeg. Secretly, and incredibly because of Freneksy's snooping secret police, a reeg here officially to negotiate for a—" She broke off and then at last in a low monotone finished, "—a separate peace between us and them." With a dark and moody expression, her eyes no longer lit by any spark whatsoever, she listlessly finished her drink. "Yes, that'll be the day. How well I can picture it. Old Virgil sits in, beaming and cackling as usual. And sees his war contracts, every fnugging last one of them, slither down the drain. Back to fake mink. Back to the bat crap days . . . when the whole factory stank to high heaven." She laughed shortly, a brisk bark of derision. "Any minute now, doctor. Oh *sure.*"

"Freneksy's cops," Eric said, sharing her mood, "as you pointed out yourself, would swoop down on Wash-35 so dalb fast—"

"I know. It's a fantasy, a wish-fulfillment dream. Born out of hopeless longing. So it hardly matters whether Virgil would decide to mastermind—and try to carry off—such an encounter or not, does it? Because it couldn't be done successfully in a million light-years. It could be tried. But not done."

"Too bad," Eric said, half to himself, deep in thought.

"Traitor! You want to be popped into the slave-labor pool?"

Eric, after pondering, said cautiously, "I want—"

"You don't know what you want, Sweetscent; every man involved in an unhappy marriage loses the metabiological capacity to know what he does want—it's been taken away from him. You're a smelly little shell, trying to do the correct thing but never quite making it because your miserable little long-suffering heart isn't in it. Look at you now! You've managed to squirm away from me."

"Have not."

"—So we're no longer touching physically. Especially

thighwise. Oh, perish thighwise from the universe. But it is hard, is it not, to do it, to squirm away in such close quarters . . . here in the lounge. And yet you've managed to do it, haven't you?"

To change the subject Eric said, "I heard on TV last night that the quatreologist with the funny beard, that Professor Wald, is back from—"

"No. He's not Virgil's guest."

"Marm Hastings, then?"

"That Taoist spellbinding nut and crank and fool? You manufacturing a joke, Sweetscent? Is that it? You suppose Virgil would tolerate a marginal fake, that—" She made an obscene upward-jerking gesture with her thumb, at the same time grinning in a show of her white, clean, and very impressive clear teeth. "Maybe," she said, "it's Ian Norse."

"Who's he?" He had heard the name; it had a vaguely familiar sound to it, and he knew that in asking her he was making a tactical error; still he did it: this, if anything, was his weakness in regard to women. He led where they followed—sometimes. But more than once, especially at critical times in his life, in the major junctions, he followed guilelessly where they led.

Phyllis sighed. "Ian's firm makes all those shiny sterile new very expensive artifical organs you cleverly graft into rich dying people; you mean, doctor, you're not clear as to whom you're indebted?"

"I know," Eric said, irritably, feeling chagrin. "With everything else on my mind I forgot momentarily; that's all."

"Maybe it's a composer. As in the days of Kennedy; maybe it's Pablo Casals. God, he *would* be old. Maybe it's Beethoven. Hmm." She pretended to ponder. "By God, I do think he said something about that. Ludwig von *somebody;* is there a Ludwig von Somebodyelse other than—"

"Christ," Eric said angrily, weary of being teased. "Stop it."

"Don't pull rank; you're not so great. Keeping one creepy old man alive century after century." She giggled her low, sweet, and very intimate warm giggle of delighted mirth.

Eric said, with as much dignity as he could manage, "I also maintain TF&D's entire work force of eighty thousand key individuals. And as a matter of fact, I can't do that from Mars, so I resent all this. I resent it very much." You included, he thought bitterly to himself.

"What a ratio," Phyllis said. "One artiforg surgeon to eighty thousand patients—eighty thousand and one. But you have your team of robants to help you . . . perhaps they can make do while you're absent."

"A robant is an it that stinks," he said, paraphrasing T. S. Eliot.

"And an artiforg surgeon," Phyllis said; "is an it that grovels."

He glowered at her; she sipped her drink and showed no contrition. He could not get to her; she simply had too much psychic strength for him.

The omphalos of Wash-35, a five-story brick apartment building where Virgil had lived as a boy, contained a truly modern apartment of their year 2055 with every detail of convenience which Virgil could obtain during these war years. Several blocks away lay Connecticut Avenue, and, along it, stores which Virgil remembered. Here was Gammage's, a shop at which Virgil had bought Tip Top comics and penny candy. Next to it Eric made out the familiar shape of People's Drugstore; the old man during his childhood had bought a cigarette lighter here once and chemicals for his Gilbert Number Five glass-blowing and chemistry set.

"What's the Uptown Theater showing this week?" Harv Ackerman murmured as their ship coasted along Connecticut Avenue so that Virgil could review these treasured sights. He peered.

It was Jean Harlow in *Hell's Angels,* which all of them had seen at least twice. Harv groaned.

"But don't forget that lovely scene," Phyllis reminded him, "where Harlow says, 'I think I'll go slip into something more comfortable,' and then when she returns—"

"I know, I know," Harv said irritably. "Okay, that I like."

The ship taxied from Connecticut Avenue onto McComb Street and soon was parking before 3039 with its black wrought-iron fence and tiny lawn. When the hatch slid back, however, Eric smelled—not the city air of a long-gone Terran capital—but the bitterly thin and cold atmosphere of Mars; he could hardly get his lungs full of it and he stood gasping, feeling disoriented and sick.

"I'll have to goose them about the air machinery," Virgil complained as he descended the ramp to the sidewalk, assisted by Jonas and Harv. It did not seem to bother him, however; he spryly hiked toward the doorway of the apartment building.

Robants in the shape of small boys hopped to their feet and one of them yelled authentically, "Hey Virg! Where you been?"

"Had to do an errand for my mother," Virgil cackled, his face shining with delight. "How are ya, Earl? Hey, I got some good Chinese stamps my dad gave me; he got them at his office. There's duplicates; I'll trade you." He fished in his pocket, halting on the porch of the building.

"Hey, you know what I have?" a second robant child shrilled. "Some dry ice; I let Bob Rougy use my Flexie for it; you can hold it if you want."

"I'll trade you a big-little book for it," Virgil said as he produced his key and unlocked the front door of the building. "How about *Buck Rogers and the Doom Comet*? That's real keen."

As the rest of the party descended from the ship, Phyllis said to Eric, "Offer the children a mint-condition 1952 Marilyn Monroe nude calendar and see what they'll give you for it. At least half a popsicle."

As the apartment house door swung aside, a TF&D guard belatedly appeared. "Oh, Mr. Ackerman; I didn't realize you'd arrived." The guard ushered them into the dark, carpeted hall.

"Is he here yet?" Virgil asked, with sudden apparent tension.

"Yes sir. In the apt resting. He asked not to be disturbed for several hours." The guard, too, seemed nervous.

Halting, Virgil said, "How large is his party?"

"Just himself, an aide, and two Secret Service men."

"Who's for a glass of ice-cold Kool-Aid?" Virgil said reflexively over his shoulder as he led the way.

"Me, me," Phyllis said, mimicking Virgil's enthusiastic tone. "I want imitation fruit raspberry lime; what about you, Eric? How about gin bourbon lime or cherry Scotch vodka? Or didn't they sell those flavors back in 1935?"

To Eric, Harv said, "I'd like a place to lie down and rest, myself. This Martian air makes me weak as a kitten." His face had become mottled and ill-looking. "Why doesn't he build a dome? Keep *real* air in here?"

"Maybe," Eric pointed out, "there's a purpose in this. Prevents him from retiring here for good; makes him leave after a short while."

Coming up to them, Jonas said, "Personally I enjoy coming to this anachronistic place, Harv. It's a fnugging museum." To Eric he said, "In all fairness, your wife does a superb job of providing artifacts for this period. Listen to that—what's it called?—that radio playing in that apt." Dutifully they listened. It was "Betty and Bob," the ancient soap opera, emanating from the long-departed past. And even Eric found himself impressed; the voices seemed alive and totally real. They were here *now,* not mere echoes of themselves. How Kathy had achieved this he didn't know.

Steve, the huge and handsome, masculine Negro janitor of the building—or rather his robant simulacrum—appeared then, smoking his pipe and nodding cordially to them all. "Morning, doctor. Little nip of cold we having these days. Kids be getting they sled out soonly. My own boy, Georgie, he saving for a sled, he say little while ago to me."

"I'll chip in a 1934 dollar," Ralf Ackerman said, reaching for his wallet. In a *sotto voce* aside to Eric he said, "Or does old papa Virgil have it that the colored kid isn't entitled to a sled?"

"That no nevermind, Mr. Ackerman," Steve assured him. "Georgie, he earn he sled; he not want tips but real and troo pay." The dignified dark robant moved off then and was gone.

"Damn convincing," Harv said presently.

"Really is," Jonas agreed. He shivered. "God, to think that the actual man's been dead a century. It's distinctly hard to keep in mind that we're on Mars, not even on Earth in our own time—I don't like it. I like things to appear what they really are."

A thought came to Eric. "Do you object to a stereo tape of a symphony played back in the evening when you're at home in your apt?"

"No," Jonas said. "But that's totally different."

"It's not," Eric disagreed. "The orchestra isn't there, the original sound has departed, the hall in which it was recorded is now silent; all you possess is twelve hundred feet of iron oxide tape that's been magnetized in a specific pattern . . . it's an illusion just like this. Only this is complete." Q.E.D., he thought, and walked on then, toward the stairs. We live with illusion daily, he reflected. When the first bard rattled off the first epic of a sometime battle, illusion entered our lives; the *Iliad* is as much a "fake" as those robant children trading postage stamps on the porch of the building. Humans have always striven to retain the past, to keep it convincing; there's nothing wicked in that. Without it we have no continuity; we have only the moment. And, deprived of the past, the moment—the present—has little meaning, if any.

Maybe, he pondered as he ascended the stairs, that's my problem with Kathy. I can't remember our combined past: can't recall the days when we voluntarily lived with each other . . . now it's become an involuntary arrangement, derived God knows how from the past.

And neither of us understands it. Neither of us can puzzle out its meaning or its motivating mechanism. With a better memory we could turn it back into something we could fathom.

He thought, Maybe this is the first sign of old age making its dread appearance. And for me at thirty-four!

Phyllis, halting on the stair, waiting for him, said, "Have an affair with me, doctor."

Inwardly he quailed, felt hot, felt terror, felt excitement, felt hope, felt hopelessness, felt guilt, felt eagerness.

He said, "You have the most perfect teeth known to man."

"Answer."

"I—" He tried to think of an answer. Could words respond to this? But this had come in the form of words, had it not? "And be roasted into a cinder by Kathy—who sees everything that goes on?" He felt the woman staring at him, staring and staring with her huge, star-fixed eyes. "Hmm," he said, not too cleverly, and felt miserable and small and exactly precisely right to the last jot and tittle what he ought not to be.

Phyllis said, "But you need it."

"Umm," he said, wilting under this unwanted, undeserved female psychiatric examination of his evil, inner soul; she had it—his soul—and she was turning it over and over on her tongue. Goddam her! She had figured it out; she spoke the truth; he hated her, he longed to go to bed with her. And of course she knew—saw on his face—all this, saw it with her accursed huge eyes, eyes which no mortal woman ought to possess.

"You're going to perish without it," Phyllis said. "Without true, spontaneous, relaxed, physical sheer—"

"One chance," he said hoarsely. "In a billion. Of getting away with it." He managed, then, actually to laugh. "In fact our standing here right now on these damn stairs is folly. But what the——do you care?" He started on, then, actually passed her, continued on up to the second floor. What do you have to lose? he thought. It's me; I'd be the one. You can handle Kathy just as easily as you can yank me around at the end of that line you keep paying out and reeling back.

The door of Virgil's private, modern apt stood open; Virgil had gone inside. The balance of the party straggled after him, the blood clan first, of course, then the mere titled officers of the firm.

Eric entered—and saw Virgil's guest.

The guest; the man they had come here to see. Reclining, his face empty and slack, lips bulging dark purple and irregular, eyes fixed absently on nothing, was Gino Molinari. Supreme elected leader of Terra's unified planetary culture, and the supreme commander of its armed forces in the war against the reegs.

His fly was unbuttoned.

3

At his lunch break Bruce Himmel technician in charge of
the final stage of quality control at Tijuana Fur & Dye Corporation's central installation, left his post and shuffled down
the streets of Tijuana toward the café at which he traditionally
ate, due to its being cheap plus making the fewest possible
social demands on him. The Xanthus, a small yellow wooden
building squeezed between two adobe dry-goods shops, attracted a variable trade of workmen and peculiar male types,
mostly in their late twenties, who indicated no particular
method of earning a living. But they left Himmel alone and
that was all he asked. In fact this essentially was all he asked
from life itself. And, oddly, life was willing to consummate
a deal of this sort with him.

As he sat in the rear, spooning up the amorphous chili and
tearing out chunks of the sticky, pale, thick bread which
accompanied it, Himmel saw a shape bearing down on him,
a tangle-haired Anglo-Saxon wearing a leather jacket, jeans,
boots, and gloves, an altogether obsoletely attired individual
seemingly from some other era entirely. This was Christian
Plout, who drove an ancient turbine-powered taxi in Tijuana;
he had hidden out in Lower California for a decade now,
being in disagreement with the Los Angeles authorities over
an issue involving the sale of capstene, a drug derived from

the fly agaric mushroom. Himmel knew him slightly because Plout, like himself, gleeked Taoism.

"Salve, amicus," Plout intoned, sliding into the booth to face Himmel.

"Greetings," Himmel mumbled, his mouth full of burdeningly hot chili. "What's new?" Plout always had in his possession the latest. During the course of his day cruising about Tijuana in his cab, he happened across everyone. If it existed, Chris Plout was on hand to witness it and, if possible, extract some gain. Plout, basically, was a bundle of sidelines.

"Listen," Plout said, leaning toward him, his sand-colored dry face wrinkled in concentration. "See this?" From his clenched fist he rolled across the table a capsule; instantly his palm covered the capsule and it had disappeared once more as suddenly as it had manifested itself.

"I see it," Himmel said, continuing to eat.

Twitching, Plout whispered, "Hey, hee-hoo. This is JJ-180."

"What's that?" Himmel felt sullenly suspicious; he wished Plout would shamble back out of the Xanthus in search of other prospects.

"JJ-180," Plout said in an almost inaudible voice, sitting hunched forward so that his face nearly touched Himmel's, "is the German name for the drug that's about to be marketed in South America as Frohedadrine. A German chemical firm invented it; the pharmaceutical house in Argentina is their cover. They can't get it into the USA; in fact it isn't even easy to get it here in Mexico, if you can believe that." He grinned, showing his irregular, stained teeth. Even his tongue, Himmel noted once again with disgust, had a peculiar tinge, as if corrupted by some unnatural substance. He drew away in aversion.

"I thought everything was available here in Tijuana," Himmel said.

"So did I. That's what interesed me in this JJ-180. So I picked up some."

"Have you taken it yet?"

"Tonight," Plout said. "At my place. I got five caps, one of them for you. If you're interested."

"What's it do?" Somehow that seemed pertinent.

Plout, undulating with an internal rhythm, said, "Hallucinogenic. But more than that. Whee, whoo, fic-fic." His eyes glazed over and he retreated into himself, grinning with beatitude. Himmel waited; at last Plout returned. "Varies from person to person. Somehow involved with your sense of what Kant called the 'categories of perception.' Get it?"

"That would be your sense of time and space," Himmel said, having read the *Critique of Pure Reason,* it being his style of prose as well as thought. In his small conapt he kept a paperbook copy of it, well marked.

"Right! It alters your perception of time in particular, so it ought to be called a tempogogic drug—correct?" Plout seemed transported by his insight. "The first tempogogic drug . . . or rather maltempogogic, to be precise. Unless you *believe* what you experience."

Himmel said, "I have to get back to TF&D." He started to rise.

Pressing him back down, Plout said, "Fifty bucks. US."

"W-what?"

"For a cap. Creaker, it's *rare.* First I've seen." Once more Plout allowed the capsule to roll briefly across the table. "I hate to give it up but it'll be an experience; we'll find the Tao, the five of us. Isn't it worth fifty US dollars to find the Tao during this nurty war? You may never see JJ-180 again; the Mex coonks are getting ready to crack down on shipments from Argentina or wherever it comes from. And they're good."

"It's really that different from—"

"Oh yes! Listen, Himmel. You know what I almost ran over with my cab just now? One of your little carts. I could have squashed it but I didn't. I see them all the time; I could squash hundreds of them . . . I go by TF&D every few hours. I'll tell you something else: The Tijuana authorities are asking me if I know where those goddam little carts are coming from. I told 'em I don't know . . . but so help me, if we don't all merge with the Tao tonight I might—"

"Okay," Himmel said with a groan. "I'll buy a capsule from you." He dug for his wallet, considering this a shakedown, expecting nothing, really, for his money. Tonight would be a hollow fraud.

He couldn't have been further wrong.

Gino Molinari, supreme leader of Terra in its war against the reegs, wore khaki, as usual, with his sole military decoration on his breast, his Golden Cross First Class, awarded by the UN General Assembly fifteen years before. Molinari, Dr. Eric Sweetscent noted, badly needed a shave; the lower portion of his face was stubbled, stained by a grime and sootlike blackness that had risen massively to the surface from deep within. His shoelaces, after the manner of his fly, were undone.

The appearance of the man, Eric thought, is appalling.

Molinari did not raise his head and his expression remained dull and unfocused as Virgil's party filed one by one into the room, saw him, and gulped in dumbfoundment. He was very obviously a sick and worn-out man; the general public impression was, it would seem, quite accurate.

To Eric's surprise he saw that in real life the Mole looked exactly as he had of late on TV, no greater, no sturdier, no more in command. It seemed impossible but it was so, and yet he *was* in command; in every legal sense he had retained his positions of power, yielding to no one—at any rate, no one on Terra. Nor, Eric realized suddenly, did Molinari intend to step down, despite his obviously deteriorated psychophysical condition. Somehow that was clear, made so by the man's utterly slack stance, his willingness to appear this natural way to a collection of rather potent personages. The Mole remained as he was, with no poise, no posture of the militant heroic. Either he was too far gone to care, or—Eric thought, Or there is too much of genuine importance at stake for him to waste his waning strength at merely impressing people, and especially those of his own planet. The Mole had passed beyond that.

For better or worse.

To Eric, Virgil Ackerman said in a low voice, "You're a doctor. You are going to have to ask him if he needs medical attention." He, too, seemed concerned.

Eric looked toward Virgil and thought, I was brought here for this. It all has been arranged for this, for me to meet Molinari. Everything else, all the other people—a cover. To fool the 'Starmen. I see that now; I see what this is and what they want me to do. I see, he realized, whom I must heal; this is the man whom my skills and talents must, from this point on, exist for. The *must;* it is put that way. The must of the situation: this is it.

Bending, he said haltingly, "Mr. Secretary General—" His voice shook. But it was not awe that stopped him—the reclining man certainly did not promote *that* emotion—but ignorance; he simply did not know what to say to a man holding such an office. "I'm a GP," he said finally, and rather emptily, he realized. "As well as an org-trans surgeon." He paused; there came no response, visible or audible. "While you're here at Wash—"

All at once Molinari raised his head; his eyes cleared. He focused on Eric Sweetscent, then abruptly, startlingly, boomed in his familiar low-toned voice, "Hell on that, doctor. I'm okay." He smiled; it was a brief but innately human smile, one of understanding at Eric's clumsy, labored efforts. "Enjoy yourself! Live it up 1935 style! Was that during prohibition? No, I guess that was earlier. Have a Pepsi-Cola."

"I was about to try a raspberry Kool-Aid," Eric said, regaining some of his aplomb; his heart rate returned now to normal.

Molinari said jovially, "Quite a construct old Virgil has here. I took the opportunity to glim it over. I ought to nationalize the fnuggin' thing; too much private capital invested here, should be in the planet's war effort." His half-joking tone was, underneath, starkly serious; obviously this elaborate artifact distressed him. Molinari, as all citizens of Terra knew, lived an ascetic life, yet oddly intersticed with infrequent interludes of priapsistic, little-revealed sybaritic indulgence. Of late, however, the binges were said to have tapered off.

"This individual is Dr. Eric Sweetscent," Virgil said. "The goddam finest nugging org-trans surgeon on Terra, as you well know from the GHQ personnel dossiers; he's put twenty-five—or is it -six?—separate artiforgs in me during the last decade, but I've paid for it; he rakes in a fat haul every month. Not quite so fat a haul, though, as his ever-loving wife." He grinned at Eric, his fleshless, elongated face genial in a fatherly way.

After a pause Eric said to Molinari, "What I'm waiting for is the day when I trans a new brain for Virgil." The irritability in his own voice surprised him; probably it had been the mention of Kathy that had set it off. "I've got several on stand-by. One is a real goozler."

" 'Goozler,' " Molinari murmured. "I've missed out on the argot of recent months . . . just plain too busy. Too many official documents to prepare; too much establishment talk. It's a goozlery war, isn't it, doctor?" His great, dark, pain-impregnated eyes fixed on Eric, and Eric saw something he had never come across before; he saw an intensity that was not normal or human. And it was a physiological phenomenon, a swiftness of reflex, due surely to a unique and superior laying-down of the neural pathways during childhood. The Mole's gaze exceeded in its authority and astuteness, its power alone, anything possessed by ordinary persons, and in it Eric saw the difference between them all and the Mole. The primary conduit linking the mind with external reality, the sense of sight, was, in the Mole, so far more developed than one anticipated that by it the man caught and held whatever happened to venture across his path. And, beyond all else, this enormity of visual prowess possessed the aspect of *wariness*. Of recognition of the imminence of *harm*.

By this faculty the Mole remained alive.

Eric realized something then, something that had never

occurred to him in all the weary, dreadful years of the war.

The Mole would have been their leader at any time, at any stage in human society. And—anywhere.

"Every war," Eric said with utmost caution and tact, "is a hard war for those involved in it, Secretary." He paused, reflected, and then added, "We all understood this, sir, when we got into it. It's the risk a people, a planet, takes when it voluntarily enters a severe and ancient conflict that's been going on a long time between two other peoples."

There was silence; Molinari scrutinized him wordlessly.

"And the 'Starmen," Eric said, "are of our stock. We are related to them genetically, are we not?"

Against that there was only a silence, a wordless void which no one cared to fill. At last, reflectively, Molinari farted.

"Tell Eric about your stomach pains," Virgil said to Molinari.

"My pains," Molinari said, and grimaced.

"The whole point in bringing you together—" Virgil began.

"Yes," Molinari growled brusquely, nodding his massive head. "I know. And you all know. It was for *exactly* this."

"I'm as certain as I am of taxes and labor unions that Dr. Sweetscent can help you, Secretary," Virgil continued. "The rest of us will go across the hall to the suite of rooms there, so you two can talk in private." With unusual circumspection he moved away, and, one by one, the blood clan and firm officers filed out of the room, leaving Eric Sweetscent alone with the Secretary General.

After a pause Eric said, "All right, sir; tell me about your abdominal complaint, Secretary." In any case a sick man was a sick man; he seated himself in the form-binding armchair across from the UN Secretary General and, in this reflexively assumed professional posture, waited.

4

That evening as Bruce Himmel tromped up the rickety wooden stairs to Chris Plout's conapt in the dismal Mexican section of Tijuana, a female voice said from the darkness behind him, "Hello, Brucie. It looks as if this is an all-TF&D night; Simon Ild is here, too."

On the porch the woman caught up with him. It was sexy, sharp-tongued Katherine Sweetscent; he had run into her at Plout's gatherings a number of times before and so it hardly surprised him to see her now. Mrs. Sweetscent wore a somewhat modified costume from that which she employed on the job; this also failed to surprise him. For tonight's mysterious undertaking Kathy had arrived naked from the waist up, except, of course, for her nipples. They had been—not gilded in the strict sense—but rather treated with a coating of living matter, sentient, a Martian life form, so that each possessed a consciousness. Hence each nipple responded in an alert fashion to everything going on.

The effect on Himmel was immense.

Behind Kathy Sweetscent ascended Simon Ild; in the dim light he had a vacant expression on his sappy, pimply, uneducated face. This was a person whom Himmel could do without; Simon—unfortunately—reminded him of nothing so much as a bad simulacrum of himself. And there was nothing for him quite so unbearable.

The fourth person gathered here in the unheated, low-ceilinged room of Chris Plout's littered, stale-food-smelling conapt was an individual whom Himmel at once recognized— recognized and stared at, because this was a man known to him through pics on the back of book jackets. Pale, with glases, his long hair carefully combed, wearing expensive, tasteful Io-fabric clothing, seemingly a trifle ill-at-ease, stood the Taoist authority from San Francisco, Marm Hastings, a slight man but extremely handsome, in his mid-forties, and, as Himmel knew, quite well-to-do from his many books on the subject of oriental mysticism. Why was Hastings here? Obviously to sample JJ-180; Hastings had a reputation for essaying an experience with every hallucinogenic drug that came into being, legal or otherwise. To Hastings this was allied with religion.

But as far as Himmel knew, Marm Hastings had never shown up here in Tijuana at Chris Plout's conapt. What did this indicate about JJ-180? He pondered as he stood off in a corner, surveying the goings-on. Hastings was occupied in examining Plout's library on the subject of drugs and religion; he seemed uninterested in the others present, even contemptuous of their existence. Simon Ild, as usual, curled up on the floor, on a pillow, and lit a twisted brown marijuana cigarette; he puffed vacantly, waiting for Chris to appear. And Kathy Sweetscent—she crouched down, stroking reflexively at her hocks, as if grooming herself flywise, putting her slender, muscular body into a state of alertness. Teasing it, he decided, by deliberate, almost yogalike efforts.

Such physicalness disturbed him; he glanced away. It was not in keeping with the spiritual emphasis of the evening. But no one could tell Mrs. Sweetscent anything; she was nearly autistic.

Now Chris Plout, wearing a red bathrobe, his feet bare, entered from the kitchen; through dark glasses he peered to see if it was time to begin. "Marm," he said. "Kathy, Bruce,

Simon, and I, Christian; the five of us. An adventure into the unexplored by means of a new substance which has just arrived from Tampico aboard a banana boat . . . I hold it here." He extended his open palm; within lay the five capsules. "One for each of us—Kathy, Bruce, Simon, Marm, and me, Christian; our first journey of the mind together. Will we all return? And will we be translated, as Bottom says?"

Himmel thought, As Peter Quince says to Bottom, actually.

Aloud, he said, " 'Bottom, thou art translated.' "

"Pardon?" Chris Plout said, frowning.

"I'm quoting," Himmel explained.

"Come on, Chris," Kathy Sweetscent said crossly. "Give us the jink and let's get started." She snatched—successfully—one of the capsules from Chris's palm. "Here I go," she said. "And without water."

Mildly, Marm Hastings said with his quasi-English accent, "Is it the same, I wonder, taken without water?" Without movement of his eye muscles he clearly succeeded in making a survey of the woman; there was that sudden stricture of his body which gave him away. Himmel felt outraged; wasn't this whole affair designed to raise them all above the flesh?

"It's the same," Kathy informed him. "Everything's the same, when you break through to absolute reality; it's all one vast blur." She then swallowed, coughed. The capsule was gone.

Reaching, Himmel took his. The others followed.

"If the Mole's police caught us," Simon said, to no one in particular, "we'd all be in the Army, serving out at the front."

"Or working in vol-labe camps at Lilistar," Himmel added. They were all tense, waiting for the drug to take effect; it always ran this way, these short seconds before the jink got to them. "For good old Freneksy, as it's translated into English. Bottom, thou art translated as Freneksy." He giggled shakily. Katherine Sweetscent glared at him.

"Miss," Marm Hastings said to her in an unperturbed voice, "I wonder if I haven't met you before; you do seem familiar. Do you spend much time in the Bay area? I have a studio and architect-designed home in the hills of West Marin, near the ocean . . . we hold seminars there often; people come and go freely. But I would remember you. Oh yes."

Katherine Sweetscent said, "My damn husband—he wouldn't ever let me. I'm self-supporting—I'm more than economically independent—and yet I have to put up with the rasping little noises and squeaks he makes whenever I try to do something original on my own." She added, "I'm an antique buyer, but old things become boring; I'd love to—"

Marm Hastings interrupted, speaking to Chris Plout, "Where does this JJ-180 originate, Plout? You said Germany, I think. But you see, I have a number of contacts in pharmaceutical institutes, both public and private, in Germany, and none of them has so much as mentioned anything called JJ-180." He smiled, but it was a sharply formed astute smile, demanding an answer.

Chris shrugged. "That's the poog as I get it, Hastings. Take it or leave it." He was not bothered; he knew, as they all did, that under these circumstances no brief of warranty was incumbent on him.

"Then it's not actually German," Hastings said, with a faint nod. "I see. Could this JJ-180, or Frohedadrine as it's also called . . . *could it possibly originate entirely off Terra?*"

After a pause Chris said, "I dunno, Hastings. I dunno."

To all of them Hastings said in his educated, severe voice, "There have been cases of illegal non-terrestrial drugs before. None of them of any importance. Derived from Martian flora, mostly, and occasionally from Ganymedean lichens. I suppose you've heard; you all *seem* informed of this topic, as you should be. Or at least—" His smile grew, but his eyes, behind his rimless glasses, were codlike. "At the very least you seem satisfied as to the pedigree of this JJ-180 for which you've paid this man fifty US dollars."

"I'm satisfied," Simon Ild said in his stupid way. "Anyhow it's too late; we paid Chris and we've all taken the caps."

"True," Hastings agreed reasonably. He seated himself in one of Chris's tottering easy chairs. "Does anyone feel any change yet? Please speak up as soon as you do." He glanced at Katherine Sweetscent. "Your nipples seem to be watching me, or is that just my imagination? In any case it makes me decidedly uncomfortable."

"As a matter of fact," Chris Plout said in a strained voice, "I feel something, Hastings." He licked his lips, trying to wet them. "Excuse me, I—to be frank, I'm here alone. None of you are with me."

Marm Hastings studied him.

"Yes," Chris went on. "I'm all alone in my conapt. None of you even exist. But the books and chairs, everything else exists. Then who'm I talking to? Have you answered?" He peered about, and it was obvious that he could not see any of them; his gaze passed by them all.

"My nipples are not watching you or anybody else," Kathy Sweetscent said to Hastings.

"I can't hear you," Chris said in panic. "Answer!"

"We're here," Simon Ild said, and sniggered.

"Please," Chris said, and now his voice was pleading. "Say something; it's just shadows. It's—lifeless. Nothing but dead things. And it's only starting—I'm scared of how it's going on; it's still happening."

Marm Hastings laid his hand on Chris Plout's shoulder.

The hand passed through Plout.

"Well, we've gotten our fifty dollars' worth," Kathy Sweetscent said in a low voice, void of amusement. She walked toward Chris, closer and closer.

"Don't try it," Hastings said to her in a gentle tone.

"I will," she said. And walked through Chris Plout. But she did not reappear on the other side. She had vanished; only Plout remained, still bleating for someone to answer him, still flailing the air in search of companions he could no longer perceive.

Isolation, Bruce Himmel thought to himself. Each of us cut off from all others. Dreadful. But—it'll wear off. *Won't it?*

As yet he did not know. And for him it had not even started.

"These pains," UN Secretary General Gino Molinari rasped, lying back on the large, red, hand-wrought couch in the living room of Virgil Ackerman's Wash-35 apartment, "generally become most difficult for me at night." He had shut his eyes; his great fleshy face sagged forlornly, the grimy jowls wobbling as he spoke. "I've been examined; Dr. Teagarden is my chief GP. They've made infinite tests, with particular attention directed toward malignancy."

Eric thought, The man's speaking by rote; it's not his natural speech pattern. This has become that ingrained in his mind, this preoccupation; he's gone through this ritual a thousand times, with as many physicians. And—he still suffers.

"There's no malignancy," Molinari added. "That seems to have been authoritatively verified." His words constituted a satire of pompous medical diction, Eric realized suddenly. The Mole had immense hostility toward doctors, since they had failed to help him. "Generally the diagnosis is acute gastritis. Or spasms of the pyloric valve. Or even an hysterical re-enactment of my wife's labor pains, which she experienced three years ago." He finished, half to himself, "Shortly before her death."

"What about your diet?" Eric asked.

The Mole opened his eyes wearily. "My diet. I don't eat, doctor. Nothing at all. The air sustains me; didn't you read that in the homeopapes? I don't need food, like you simple schulps do. I'm different." His tone was urgently, acutely embittered.

"And it interferes with your duties?" Eric asked.

The Mole scrutinized him. "You think it's psychosomatic, that outmoded pseudo science that tried to make people morally responsible for their ailments?" He spat in anger; his face writhed and now the flesh was no longer hanging and loose—it was stretched taut, as if ballooned out from within. "So I can escape my responsibilities? Listen, doctor;

I still have my responsibilities—*and* the pain. Can that be called secondary neurotic psychological gain?"

"No," Eric admitted. "But anyhow I'm not qualified to deal with psychosomatic medicine; you'd have to go to—"

"I've seen them," the Mole said. All at once he dragged himself to his feet, stood swaying, facing Eric. "Get Virgil back here; there's no point in your wasting your time interrogating me. And anyhow I don't choose to be interrogated. I don't care for it." He strode unsteadily toward the door, hitching up his sagging khaki trousers as he went.

Eric said, "Secretary, you could have your stomach removed, you realize. At any time. And an artiforg planted in replacement. The operation is simple and almost always successful. Without examining your case records I shouldn't say this, but you may *have* to have your stomach replaced one of these days. Risk or no risk." He was certain that Molinari would survive; the man's fear was palpably phobic.

"No," Molinari said quietly. "I don't have to; it's my choice. I can die instead."

Eric stared at him.

"Sure," Molinari said. "Even though I'm the UN Secretary General. Hasn't it occurred to you that I want to die, that these pains, this developing physical—or psychosomatic—illness is a way out for me? I don't want to go on. Maybe. Who knows? What difference does it make, to anybody? But the hell with it." He tore open the hall door. "Virgil," he boomed in a surprisingly virile voice. "For chrissake, let's pour and get this party started." Over his shoulder he said to Eric, "Did you know this was a party? I bet the old man told you it was a serious conference for solving Terra's military, political, and economic problems. In one half hour." He grinned, showing his big, white teeth.

"Frankly," Eric said, "I'm glad to hear it's a party." The session with Molinari had been as difficult for him as it had been for the Secretary. And yet—he had an intuition that Virgil Ackerman would not let it end there. Virgil wanted something done for the Mole; he desired to see the man's distress eased, and for a good, practical reason.

The collapse of Gino Molinari would signify an end to Virgil's possession of TF&D. Management of Terra's economic syndromes no doubt held priority for Freneksy's officials; their agenda had probably been drawn up in detail.

Virgil Ackerman was a shrewd businessman.

"How much," Molinari asked suddenly, "does the old fruit pay you?"

"V-very well," Eric said, taken by surprise.

Molinari, eyeing him, said, "He's talked to me about you. Before this get-together. Sold me on you, how good you are. Because of you he's still alive long after he ought to be dead, all that crap." They both smiled. "What's your choice in liquor, doctor? I like anything. And I like fried chops and Mexican food and spare ribs and fried prawns dipped in horse-radish and mustard. . . . I treat my stomach kind."

"Bourbon," Eric said.

A man entered the room, glanced at Eric. He had a gray, grim expression and Eric realized that this was one of the Mole's Secret Service men.

"This is Tom Johannson," the Mole explained to Eric. "He keeps *me* alive; he's my Dr. Eric Sweetscent. But he does it with his pistol. Show doc your pistol, Tom; show him how you can nam anybody, any time you want, at any distance. Plug Virgil as he comes across the hall, right in the fnugging heart; then doc can paste a new heart in its place. How long does it take, doc? Ten, fifteen minutes?" The Mole laughed loudly. And then he motioned to Johannson. "Shut the door."

His bodyguard did so; the Mole stood facing Eric Sweetscent.

"Listen, doctor. Here's what I want to ask you. Suppose you began to perform an org-trans operation on me, taking out my old stomach and putting in a new one, and something went wrong. It wouldn't hurt, would it? Because I'd be out. Could you do that?" He watched Eric's face. "You understand me, don't you? I see you do." Behind them, at the closed door, the bodyguard stood impassively, keeping everyone else out, preventing them from hearing. This was for Eric alone. In utmost confidence.

"Why?" Eric said, after a time. "Why not simply use Johannson's loger-magnum pistol? If this is what you want . . ."

"I don't know why, actually," the Mole said. "No one particular reason. The death of my wife, perhaps. Call it the responsibility I have to bear . . . and which I'm not managing to discharge properly, at least according to many people. I don't agree; I think I'm succeeding. But they don't understand all the factors in the situation." He admitted, then, "And I'm tired."

"It—could be done," Eric said truthfully.

"And *you* could do it?" The man's eyes blazed, keen and fixed on him. Sizing him up as each second ticked away.

"Yes, I could do it." He held, personally, an odd view regarding suicide. Despite his code, the ethical understructure of medicine, he believed—and it was based on certain very real experiences in his own life—that if a man wanted to die he had the right to die. He did not possess an elaborated rationalization to justify this belief; he had not even tried to construct one. The proposition, to him, seemed self-evident. There was no body of evidence which proved that life in the first place was a boon. Perhaps it was for some persons; obviously it was not for others. For Gino Molinari it was a nightmare. The man was sick, guilt-ridden, saddled with an enormous, really hopeless task: he did not have the confidence of his own people, the Terran population, and he did not enjoy the respect or trust or admiration of the people of Lilistar. And then, above and beyond all that, lay the personal consideration, the events in his own private life, starting with the sudden, unexpected death of his wife and ending up with the pains in his belly. And then, too, Eric realized with acute comprehension, there was probably more. Factors known only to the Mole. Deciding factors which he did not intend to tell.

"*Would* you do such a thing?" Molinari asked.

After a long, long pause Eric said, "Yes I would. It would be an agreement between the two of us. You'd ask for it and I'd give it to you and it would end there. It would be no one's business but our own."

"Yes." The Mole nodded and on his face relief showed; he seemed now to relax a little, to experience some peace. "I can see why Virgil recommended you."

"I was going to do it to myself, once," Eric said. "Not so long ago."

The Mole's head jerked; he stared at Eric Sweetscent with a look so keen that it cut through his physical self and into that which lay at the deepest, most silent part of him. "Really?" the Mole said then.

"Yes." He nodded. So I can understand, he thought to himself, can empathize with you even without having to know the exact reasons.

"But I," the Mole said, "want to know the reasons." It was so close to a telepathic reading of his mind that Eric felt stunned; he found himself unable to look away from the penetrating eyes and he realized, then, that it had been no parapsychological talent on the Mole's part; it had been swifter and stronger than that.

The Mole extended his hand; reflexively, Eric accepted it. And, once he had done so, he found the grip remaining; the Mole did not release his hand but tightened his grip so that pain flew up Eric's arm. The Mole was trying to see him better, trying, as Phyllis Ackerman had done not so long ago, to discover everything that could be discovered about him. But out of the Mole's mind came no glib, flip theories; the Mole insisted on the truth, and articulated by Eric Sweetscent himself. He had to tell the Mole what it had been; he had no choice.

Actually, in his case it had been a very small matter. Something which if told—and he had never been so foolish as to tell it, even to his professional headbasher—would have proved absurd, would have made him appear, and rightly so, an idiot. Or, even worse, mentally deranged.

It had been an incident between himself and—

"Your wife," the Mole said, staring at him, never taking his eyes from him. And still the steady grip of his hand.

"Yes." Eric nodded. "My Ampex video tapes . . . of the great mid-twentieth century comedian Jonathan Winters."

The pretext for his first invitation of Kathy Lingrom had been his fabulous collection. She had expressed a desire to see them, to drop by his apt—at his invitation—to witness a few choice shots.

The Mole said, "And she read something psychological into your having the tapes. Something 'meaningful' about you."

"Yes." Eric nodded somberly.

After Kathy had sat curled up one night in his living room, as long-legged and smooth as a cat, her bare breasts faintly green from the light coating of polish she had given them (in the latest style), watching the screen fixedly and of course, laughing—who could fail to?—she had said contemplatively, "You know, what's great about Winters was his talent for role-playing. And, once in a role, he was submerged; he seemed actually to believe in it."

"Is that bad?" Eric had said.

"No. But it tells me why you gravitate to Winters." Kathy fondled the damp, cold glass of her drink, her long lashes lowered in thought. "It's that residual quality in him that could never be submerged in his role. It means you resist life, the role that you play out—being an org-trans surgeon, I suppose. Some childish, unconscious part of you won't enter human society."

"Well, is *that* bad?" He had tried to ask jokingly, wanting—even then—to turn this pseudopsychiatric, ponderous discussion to more convivial areas . . . areas clearly defined in his mind as he surveyed her pure, bare, pale-green breasts flickering with their own luminosity.

"It's deceitful," Kathy said.

Hearing that, then, something in him had groaned, and something in him groaned now. The Mole seemed to hear it, to take note.

"You're cheating other people," Kathy said. "Me, for instance." At that point—mercifully—she changed the topic. For that he felt gratitude. And yet—why did it bother him so?

Later, when they had married, Kathy primly requested that he keep his tape collection in his study and not out in the shared portion of their conapt. The collection vaguely vexed her, she said. But she did not know—or anyhow did not say—why. And when in the evenings he felt the old urge to play a section of tape, Kathy complained.

"Why?" the Mole asked.

He did not know; he had not then and did not now understand it. But it had been an ominous harbinger; he saw her aversion but the significance of it eluded him, and this inability to grasp the meaning of what was taking place in his married life made him deeply uneasy.

Meanwhile, through Kathy's intercession, he had been hired by Virgil Ackerman. His wife had made it possible for him to take a notable leap in the hierarchy of econ and sose—economic and social—life. And of course he felt gratitude toward her; how could he not? His basic ambition had been fulfilled.

The means by which it had been accomplished had not struck him as overpoweringly important: many wives helped their husbands up the long steps in their careers. And vice versa. And yet—

It bothered Kathy. Even though it had been her idea.

"*She* got you your job here?" the Mole demanded, scowling. "And then after that she held it against you? I seem to get the picture, very clear." He plucked at a front tooth, still scowling, his face dark.

"One night in bed—" He stopped, feeling the difficulty of going on. It had been too private. And too awfully unpleasant.

"I want to know," the Mole said, "the rest of it."

He shrugged. "Anyhow—she said something about being 'tired of the sham we're living.' The 'sham,' of course, being my job."

Lying in bed, naked, her soft hair curling about her shoulders—in those days she had worn it longer—Kathy had said, "You married me to get your job. And you're not striving on your own; a man should make his own way." Tears filled her eyes, and she flopped over on her face to cry—or appear, anyhow—to cry.

" 'Strive'?" he had said, baffled.

The Mole interrupted, "Rise higher. Get a better job. That's what they mean when they say that."

"But I like my job," he answered.

"So you're content," Kathy said, in a muffled, bitter voice, "to *appear* to be successful. When you really aren't." And then, sniffling and snuffling, she added, "And you're terrible in bed."

He got up and went into the living room of their conapt and sat alone for a time and then, instinctively, he made his way into his study and placed one of his treasured Johnny Winters tapes into the projector. For a while he sat in misery watching Johnny put on one hat after another and become a different person under each. And then—

At the doorway Kathy appeared, smooth and naked and slim, her face contorted. "Have you found it?"

"Found what?" He shut the tape projector off.

"The tape," she stated, "that I destroyed."

He stared at her, unable to take in what he had heard.

"A few days ago." Her tone, defiant, shrilled at him. "I was all alone here in the conapt; I felt blue—you were busy doing some drafk nothing thing for Virgil—and I put on a reel; I put it on exactly right; I followed all the instructions. But *it* did something wrong. So it got erased."

The Mole grunted somberly. "You were supposed to say 'It doesn't matter.' "

He had known that; known it then, knew it now. But in a strangled, thick voice he had said, "Which tape?"

"I don't remember."

His voice rose; it escaped him. "Goddam it, *which tape?*" He ran to the shelf of tapes; grabbed the first box; tore it open; carried it at once to the projector.

"I knew," Kathy said, in a harsh, bleak voice as she watched him with withering contempt, "that your——tapes meant more to you than I do or ever did."

"Tell me which tape!" he pleaded. *"Please!"*

"No, she wouldn't say," the Mole murmured thoughtfully. "That would be the entire point. You'd have to play every one of them before you could find out. A couple days of playing tapes. Clever dame; damn clever."

"No," Kathy said in a low, embittered, almost frail voice. Now her face was peaked with hatred for him. "I'm *glad* I did it. You know what I'm going to do? I'm going to ruin all of them."

He stared at her. Numbly.

"You deserve it," Kathy said, "for holding back and not giving me all your love. *This* is where you belong, scrabbling like an animal, a panic-ridden animal. Look at you! Contemptible—trembling and about to burst into tears. Because someone ruined one of your INCREDIBLY important tapes."

"But," he said, "it's my hobby. My lifetime hobby."

"Like a kid pulling its pud," Kathy said.

"They—can't be replaced. I have the only copies of some of them. The one from the Jack Paar show—"

"So what? You know something, Eric? Do you know, really know, why you like watching men on tape?"

The Mole grunted; his heavy, fleshy, middle-aged face flinched as he listened.

"Because," Kathy said, "you're a fairy."

"Ouch," the Mole murmured, and blinked.

"You're a repressed homosexual. I sincerely doubt if you're aware of it on a conscious level, but it's there. Look at me; look. Here I am; a perfectly attractive woman, available to you any time you want me."

The Mole said, aside, wryly, "And at no cost."

"And yet you're in here with these tapes and not in the bedroom screwbling with me. I hope—Eric, I hope to *God* I ruined one that—" She turned away from the door then. "Good night. And have fun playing with yourself." Her voice—actually and unbelievably—had become controlled, even placid.

From a crouched position he bolted toward her. Reached for her as she retreated smooth and white and naked down the hall, her back to him. He grabbed her, grabbed firm hold, sank his fingers into her soft arm. Spun her around. Blinking, startled, she faced him.

"I'm going to—" He broke off. *I'm going to kill you,* he had started to say. But already in the unstirred depths of his mind, slumbering beneath the frenzy of his hysterical antics, a cold and rational fraction of him whispered its ice-God voice: Don't say it. Because if you do, then she's got you. She'll never forget. As long as you live she'll make you suffer. This is a woman that one must not hurt because she knows techniques; she knows how to hurt back. A thousandfold. Yes, this is her wisdom, this knowing how to do this. Above all other things.

"Let—go—of—me." Her eyes blazed smokily.

He released her.

After a pause, while she rubbed her arm, Kathy said, "I want that collection of tapes out of this apartment by tomorrow night. Otherwise we're finished, Eric."

"Okay," he said, nodding.

"And then," Kathy said, "I'll tell you what else I want. I want you to start looking for a higher paying job. At another company. So I won't run into you every time I turn around. And then . . . we'll see. Possibly we can stay together. On a new basis, one fairer to me. One in which you make some attempt to pay attention to my needs in addition to your own." Astonishingly, she sounded perfectly rational and in control of herself. Remarkable.

"You got rid of the tapes?" the Mole asked him.

He nodded.

"And you spent the next few years directing your efforts toward controlling your hatred for your wife."

Again he nodded.

"And the hatred for her," Mole said, "became hatred for yourself. Because you couldn't stand being afraid of one small woman. But a very powerful person—notice I said 'person,' not 'woman.' "

"Those low blows," Eric said. "Like her erasing my tape—"

"The low blow," the Mole interrupted, "was not her erasing the tape. It was her refusing to tell you which one she had erased. And her making it so clear that she enjoyed the situation. If she had been sorry—but a woman, a person, like that; they never become sorry. Never." He was silent for a time. "And you can't leave her."

"We're fused," Eric said. "The damage is done." The mutually inflicted pain delivered at night without the possibility of anyone intervening, overhearing and coming to help. Help, Eric thought. We both need help. Because this will go on, get worse, corrode us further and further until at last, mercifully—

But that might take decades.

So Eric could understand Gino Molinari's yearning for death. He, like the Mole, could envision it as a release—the only dependable release that existed . . . or appeared to exist, given the ignorance, habit patterns, and foolishness of the participants. Given the timeless human equation.

In fact he felt a considerable bond with Molinari.

"One of us," the Mole said, with perception, "suffering unbearably on the private level, hidden from the public, small and unimportant. The other suffering in the grand Roman public manner, like a speared and dying god. Strange. Completely opposite. The microcosm and the macro."

Eric nodded.

"Anyhow," the Mole said, releasing Eric's hand and slapping him on the shoulder, "I'm making you feel bad. Sorry, Dr. Sweetscent; let's drop the topic." To his bodyguard he said, "Open the door now. We're done."

"Wait," Eric said. But then he did not know how to go on, to say it.

The Mole did it for him. "How would you like to be attached to my staff?" Molinari said abruptly, breaking the silence. "It can be arranged; technically you'd be drafted into military service." He added, "You may take it for granted you'd be my personal physician."

Trying to sound casual, Eric said, "I'm interested."

"You wouldn't be running into her all the time. This might

be a beginning. A start toward prying the two of you apart."

"True." He nodded. Very true. And very attractive, when thought of that way. But the irony—this consisted of precisely that which Kathy had goaded him toward all these years. "I'd have to talk it over with my wife," he began, and then flushed. "Virgil, anyhow," he muttered. "In any case. He'd have to approve."

Regarding him with brooding severity, the Mole said in a slow, dark voice, "There is one drawback. You would not see so much of Kathy; true. But by being with me you'd see a great deal of our—" He grimaced. "The ally. How do you suppose you'd enjoy yourself surrounded by 'Starmen? You might find yourself having a few spasms of the gut late at night yourself . . . and perhaps worse—other—psychosomatic disorders, some you may not anticipate, despite your profession."

Eric said, "It's bad enough for me late at night as it is. This way I might have some company."

"Me?" Molinari said. "I wouldn't be company, Sweetscent, for you or anybody else. I'm a creature that's flayed alive at night. I retire at ten o'clock and then I'm back up, usually by eleven; I—" He broke off, meditatively. "No, night is not a good time for me; not at all."

It could clearly be seen in the man's face.

5

On the night of his return from Wash-35 Eric Sweetscent encountered his wife at their conapt across the border in San Diego. Kathy had arrived before him. The meeting, of course, was inevitable.

"Back from little red Mars," she observed as he shut the living room door after him. "Two days doing what? Shooting your agate into the ring and beating all the other boys and girls? Or exposing sun pictures of Tom Mix?" Kathy sat in the center of the couch, a drink in one hand, her hair swept back and tied, giving her the look of a teen-ager; she wore a plain black dress and her legs were long and smooth, strikingly tapered at the ankles. Her feet were bare and each toenail bore a shiny decal depicting—he bent to see—a scene in color of the Norman Conquest. The smallest nail on each foot glittered with a picture too obscene for him to contemplate; he went to hang his coat in the closet.

"We pulled out of the war," he said.

"Did we? You and Phyllis Ackerman? Or you and someone else?"

"Everybody was there. Not just Phyllis." He wondered what he could fix for dinner; his stomach was empty and in a state of complaint. As yet, however, there were no pains. Perhaps that came later.

"Any special reason why I wasn't asked along?" Her voice snapped like a lethal whip, making his flesh cringe; the natural biochemical animal in him dreaded the exchange which was in store for him—and also for her. Obviously she, like himself, was compelled to press head-on; she was as much caught up and helpless as he.

"No special reason." He wandered into the kitchen, feeling a little dulled, as if Kathy's opening had flattened his senses. Many such encounters had taught him to shield himself on the somatic level, if at all possible. Only old husbands, tired, experienced husbands, knew to do this. The newcomers . . . they're forced on by diencephalic responses, he reflected. And it's harder on them.

"I want an answer," Kathy said, appearing at the door. "As to why I was deliberately excluded."

God, how physically appealing his wife was; she wore nothing, of course, under the black dress and each curved line of her confronted him with its savory familiarity. But where was the smooth, yielding, familiar mentality to go with this tactile form? The furies had seen to it that the curse—the curse in the house of Sweetscent, as he occasionally thought of it—had arrived full force; he faced a creature which on a physiological level was sexual perfection itself and on the mental level—

Someday the hardness, the inflexibility, would pervade her; the anatomical bounty would calcify. And then what? Already her voice contained it, different now from what he remembered of a few years back, even a few months. Poor Kathy, he thought. Because when the death-dealing powers of ice and cold reach your loins, your breasts and hips and buttocks as well as your heart—it was already deep in her heart, surely—then there will be no more woman. And you won't survive that. No matter what I or any man chooses to do.

"You were excluded," he said carefully, "because you're a pest."

Her eyes flew open wide; for an instant they filled with

alarm and simple wonder. She did not understand. Fleetingly, she had been brought back to the level of the merely human; the goading ancestral pressure in her had abated.

"Like you are now," he said. "So leave me alone; I want to fix myself some dinner."

"Get Phyllis Ackerman to fix it for you," Kathy said. The super-personal authority, the derision conjured up from the malformed crypto-wisdom of the ages, had returned. Almost psionically, with a woman's talent, she had intuited his slight romantic brush with Phyllis on the trip to Mars. And on Mars itself, during their overnight stay—

Calmly, he assumed that her heightened faculties could not genuinely ferret out that. Ignoring her, he began, in a methodical manner, to heat a frozen chicken dinner in the infrared oven, his back to his wife.

"Guess what I did," Kathy said. "While you were gone."

"You took on a lover."

"I tried a new hallucinogenic drug. I got it from Chris Plout; we had a jink session at his place and none other than the world-famous Marm Hastings was there. He made a pass at me while we were under the influence of the drug and it was—well, it was a pure vision."

"Did he," Eric said, setting a place for himself at the table.

"How I'd adore to bear his child," Kathy said.

" 'Adore to.' Christ, what decadent English." Ensnared, he turned to face her. "Did you and he—"

Kathy smiled. "Well, maybe it was a hallucination. But I don't think so. I'll tell you why. When I got home—"

"Spare me!" He found himself shaking.

In the living room the vidphone chimed.

Eric went to get it and when he lifted the receiver he saw on the small gray screen the features of a man named Captain Otto Dorf, a military adviser to Gino Molinari. Dorf had been at Wash-35, assisting in security measures; he was a thin-faced man with narrow, melancholy eyes, a man utterly dedicated to the protection of the Secretary. "Dr. Sweetscent?"

"Yes," Eric said. "But I haven't—"

"Will an hour be enough? We'd like to send a 'copter to pick you up at eight o'clock your time."

"An hour will do," Eric said. "I'll have my things packed and will be waiting in the lobby of my conapt building."

After he had rung off he returned to the kitchen.

Kathy said, "Oh my God. Oh Eric—can't we talk? Oh dear." She slumped at the table and buried her head in her arms. "I didn't do anything with Marm Hastings; he is handsome and I did take the drug, but—"

"Listen," he said, continuing to prepare his meal. "This was all arranged earlier today at Wash-35. Virgil wants me to do it. We had a long, quiet talk. Molinari's needs are at present greater than Virgil's. And actually I can still serve Virgil in org-trans situations but I'll be stationed at Cheyenne." He added, "I've been drafted; as of tomorrow I'm a medic in the UN military forces, attached to Secretary Molinari's staff. There's nothing I can do to change it; Molinari signed the decree to that effect last night."

"Why?" Terror-stricken, she gazed up at him.

"So I can get out of this. Before one of us—"

"I won't spend any more money."

"There's a war on. Men are being killed. Molinari is sick and he needs medical help. Whether you spend money or not—"

"But you *asked* for this job."

Presently he said, "I begged for it, as a matter of fact. I gave Virgil the greatest line of hot fizz ever strung together at one time in one place."

She had drawn herself together now; she had become poised. "What sort of pay will you receive?"

"Plenty. And I'll continue to draw a salary from TF&D, too."

"Is there a way I can come with you?"

"No." He had seen to that.

"I knew you'd dump me when you finally became a success—you've been trying to extricate yourself ever since we met." Kathy's eyes filled with tears. "Listen, Eric; I'm afraid that that drug I took is addictive. I'm terribly scared. You have no idea what it does; I think it comes from somewhere off Earth, maybe Lilistar. What if I keep taking it? What if because of your leaving—"

Bending, he picked her up in his arms. "You ought to keep away from those people; I've told you so goddam many times—" It was futile talking to her; he could see what lay ahead for both of them. Kathy had a weapon by which she could draw him back to her once more. Without him she would be destoyed by her involvement with Plout, Hastings, and company; leaving her would simply make her situation worse. The sickness that had entered them over the years could not be nullified by the act he had in mind, and only in the Martian babyland could he have imagined otherwise.

He carried her into the bedroom and set her gently on the bed.

"Ah," she said, and shut her eyes. "Oh Eric—" She sighed.

However, he couldn't. This, too. Miserably, he moved from her, sat on the edge of the bed. "I have to leave TF&D," he said presently. "And you have to accept it." He stroked her hair. "Molinari is cracking up; maybe I can't help him but at least I can try. See? That's the real—"

Kathy said, "You're lying."

"When? In what way?" He continued stroking her hair but it had become a mechanical action, without volition or desire.

"You would have made love to me just now, if that was why you were leaving." She rebuttoned her dress. "You don't care about me." Her voice held certitude; he recognized the drab, thin tone. Always this barrier, this impossibility of getting through. This time he did not waste his time trying; he simply went on stroking her, thinking, It'll be on my conscience, whatever happens to her. And she knows it, too. So she's absolved of the burden of responsibility, and that, for her, is the worst thing possible.

Too bad, he thought, I wasn't able to make love to her.

"My dinner's ready," he said, rising.

She sat up. "Eric, I'm going to pay you back for leaving me." She smoothed her dress. "You understand?"

"Yes," he said, and walked into the kitchen.

"I'll devote my life to it," Kathy said, from the bedroom. "Now I have a reason for living. It's wonderful to have a purpose at last; it's thrilling. After all these pointless ugly years with you. God, it's like being born all over again."

"Lots of luck," he said.

"Luck? I don't need luck; I need skill, and I think I have skill. I learned a lot during that episode under the effects of that drug. I wish I could tell you what it is; it's an incredible drug, Eric—it changes your entire perception of the universe and especially of other people. You don't ever view them the same again. You ought to try it. It would help you."

"Nothing," he said, "would help me."

His words, in his ears, sounded like an epitaph.

He had almost finished packing—and had long since eaten—when the doorbell of the conapt rang. It was Otto Dorf, already here with the military 'copter, and Eric soberly went to open the door for him.

Glancing about the conapt, Dorf said, "Did you have an opportunity to say goodbye to your wife, doctor?"

"Yes." He added, "She's gone now; I'm alone." He closed his suitcase and carried it and its companion to the door. "I'm ready." Dorf picked up one suitcase and together they walked to the elevator. "She did not take it very well," he remarked to Dorf as they presently descended.

"I'm unmarried, doctor," Dorf said. "I wouldn't know." His manner was correct and formal.

In the parked 'copter another man waited. He held out his hand as Eric ascended the rungs. "Doctor; it's good to meet you." The man, hidden in the shadows, explained, "I'm Harry Teagarden, chief of the Secretary's medical staff. I'm glad you're joining us; the Secretary hadn't informed me in advance but that's no matter—he invariably acts on impulse."

Eric shook hands with him, his mind still on Kathy. "Sweetscent."

"How did Molinari's condition strike you when you met him?"

"He seemed tired."

Teagarden said, "He's dying."

Glancing at him swiftly, Eric said, "From what? In this day and age, with artiforgs available—"

"I am familiar with current surgical techniques; believe me." Teagarden's tone was dry. "You saw how fatalistic he is. He wants to be punished, obviously, for leading us into this war." Teagarden was silent as the 'copter ascended into the night sky and then he continued, "Did it ever occur to you that Molinari *engineered* the losing of this war? That he wants to fail? I don't think even his most rabid political enemies have tried that idea out. The reason I'm saying this to you is that we don't have bales of time. Right at this moment Molinari is in Cheyenne suffering from a massive attack of his acute gastritis—or whatever you care to call it. From your holiday at Wash-35. He's flat on his back."

"Any internal bleeding?"

"Not yet. Or perhaps there has been and Molinari hasn't told us. With him it's possible; he's naturally secretive. Essentially he trusts nobody."

"And you're positive there's no malignancy?"

"We can't find any. But Molinari doesn't allow us to conduct as many tests as we'd like; he bolts. Too busy. Papers to sign, speeches to write, bills to present to the General Assembly. He tries to run everything singlehandedly. He can't seem to delegate authority and then when he does he sets up overlapping organizations that immediately compete—it's his way of protecting himself." Teagarden glanced curiously at Eric. "What did he say to you at Wash-35?"

"Not much." He did not intend to disclose the contents of their discussion. Molinari had beyond doubt meant it for his ears exclusively. In fact, Eric realized, that was the cardinal reason for his being brought to Cheyenne. He had something to offer Molinari that the other medics did not, a strange contribution for a doctor to be making . . . he wondered how Teagarden would react if he were to tell him.

Probably—and for good reason—Teagarden would have him put under arrest. And shot.

"I know why you're going to be with us," Teagarden said.

Eric grunted. "You do?" He doubted it.

"Molinari is simply following his instinctive bias, having us double-checked by infusing new blood into our staff. But no one objects; in fact we're grateful—we're all overworked. You know, of course, that the Secretary has a huge family, even larger than that of Virgil Ackerman, your paterfamilias-style former employer."

"I believe I've read it's three uncles, six cousins, an aunt, a sister, an elderly brother who—"

"And they're all in residence at Cheyenne," Teagarden said. "Constantly so. Hanging around him, trying to wangle little favors, better meals, quarters, servants—you get the pic. And—" He paused. "I should add there's a mistress."

That, Eric did not know. It had never been mentioned, even in the press hostile to the Secretary.

"Her name is Mary Reineke. He met her before his wife's death. On paper Mary's listed as a personal secretary. I like her. She's done a lot for him, both before and after his wife's death. Without her he probably wouldn't have survived. The 'Starmen loathe her . . . I don't quite know why. Perhaps I've missed out on some fact."

"How old is she?" The Secretary, Eric guessed, was in his late forties or early fifties.

"As young as its humanly possible to be. Prepare yourself, doctor." Teagarden chuckled. "When he met her she was in high school. Working in the late afternoons as a typist. Perhaps she handed him a document . . . nobody knows for sure, but they did meet over some routine business matter."

"Can his illness be discussed with her?"

"Absolutely. She's the one—the only one—who's been able to get him to take phenobarbital and, when we tried it, pathabamate. Phenobarb made him sleepy, he said, and path made his mouth dry. So of course he dropped them down a waste chute; he quit. Mary made him go back on. She's Italian. As he is. She can bawl him out in a way he remembers from his childhood, from his mama, perhaps . . . or his sister or aunt; they all bawl him out and he tolerates it, but he doesn't listen, except to Mary. She lives in a concealed apt in Cheyenne guarded by lines of Secret Service men—because of the 'Star people. Molinari dreads the day they'll—" Teagarden broke off.

"They'll what?"

"Kill her or maim her. Or weed out half her mental processes, turn her into a debrained vegetable; they've got a spectrum of techniques they can make use of. You didn't know our dealings with the ally were so rough at the top, did you?" Teagarden smiled. "It's a rough war. That's how Lilistar acts toward us, our superior ally beside which we're a flea. So imagine how the enemy, the reegs, would treat us if our defense line cracked and they managed to pour in."

For a time they rode in silence; no one cared to speak.

"What do you think would happen," Eric said finally, "if Molinari passed out of the pic?"

"Well, it would go one of two ways. Either we'd get someone more pro-Lilistar or we wouldn't. What other choices are there, and why do you ask? Do you believe we're going to lose our patient? If we do, doctor, we also lose our jobs and possibly our lives. Your one justification for existence—and mine—is the continual viable presence of one overweight, middle-aged Italian who lives in Cheyenne, Wyoming, with his enormous family and his eighteen-year-old mistress, who has stomach pains and enjoys eating a late-evening snack of batter-fried giant prawns with mustard and horseradish. I don't care what they told you or what you signed; you're not going to be inserting any more artiforgs into Virgil Ackerman for a long time; there won't be the opportunity *because keeping Gino Molinari alive is a full-time task.*" Teagarden seemed irritable and upset now; his voice, in the darkness of the 'copter cab, was jerky. "It's too much for me, Sweetscent. You won't have any other life but Molinari; he'll talk your ear off, deliver practice speeches to you on every topic on Earth—ask your opinion about everything from contraception to mushrooms—how to cook them—to God to what would you do *if,* and so forth. For a dictator—and you realize that's what he is, only we don't like to use the name—he's an anomaly. First of all he's probably the greatest political strategist alive; how else do you suppose he rose to be UN Secretary General? It took him twenty years, and fighting all the way; he dislodged every political opponent he met, from every country on Terra. Then he got mixed up with Lilistar. That's called foreign policy. On foreign policy the master strategist failed, because at that point a strange occlusion entered his mind. You know what it's called? Ignorance. Molinari spent all his time learning how to knee people in the groin, and with Freneksy that isn't called for. He could no more deal with Freneksy than you or I could—possibly worse."

"I see," Eric said.

"But Molinari went ahead anyhow. He bluffed. He signed the Pact of Peace which got us into the war. And here's where Molinari differs from all the fat, overblown, strutting dictators in the past. *He took the blame on his own shoulders;* he didn't fire a foreign minister here or shoot a policy adviser from the State there. *He* did it and he knows it. And it's killing him, by quarter inches, day in, day out. Starting from the gut. He loves Terra. He loves people, all of them, washed and unwashed; he loves his wretched pack of sponging relatives. He shoots people, arrests people, but he doesn't like it. Molinari is a complex man, doctor. So complex that—"

Dorf interrupted drily, "A mixture of Lincoln and Mussolini."

"He's a different person with everyone he meets," Teagarden continued. "Christ, he's done things so rotten, so goddam wicked that they'd make your hair stand on end. He's had to. Some of them will never be made public, even by his political foes. And he's suffered because of doing them. Did you ever know anyone who *really* accepted responsibility, guilt and blame, before? Do *you*? Does your wife?"

"Probably not," Eric admitted.

"If you or I ever really accepted the moral responsibility

for what we've done in our lifetime—we'd drop dead or go mad. Living creatures weren't made to understand what they do. Take the animals we've run over on the road, or the animals we eat. When I was a kid it was my monthly job to go out and poison rats. Did you ever watch a poisoned animal die? And not just one but scores of them, month after month. I don't *feel* it. The blame. The load. Fortunately it doesn't register—it can't, because if it did there'd be no way I could go on. And that's how the entire human race gets by. All but the Mole. As they call him." Teagarden added, " 'Lincoln and Mussolini.' I was thinking more of One Other, back about two thousand years."

"This is the first time," Eric said, "I ever heard anyone compare Gino Molinari to Christ. Even in his captive press."

"Perhaps," Teagarden said, "it's because I'm the first person you've ever talked to who's been around the Mole twenty-four hours a day."

ˋ "Don't tell Mary Reineke about your comparison," Dorf said. "She'll tell you he's a bastard. A pig in bed and at the table, a lewd middle-aged man with rape in his eye, who ought to be in jail. She tolerates him . . . because she's charitable." Dorf laughed sharply.

"No," Teagarden said, "that's not what Mary would say . . . except when she's sore, which is about a fourth of the time. I don't know what Mary Reineke would say; maybe she wouldn't even try. She just accepts him as he is; she tries to improve him, but even if he doesn't improve—and he won't—she loves him anyhow. Have you ever known that other kind of woman? Who saw *possibilities* in you? And with the right kind of help from her—"

"Yes," Eric said. He wished to see the subject changed; it made him think about Kathy. And he did not care to.

The 'copter droned on toward Cheyenne.

In bed alone Kathy lay half sleeping as morning sunlight ignited the variegated textures of her bedroom. All the colors so familiar to her in her married life with Eric now became distinguished one from another as the light advanced. Here, where she lived, Kathy had established potent spirits of the past, trapped within the concoctions of other periods: a lamp from early New England, a chest of drawers that was authentic bird's-eye maple, a Hepplewhite cabinet. . . . She lay with her eyes half open, aware of each object and all the connecting strands involved in her acquisition of them. Each was a triumph over a rival; some competing collector had failed, and it did not seem farfetched to regard this collection as a graveyard, with the ghosts of the defeated persisting in the vicinity. She did not mind their activity in her home life; after all, she was tougher than they.

"Eric," she said sleepily, "for chrissake get up and put on the coffee. And help me out of bed. Push or speak." She turned toward him, but no one was there. Instantly she sat up. Then she got up from the bed, walked barefoot to the closet for her robe, shivering.

She was putting on a light gray sweater, tugging it with difficulty over her head, when she realized that a man stood watching her. As she had dressed he had lounged in the doorway, making no move to announce his presence; he was enjoying the sight of her dressing, but now he shifted, stood upright and said, "Mrs. Sweetscent?" He was perhaps thirty, with a dark, rough muzzle and eyes which did not encourage her sense of well-being. In addition he wore a drab-gray uniform and she knew what he was: a member of Lilistar's secret police operating on Terra. It was the first time in her life that she had ever run into one of them.

"Yes," she said, almost soundlessly. She continued dressing, sitting on the bed to slip on her shoes, not taking her eyes from him. "I'm Kathy Sweetscent, Dr. Eric Sweetscent's wife, and if you don't—"

"Your husband is in Cheyenne."

"Is he?" She rose to her feet. "I have to fix breakfast; please let me by. And let me see your warrant for coming in here." She held out her hand, waiting.

"My warrant," the Lilistar grayman said, "calls for me to search this conapt for an illegal drug, JJ-180. Frohedadrine.

If you have any, hand it over and we'll go directly to the police barracks at Santa Monica." He consulted his notebook. "Last night in Tijuana at 45 Avila Street you used the drug orally in the company of—"

"May I call my attorney?"

"No."

"You mean I have no legal rights at all?"

"This is wartime."

She felt afraid. Nevertheless she managed to speak with reasonable calm. "May I call my employer and tell him I won't be in?"

The gray policeman nodded. So she went to the vidphone and dialed Virgil Ackerman at his home in San Fernando. Presently his birdlike, weathered face appeared, owlishly waking in a fuss of confusion. "Oh, Kathy. Where's the clock?" Virgil peered about.

Kathy said, "Help me, Mr. Ackerman. The Lilistar—" She ceased, because the grayman had broken the connection with a swift movement of his hand. Shrugging, she hung up.

"Mrs. Sweetscent," the grayman said, "I'd like to introduce Mr. Roger Corning to you." He made a motion and into the apartment, from the hall, came a 'Starman dressed in an ordinary business suit, a briefcase under his arm. "Mr. Corning, this is Kathy Sweetscent, Dr. Sweetscent's wife."

"Who are you?" Kathy said.

"Someone who can get you off the hook, dear," Corning said pleasantly. "May we sit down in your living room and discuss this?"

Going into the kitchen, she twisted the knob for soft-boiled eggs, toast, and coffee without cream. "There's no JJ-180 in this apt. Unless you put it here yourself during the night." The food was ready; she carried it to the table on its throwaway tray and seated herself. The smell of the coffee vanquished the remnants of fear and bewilderment in her; she felt capable again and not so intimidated.

Corning said, "We have a permanent photographic sequence of your evening at 45 Avila Street. From the moment you followed Bruce Himmel up the stairs and inside. Your initial words were, 'Hello, Bruce. It looks as if this is an all-TF&D—' "

"Not quite," Kathy said. "I called him *Brucie*. I always call him Brucie because he's so hebephrenic and dumb." She drank her coffee, her hand steady as it held the throw-away cup. "Does your photographic sequence prove what was in the capsules we took, Mr. Gorning?"

"Corning," he corrected good-naturedly. "No, Katherine, it doesn't. But the testimony of two of the other participants does. Or will when it's entered under oath before a military tribunal." He explained, "This falls outside the jurisdiction of your civilian courts. We ourselves will handle all details of the prosecution."

"Why is that?" she inquired.

"JJ-180 can only be acquired from the enemy. Therefore your use of it—and we can establish this before our tribunal—constitutes intercourse with the enemy. In time of war the tribunal's demand naturally would be death." To the gray-uniformed policeman Corning said, "Do you have Mr. Plout's deposition with you?"

"It's in the 'copter." The grayman started toward the door.

"I thought there was something subhuman about Chris Plout," Kathy said. "Now I'm meditating about the others . . . who else last night had a subhuman quality? Hastings? No. Simon Ild? No, he—"

"All this can be avoided," Corning said.

"But I don't want to avoid it," Kathy said. "Mr. Ackerman heard me on the vidphone; TF&D will send an attorney. Mr. Ackerman is a friend of Secretary Molinari; I don't think—"

"We can kill you, Kathy," Corning said. "By nightfall, The tribunal can meet this morning; it's all arranged."

After a time—she had ceased eating—Kathy said, "Why? I'm that important? What is there in JJ-180? I—" She hesitated. "What I tried last night didn't do so very much." All at once she wished like hell that Eric had not left. This wouldn't have happened with him here, she realized. They would have been afraid.

Soundlessly, she began to cry; she sat hunched over at her plate, tears sliding down her cheeks and dropping to disappear. She did not even try to cover her face; she put her hand to her forehead, rested leaning against her arm, saying nothing. ——it, she thought.

"Your position," Corning said, "is serious but not hopeless; there's a difference. We can work out something . . . that's why I'm here. Stop crying and sit up straight and listen to me and I'll try to explain." He unzipped his briefcase.

"I know," Kathy said. "You want me to spy on Marm Hastings. You're after him because he advocated signing a separate peace with the reegs that time on TV. Jesus, you've infiltrated this whole planet. Nobody's safe." She got up, groaned with despair, went to the bedroom for a handkerchief, still sniffling.

"Would you watch Hastings for us?" Corning said, when she returned.

"No." She shook her head. Better to be dead, she thought.

"It's not Hastings," the uniformed Lilistar policeman said.

Corning said, "We want your husband. We'd like you to follow him to Cheyenne and take up where you left off. Bed and board, I think the Terran phrase is. As soon as it possibly can be arranged."

She stared at him. "I can't."

"Why can't you?"

"We broke up. He left me." She could not understand why, if they knew everything else, they didn't know that.

"Resolutions of that type in a marriage," Corning said, as if speaking with the weary wisdom of an infinity of ages, "can always be reduced to the status of a temporary misunderstanding. We'll take you to one of our psychologists—we have several excellent ones in residence here on this planet—and he'll brief you on the techniques to use in healing this rift with Eric. Don't worry, Kathy; we know what went on here last night. Actually it works out to our advantage; it gives us an opportunity to talk with you alone."

"No." She shook her head. "We'll never be back together. I don't *want* to be with Eric. No psychologist, even one of yours, can change that. I hate Eric and I hate all this crap you're mixed up in. I hate you 'Starmen, and everyone on Terra feels the same way—I wish you'd get off the planet, I wish we'd never gotten into the war." Impotently, with frenzy, she glared at him.

"Cool off, Kathy." Corning remained unruffled.

"God, I wish Virgil were here; he's not afraid of you—he's one of the few people on Terra—"

"No one on Terra," Corning said absently, "has that status. It's time you faced reality; we could, you know, take you to Lilistar, instead of killing you . . . had you thought about that, Kathy?"

"Oh God." She shuddered. Don't take me to Lilistar, she said to herself, praying in silence. At least let me stay here on Terra with people I know. I'll go back to Eric; I'll *beg* him to take me back. "Listen," she said aloud. "I'm not worrying about Eric. It isn't what you might do to him that frightens me." It's myself, she thought.

"We know that, Kathy," Corning said, nodding. "So this really ought to please you, when you examine it without distracting emotion. By the way . . ." Dipping into the briefcase, Corning brought out a handful of capsules; he laid one on the kitchen table and the capsule rolled off and fell to the floor. "No offense meant, Kathy, but—" He shrugged. "It is addictive. From even one exposure, such as you indulged yourself in at 45 Avila Street last night. And Chris Plout isn't going to get you any more." Picking up the capsule of JJ-180 which had fallen to the kitchen floor, he held it out to Kathy.

"It couldn't be," she said faintly, declining. "After just one try. I've taken dozens of drugs before and never—" She regarded him then. "You bastards," she said. "I don't believe it and anyhow, even if it is true, I can get unaddicted—there're clinics."

"Not for JJ-180." Returning the capsule to his briefcase, Corning added casually, "*We* can free you of your addiction, not here but at a clinic in our own system . . . perhaps later we can arrange this. Or you can stay on it and we can supply you for the rest of your life. Which won't be long."

"Even to break a drug habit," Kathy said, "I wouldn't go to Lilistar. I'll go to the reegs; it's their drug—you said so. They must know more about it than you do if they invented it." Turning her back to Corning, she walked to the living room closet and got her coat. "I'm going to work. Goodbye." She opened the door to the hall. Neither 'Starman made a move to halt her.

It must be true, then, she thought. JJ-180 must be as addictive as they say. I haven't got a goddam chance; they know it and I know it. I have to cooperate with them or try to escape all the way across to the reeg lines, where it originates, and even then I'd still be addicted; I wouldn't have gained anything. And the reegs would probably kill me.

Corning said, "Take my card, Kathy." He walked to her, extending the small white square. "When you find yourself requiring the drug, must at any cost have it—" He dropped the card into the breast pocket of her coat. "Come and see me. We'll be expecting you, dear; we'll see you're supplied." He added, as an afterthought, "Of course it's addictive, Kathy; that's why we put you on it." He smiled at her.

Shutting the door after her, Kathy made her way blindly to the elevator, numbed now to the point where she felt nothing, not even fear. Only a vague emptiness inside her, the vacuum left by the extinction of hope, of the ability even to conceive a possibility of escape.

But Virgil Ackerman could help me, she said to herself as she entered the elevator and touched the button. I'll go to him; he'll know exactly what I should do. I'll never work with the 'Starmen, addiction or not; I won't cooperate with them about Eric.

But she knew, before long, that she would.

6

It was during the early afternoon, as she sat in her office at TF&D arranging for the purchase of a 1935 artifact, a reasonably unworn Decca record of the Andrews Sisters singing "Bei Mir Bist Du Schön," that Kathy Sweetscent felt the first withdrawal symptoms.

Her hands became oddly heavy.

With extreme care she put the delicate record down. And there was a physiognomic alteration in the objects around her. While at 45 Avila Street, under the influence of JJ-180, she had experienced the world as consisting of airy, penetrable, and benign entities, like so many bubbles; she had found herself able—at least in hallucination—to pass through them at will. Now, in the familiar environment of her office, she experienced a transformation of reality along the lines of an ominous progression: ordinary things, whichever way she looked, seemed to be gaining density. They were no longer susceptible to being moved or changed, affected in any way, by her.

And, from another viewpoint, she simultaneously experienced the oppressive change as taking place within her own body. From either standpoint the ratio between herself, her physical powers, and the outside world had altered for the worst; she experienced herself as growing progressively more and more helpless in the literal physical sense—there was, with each passing moment, less which she could do. The ten-inch Decca record, for instance. It lay within touch of her fingers, but suppose she reached for it? The record would evade her. Her hand, clumsy with unnatural weight, hobbled by the internal gathering of density, would crush or break the record; the concept of performing intricate, skillful actions in reference to the record seemed out of the question. Refinements of motion were no longer a property belonging to her; only gross, sinking mass remained.

Wisely, she realized that this told her something about JJ-180; it lay in the class of thalamic stimulants. And now, in this withdrawal period, she was suffereing a deprivation of thalamic energy; these changes, experienced as taking place in the outside world and in her body, were in actuality minute alterations of the metabolism of her brain. But—

This knowledge did not help her. For these changes in herself and her world were not beliefs; they were authentic experiences, reported by the normal sensory channels, imposed on her consciousness against her will. As stimuli they could not be avoided. And—the alteration of the world's physiognomy continued; the end was not in sight. In panic she thought, How far will this go? How much worse can it get? Certainly not much worse . . . the impenetrability of even the smallest objects around her now seemed almost infinite; she sat rigidly, unable to move, incapable of thrusting her great body into any new relationship with the crushingly heavy objects that surrounded her and seemed to be pressing nearer and nearer.

And, even as the objects in her office settled massively against her, they became, on another level, remote; they receded in a meaningful, terrifying fashion. They were losing, she realized, their animation, their—so to speak—working souls. The animae which inhabited them were departing as her powers of psychological projection deteriorated. The objects had lost their heritage of the familiar; by degrees they became cold, remote, and—hostile. Into the vacuum left by the decline in her relatedness to them the things surrounding

her achieved their original isolation from the taming forces
which normally emanated from the human mind; they became raw, abrupt, with jagged edges capable of cutting, gash-
ing, inflicting fatal wounds. She did not dare stir. Death, in
potentiality, lay inherent in every object; even the hand-
wrought brass ash tray on her desk had become irregular,
and in its lack of symmetry it obtained projecting planes,
shot out surfaces which, like spines, could tear her open if
she was stupid enough to come near.

The combox on her desk buzzed. Lucile Sharp, Virgil Ackerman's secretary, said, "Mrs. Sweetscent, Mr. Ackerman
would like to see you in his office. I'd suggest you bring along
the new 'Bei Mir Bist Du Schön' record you purchased today;
he expressed interest in it."

"Yes," Kathy said, and the effort almost buried her; she
ceased breathing and sat with her rib-cage inert, the basic
physiological processes slowing under the pressure, dying by
degrees. And then, somehow, she breathed one breath; she
filled her lungs and then exhaled raggedly, noisily. For the
moment she had escaped. But it was all worsening. What
next? She rose to her feet, stood. So this is how it feels to
be hooked on JJ-180, she thought. She managed to pick up
the Decca record. Its dark edges were like knife blades sawing
into her hands as she carried it across the office to the door.
Its hostility toward her, its inanimate and yet ferocious desire
to inflict destruction on her, became overwhelming; she
cringed from the disc's touch.

And dropped it.

The record lay on the thick carpet, apparently unbroken.
But how to pick it up once more? How to drag it loose from
the nape, the backdrop, surrounding it? Because the record
no longer seemed separate; it had fused. With the carpet,
the floor, the walls, and now everything in the office, it presented a single indivisible, unchangeable surface, without
rupture. No one could come or go within this cubelike spa-
ciality; every place was already filled, complete—nothing
could change because everything was present already.

My God, Kathy thought as she stood gazing down at the

record by her feet. I can't free myself; I'm going to remain here, and they'll find me like this and know something's terribly wrong. This is catalepsy!

She was still standing there when the office door opened and Jonas Ackerman, briskly, with a jovial expression on his smooth, youthful face, entered, strode up to her, saw the record, bent unhinderedly down and gently lifted it up and placed it in her outstretched hands.

"Jonas," she said in a slow, thickened voice, "I—need medical help. I'm sick."

"Sick how?" He stared at her with concern, his face twisted up, wriggling, she thought, like nests of snakes. His emotion overpowered her; it was a sickening, fetid force. "My God," Jonas said, "what a time you picked—Eric's not here today, he's in Cheyenne, and we haven't got the new man that's replacing him yet. But I could drive you to the Tijuana Government Clinic. What is it?" He gripped her arm, pinching her flesh. "I think you're just blue because Eric's gone."

Take me upstairs," she managed to say. "To Virgil."

"Boy, you *do* sound awful," Jonas said. "Yes, I'll be glad to get you upstairs to the old man; maybe he'll know what to do." He guided her toward the office door. "Maybe I better take that record; you look like you're about to drop it again."

It could not have taken more than two minutes to reach Virgil Ackerman's office and yet to her the ordeal consumed a vast interval. When she found herself facing Virgil at last she was exhausted; she panted for breath, unable to speak. It was just too goddam much for her.

Eyeing her curiously, and then with alarm, Virgil said in his thin, penetrating voice, "Kathy, you better go home today; fix yourself up with an armful of women-type magazines and a drink, propped up in bed—"

"Leave me alone," she heard herself say. "Christ," she said, then, in despair. "*Don't* leave me alone, Mr. Ackerman; please!"

"Well, make up your mind," Virgil said, still scrutinizing her. "I can see that Eric's leaving here and going to Cheyenne to—"

"No," she said. "I'm okay." Now it had worn off a little; she felt as if she had imbibed some strength from him, perhaps because he had so much. "Here's a fine item for Wash-35." She turned to Jonas for the record. "It was one of the most popular tunes of the times. This and 'The Music Goes Round and Round.' " Taking the record, she placed it before him on his big desk. I'm not going to die, she thought; I'm going to get through this and recover my health. "I'll tell you what else I have a line on, Mr. Ackerman." She seated herself in a chair by the desk, wanting to conserve what energy she had. "A private recording which someone made, at the time, of Alexander Woollcott on his program, 'The Town Crier.' So the next time we're up at Wash-35 we'll be able to listen to Woollcott's actual voice. And not an imitation. As we're doing."

" 'The Town Crier'!" Virgil exclaimed in childish joy. "My favorite program!"

"I'm reasonably sure I can get it," Kathy said. "Of course, until I actually pay over the money there could still be a hitch. I have to fly out to Boston to make the final arrangements; the recording is there, in the possession of a rather shrewd spinster-lady named Edith B. Scruggs. It was made on a Packard-Bell Phon-o-cord, she tells me in her correspondence."

"Kathy," Virgil Ackerman said, "if you can actually turn up an authentic recording of the voice of Alexander Woollcott—I'm going to raise your salary, so help me God. Mrs. Sweetscent, sweetheart, I'm in love with you because of what you do for me. Was Woollcott's radio program over WMAL or WJSV? Research that for me, will you? Go through those '35 copies of the *Washington Post*—and by the way, that reminds me. That *American Weekly* with the article on the Sargasso Sea. I think we'll finally decide to exclude that from Wash-35 because when I was a boy my parents didn't take the Hearst papers; I only saw it when I—"

"Just a moment, Mr. Ackerman," Kathy said, raising her hand.

He cocked his head expectantly. "Yes, Kathy?"

"What if I went to Cheyenne and joined Eric?"

"But—" Virgil bleated, gesturing. "I need you!"

"For a while," she said. Maybe that will be enough, she thought. They might not demand any more. "You let *him* go," she said, "and he keeps you alive; he's a lot more vital than I am."

"But Molinari needs him. And he doesn't need you; he has no babyland he's building; he's not a bit interested in the past—he's full of gas about the future, like an adolescent." Virgil looked stricken. "I can't spare you, Kathy; losing Eric was bad enough but the deal in his case is that I can send for him any time I get into difficulty. I *had* to let him go; it was the patriotic thing, in wartime—I didn't want to; in fact I'm scared as hell without him. But not you." His tone became plaintive. "No, that's too much. Eric swore to me when we were at Wash-35 that you wouldn't want to go with him." He shot a mute, appealing glance at Jonas. "Make her stay, Jonas."

Rubbing his chin thoughtfully, Jonas said to her, "You don't love Eric, Kathy. I've talked to you and to him; you both tell me your domestic woes. You're as far apart from each other as it's possible to be and not commit an outright crime . . . I don't get this."

"I believed that," she said, "while he was here. But I kidded myself. Now I know better, and I'm sure he feels the same way."

"Are you sure?" Jonas said acutely. "Call him." He indicated the vidphone on Virgil's desk. "See what he says. Frankly I think you're better off separated, and I have no doubt Eric knows it."

Kathy said, "May I be excused to go? I want to get back down to my office." She felt sick at her stomach and achingly frightened. Her damaged, drug-addicted body yearned for relief and in its thrashings it directed her actions; it was compelling her to follow Eric to Cheyenne. Despite what the Ackermans said. She could not stop, and even now in her confusion she could read the future; she could not escape the drug JJ-180—the 'Starmen had been correct. She would have to go back to them, follow up on the card that Corning had given her. God, she thought, if I only could tell Virgil. I have to tell someone.

And then she thought, I'll tell Eric. He's a doctor; he'll be able to help me. I'll go to Cheyenne for that, *not for them.*

"Will you do me one favor?" Jonas Ackerman was saying to her. "For heaven's sake, Kathy; listen." Again he squeezed her arm.

"I'm listening," she said with irritation. "And let go." She tugged her arm away, stepped back from him, feeling rage. "Don't treat me like this; I can't stand it." She glared at him.

Carefully, in a deliberately calm voice, Jonas said to her, "We'll let you follow your husband to Cheyenne, Kathy, *if* you promise to wait twenty-four hours before you go."

"Why?" She could not understand.

"So that this initial period of shock at the separation has a chance to wear off," Jonas said. "I'm hoping that in twenty-four hours you'll see your way clear to changing your mind. And meanwhile—" He glanced at Virgil; the old man nodded in agreement. "I'll stay with you," Jonas said to her. "All day and all night, if necessary."

Appalled, she said, "Like hell you will. I won't—"

"I know there's something wrong with you," Jonas said quietly. "It's obvious. I don't think you should be left alone. I'm making it my responsibility to see that nothing happens to you." He added in a low voice, "You're too valuable to us to do something terminal." Again, and this time with harsh firmness, he took hold of her arm. "Come on; let's go downstairs to your office—it'll do you good to get wrapped up in your work, and I'll just sit quietly, not interfering. After work tonight I'll fly you up to L.A. to Spingler's for dinner; I know you like sea food." He guided her toward the door of the office.

She thought, *I'll get away.* You're not that smart, Jonas; sometime today, perhaps tonight, I'll lose you and go to Cheyenne. Or rather, she thought with nausea and an upsurge of her former terror, I'll lose you, dump you, slip away from you in the labyrinth that's the night city of Tijuana, where all kinds of things, some of them terrible, some of them wonderful and full of beauty, happen. Tijuana will be too much for you. It's almost too much for me. And I know it fairly well; I've spent so much of my time, my life, in Tijuana at night.

And look how it's worked out, she thought bitterly. I wanted to find something pure and mystical in life and instead I wound up spliced to people who hate us, who dominate our race. Our ally, she thought. We ought to be fighting them; it's clear to me now. If I ever get to see Molinari alone at Cheyenne—and maybe I will—I'll tell him that, tell him we have the wrong ally and the wrong enemy.

"Mr. Ackerman," she said, turning urgently to Virgil. "I have to go to Cheyenne to tell the Secretary something. It affects all of us; it has to do with the war effort."

Virgil Ackerman said drily, "Tell me and I'll tell him. There's a better chance that way; you'll never get to see him . . . not unless you're one of his bambinos or cousins."

"That's it," she said. "I'm his child." It made perfect sense to her; all of them on Terra were children of the UN Secretary. And they had been expecting their father to lead them to safety. But somehow he had failed.

Unresistingly, she followed Jonas Ackerman. "I know what you're doing," she said to him. "You're using this opportunity, with Eric away and me in this terrible state, to take sexual advantage of me."

Jonas laughed. "Well, we'll see." His laugh, to her, did not sound guilty; it sounded sleekly confident.

"Yes," she agreed, thinking of the 'Star policeman Corning. "We'll see how lucky you are in making out with me. Personally I wouldn't bet on it." She did not bother to remove his big, determined hand from her shoulder; it would only reappear.

"You know," Jonas said, "if I didn't know better, I'd say from the way you've been acting that you're on a substance which we call JJ-180." He added, "But you couldn't be because there's no way you could get hold of it."

Staring at him, Kathy said, "What—" She couldn't go on.

"It's a drug," Jonas said. "Developed by one of our subsidiaries."

"It wasn't developed by the reegs?"

"Frohedadrine, or JJ-180, was developed in Detroit, last year, by a firm which TF&D controls called Hazeltine Corporation. It's a major weapon in the war—or will be when it's in production, which will be later this year."

"Because," she said numbly, "it's so addictive?"

"Hell no. Many drugs are addictive, starting with the opium derivatives. Because of the nature of the hallucinations it causes its users." He explained, "It's hallucinogenic, as LSD was."

Kathy said, "Tell me about the hallucinations."

"I can't; that's classified military information."

Laughing sharply, she said, "Oh God—so the only way I could find out would be to take it."

"How can you take it? It's not available, and even when it's in production we wouldn't conceivably under any circumstances allow our own population to use it—the stuff's toxic!" He glared at her. "Don't even talk about using it; every test animal to which it was administered died. Forget I even mentioned it; I thought Eric had probably told you about it—I shouldn't have brought it up, but you have been acting strangely; it made me think of JJ-180 because I'm so scared— we all are—that someone, some way, will get hold of it on the domestic market, one of our own people."

Kathy said, "Let's hope that never happens." She felt like laughing, still; the whole thing was insane. The 'Starmen had obtained the drug on Terra but pretended to have gotten it from the reegs. Poor Terra, she thought. We can't even get credit for this, for this noxious, destructive chemical which destroys the mind—as Jonas says, a potent weapon of war. And who's using it? Our ally. And on whom? On us. The irony is complete; it forms a circle. Certainly cosmic justice that a Terran should be one of the first to become addicted to it.

Frowning, Jonas said, "You asked if JJ-180 hadn't been developed by the enemy; that suggests you have heard of it.

So Eric did mention it to you. It's all right; only knowledge of its properties is classified, not its existence. The reegs know we've been experimenting with drug warfare for decades, back into the twentieth century. It's one of Terra's specialties.'' He chuckled.

"Maybe we'll win after all," Kathy said. "That ought to cheer up Gino Molinari. Perhaps he'll be able to stay in office with the assistance of a few new miracle weapons. Is he counting on this? Does he know?''

"Of course Molinari knows; Hazeltine has kept him informed at every stage of development. But for chrissake don't go and—''

"I won't get you in trouble," Kathy said. I think I'll get you addicted to JJ-180, she said to herself. That's what you deserve; everyone who helped develop it, who knows about it. Stay with me night and day during the next twenty-four hours, she thought. Eat with me, go to bed with me, and by the time it's over you'll be earmarked for death just as I am. And then, she thought, maybe I can get Eric on it. Him most of all.

I'll carry it with me to Cheyenne, Kathy decided. Infect everyone there, the Mole and his entourage. And for a good reason.

They'll be forced to discover a method of breaking the addiction. Their own lives will depend on it, not just mine. And for me alone it wouldn't be worth seeking; even Eric wouldn't have tried, and certainly Corning and his people don't care—no one cares about me, when you get right down to it.

This was probably not at all what Corning and those above him had in mind in sending her to Cheyenne. But that was just too bad; this was what she intended to do.

"It'll go in their water supply," Jonas was explaining. "The Reegs—they maintain huge central water sources, as Mars did once. JJ-180 will be introduced there, carried throughout their planet. I admit it sounds desperate on our part, a—you know. A tour de force. But actually it's very rational and reasonable.''

"I'm not criticizing it at all," Kathy said. "In fact I think the idea sounds brilliant."

The elevator arrived; they entered and descended.

"Look what the ordinary citizen of Terra doesn't know," Kathy said. "He goes merrily on about his daily life . . . it would never occur to him that his government has developed a drug that in one exposure turns you into a—how would you put it, Jonas? Something less than a robant? Certainly less than human. I wonder where you would place it on the evolutionary ladder."

"I never told you that one exposure to JJ-180 meant addiction," Jonas said. "Eric must have told you that."

"With the lizards of the Jurassic Period," Kathy decided. "Things with tiny brains and immense tails. Creatures with almost no mentalities; just reflex machines acting out the externals of living, going through the motions but not actually there. Right?"

"Well," Jonas said, "it's reegs that'll be receiving the drug; I wouldn't waste any tears on reegs."

"I'd waste a tear on anything," Kathy said, "that got hooked by JJ-180. I hate it; I wish—" She broke off. "Don't mind me; I'm just upset by Eric's leaving. I'll be okay." To herself she wondered when she would have an opportunity to look for Corning. And get more capsules of the drug. It was clear now that she had become an addict. By now she had to face it.

She felt only resignation.

At noon, in the neat, modern, but excessively small conapt provided him by the mystifying workings of the higher governmental authorities of Cheyenne, Dr. Eric Sweetscent finished reading the medical charts on his new patient—referred to throughout the enormous body of writings merely as "Mr. Brown." Mr. Brown, he reflected as he locked the folio back in its unbreakable plastic box, is a sick man, but his sickness simply could not be diagnosed, at least in the customary way. Because—and this was the odd thing, for which Teagarden had not prepared him—the patient had shown, over the years, symptoms of major organic diseases, symptoms not associated with psychosomatic disorders. There had been at one time a malignancy in the liver which had metastasized—and yet Mr. Brown had not died. And the malignancy had gone away. Anyhow it was not there now; tests during the last two years proved that. An exploratory operation had even been performed, finally, and Mr. Brown's liver had not even shown the degeneracy anticipated in a man of his age.

It was the liver of a youth of nineteen or twenty.

And this oddity had been observed in other organs subjected to acute examination. But Mr. Brown was failing in his overall powers; palpably, he was in the process of declining—he looked considerably older than his chronological age, and the aura around him was one of ill health. It was as if his body on a purely physiological level were growing younger while his essence, his total psychobiological *Gestalt*, aged naturally—in fact failed conspicuously.

Whatever physiological force it was that maintained him organically, Mr. Brown was not receiving any benefit therefrom, except of course that he had not died of the malignant tumor in his liver or the earlier one detected in his spleen, or the surely fatal cancer of the prostate gland which had gone undetected during his third decade.

Mr. Brown was alive—but just barely so. Throughout, his body was overworked and in a state of deterioration; take his circulatory system, for instance. Brown's blood pressure was 220—despite vasodilators administered orally; already his eyesight had been materially affected. And yet, Eric reflected, Brown would undoubtedly surmount this as he had every other ailment; one day it would simply go away, even though he refused to stay on the prescribed diet and did not respond to reserpine.

The outstanding fact was simply that Mr. Brown had had at one time or another almost every serious disease known, from infarcts in his lungs to hepatitis. He was a perambulating symposium of illness, never well, never functioning properly; at any given time some vital portion of his body was affected. And then—

In some fashion he had cured himself. And without the use of artiforgs. It was as if Brown practiced some folk-style, homeopathic medicine, some idiotic herbal remedy which he had never disclosed to his attending physicians. And probably never would.

Brown needed to be sick. His hypochondriasis was real; he did not merely have hysterical symptoms—he had true diseases which usually turned the patient into a terminal case. If this was hysteria, a variety of purely psychological complaint, Eric had never run across it before. And yet, despite this, Eric had the intuition that all these illnesses had existed for a reason; they were engendered from the complexity, the undisclosed depths, of Mr. Brown's psyche.

Three times in his life Mr. Brown had given himself cancer. But how? And—why?

Perhaps it arose from his death wish. And each time, Mr. Brown halted at the brink, pulled himself back. He needed to be sick—but not to die. The suicide wish, then, was spurious.

This was important to know. If it was so, Mr. Brown would fight to survive—would fight against the very thing he had hired Eric to bring about.

Therefore Mr. Brown would be an exceedingly difficult patient. To say the least. And all this—beyond doubt—functioned at an unconscious level; Mr. Brown was certainly unaware of his twin, opposing drives.

The door chimes of the conapt sounded. He went to answer—and found himself facing an official-looking individual in a natty business suit. Producing identification, the man explained, "Secret Service, Dr. Sweetscent. Secretary Molinari needs you; he's in a good deal of pain so we'd better hurry."

"Of course." Eric dashed to the closet for his coat; a moment later he and the Secret Service man were hiking toward the parked wheel. "More abdominal pains?" Eric asked.

"Now the pains seem to have shifted over to his left side," the Secret Service man said as he piloted the wheel out into traffic. "In the region of his heart."

"He didn't describe them as feeling as if a great hand was pressing down on him, did he?"

"No, he's just lying there groaning. And asking for you." The Secret Service man seemed to take it matter-of-factly; evidently for him this was old and familiar. The Secretary, after all, was always sick.

Presently they had reached the UN White House and Eric was descending by in-track. If only I could install an artiforg, he reflected. It would end all this—

But it was clear to him, now that he had read the file, why Molinari refused artiforg transplant on principle. If he accepted a transplant he would recover; the ambiguity of his existence—hovering between illness and health—would cease. His twin drives would be resolved in favor of health. Hence the delicate psychic dynamism would be upset and Molinari would be delivered over to one of the two forces striving for mastery within him. And this he could not afford to do.

"This way, doctor." The Secret Service man led him down a corridor, to a door at which several uniformed police stood. They stepped aside and Eric entered.

In the center of the room, in a vast rumpled bed, lay Gino Molinari, on his back, watching a television set fixed to the ceiling. "I'm dying, doctor," Molinari said, turning his head. "I think these pains are coming from my heart now. It probably was my heart all the time." His face, enlarged and florid, shone with sweat.

Eric said, "We'll run an EKG on you."

"No, I had that, about ten minutes ago; it showed nothing. My illness is too goddam subtle for your instruments to detect. That doesn't mean it's not there. I've heard of people who've had massive coronaries and have taken EKGs and nothing showed up; isn't that a fact? Listen, doctor. I know something that you don't. You wonder why I have these pains. Our ally—our partner in this war. They've got a master plan which includes seizing Tijuana Fur & Dye; they showed me the document—they're that confident. They've got an agent planted in your firm already. But I'm telling you in case I die suddenly from this ailment; I could go any minute, you know that."

"Did you tell Virgil Ackerman?" Eric asked.

"I started to but—Christ, how can you tell an old man something like that? He doesn't understand what sort of things go on in an all-out war; this is nothing, this seizing of Terra's major industries. This is probably only the beginning."

"Now that I know," Eric said, "I feel I should tell Virgil."

"Okay, tell him," Molinari grated. "Maybe you can find a way. I was going to when we were at Wash-35 but—" He rolled in pain. "Do something for me, doctor; this is killing me!"

Eric gave him an intravenous injection of morprocaine and the UN Secretary quieted.

"You just don't know," Molinari mumbled in a lulled, relaxed voice, "what I'm up against with these 'Starmen. I did my best to keep them off us, doctor." He added, "I don't feel the pain now; what you did seems to have taken care of it."

Eric asked, "When are they going ahead with seizing TF&D? Soon?"

"A few days. Week. Elastic schedule. It makes a drug they're interested in . . . you probably don't know. Neither do I. In fact I don't know anything, doctor; that's the whole secret of my situation. Nobody tells me a thing. Even you; what's wrong with me, for instance—you won't tell me that, I bet."

To one of the watching Secret Service men Eric said, "Where can I find a vidphone booth?"

"Don't go off," Molinari said, from his bed, half rising. "The pain would come back right away; I can tell. What I want you to do is get Mary Reineke here; I need to talk to her, now that I'm feeling better. See, doctor, I haven't told her about it, about how sick I am. And don't you, either; she needs to hold an idealized image of me. Women are like that; to love a man they have to look up to him, glorify him. See?"

"But when she sees you lying in bed doesn't she think—"

"Oh, she knows I'm sick; she just doesn't know that it's fatal. You see?"

Eric said, "I promise I won't tell her it's fatal."

"Is it?" Molinari's eyes flew open in alarm.

"Not to my knowledge," Eric said. Cautiously he added, "Anyhow, I learn from your file that you've survived several customarily fatal illnesses, including cancer of—"

"I don't want to talk about it. I get depressed when I'm reminded how many times I've had cancer."

"I should think—"

"That it would elate me that I recovered? No, *because maybe the next time I'm not going to recover.* I mean, sooner or later it'll get me, and before my job is done. And what'll happen to Terra then? You figure it out; you make an educated guess."

"I'll go and contact Miss Reineke for you," Eric said, and started toward the door of the room. A Secret Service man detached himself to lead the way to the vidphone.

Outside in the corridor the Secret Service man said in a low voice, "Doctor, there's an illness on level three, one of the White House cooks passed out about an hour ago; Dr. Teagarden's with him and wants you for a confab."

"Certainly," Eric said. "I'll look in on him before I make my phone call." He followed the Secret Service man to the elevator.

In the White House dispensary he found Dr. Teagarden. "I needed you," Teagarden said at once, "because you're an artiforg man; this is a clear case of angina pectoris and we're going to need an org-trans right away. I assume you brought at least one heart with you."

"Yes," Eric murmured. "Had there been a history of heart trouble with this patient?"

"Not until two weeks ago," Teagarden said. "When he had a mild attack. Then of course dorminyl was administered, twice daily. And he seemed to recover. But now—"

"What's the relationship between this man's angina and the Secretary's pain?"

" 'Relationship'? Is there one?"

"Doesn't it seem strange? Both men develop severe abdominal pains at about the same time—"

"But in the case of McNeil, here," Teagarden said, leading Eric to the bed, "the diagnosis is unmistakable. Whereas with Secretary Molinari no such diagnosis as angina can be made; the symptoms are not there. So I don't see the relationship." Teagarden added, "Anyhow this is a very tense place, doctor, people get sick here regularly."

"It still seems—"

"In any case," Teagarden said, "the problem is simply a technical one; transplant the fresh heart and that's that."

"Too bad we can't do the same upstairs." Eric bent over the cot on which the patient McNeil lay. So this was the man who had the ailment which Molinari imagined *he* had. Which came first? Eric wondered. McNeil or Gino Molinari? Which is cause and which effect—assuming that such a relationship exists, and that is a mighty tenuous assumption at best. As Teagarden points out.

But it would be interesting to know, for instance, if anyone in the vicinity had cancer of the prostate gland when Gino had it . . . and the other cancers, infarcts, hepatitis, and whatever else as well.

It might be worth checking the medical records of the White House staff, he conjectured.

"Need me to assist in the org-trans?" Teagarden asked. "If not I'll go upstairs to the Secretary. There's a White House nurse who can help you; she was here a minute ago."

"I don't need you. What I'd like is a list of all the current complaints among members of the local entourage; everyone who's in physical contact with Molinari from day to day, whether these people are staff members or frequent official visitors—whatever their posts are. Can that be done?"

"With the staff, yes," Teagarden said. "But not with visitors; we have no medical files on them. Obviously." He eyed Eric.

"I have a feeling," Eric said, "that the moment a fresh heart is transplanted to McNeil here the Secretary's pains will go away. And later records will show that as of this date the Secretary recovered from severe angina pectoris."

Teagarden's expression fused over, became opaque. "Well," he said, and shrugged. "Metaphysics, along with surgery. We've obtained a rare combination in you, doctor."

"Would you say that Molinari is empathic enough to develop every ailment suffered by every person around him? And I don't mean just hysterically; I mean he genuinely experiences it. *Gets* it."

"No such empathic faculty," Teagarden said, "if you can bring yourself to dignify it by calling it a faculty, is known to exist."

"But you've seen the file," Eric pointed out quietly. He opened his instrument case and began to assemble the robant, self-guiding tools which he would need for the transplant of the artificial heart.

7

After the operation—it required only half an hour's labor on his part—Eric Sweetscent, accompanied by two Secret Service men, set off for the apartment of Mary Reineke.

"She's dumb," the man to his left said, gratuitously.

The other Secret Service man, older and grayer, said, " 'Dumb'? She knows what makes the Mole work; nobody else has been able to dope that out."

"There's nothing to dope out," the first—youthful—Secret Service man said. "It's just the meeting of two vacuums and that's the same as one big vacuum."

"Yeah, some vacuum. He rises to the UN Secretaryship; you think you or anybody else you know could do that? Here's her conapt." The older Secret Service man halted and indicated a door. "Don't act surprised when you see her," he told Eric. "I mean, when you see she's just a kid."

"I was told," Eric said. And rang the bell. "I know all about it."

" 'You know all about it,' " the Secret Service man to his left mocked. "Good for you—without even seeing her. Maybe you'll be the next UN Secretary after the Mole finally succumbs."

The door opened. An astonishingly small, dark, pretty girl

wearing a man's red silk shirt with the tails out and tapered, tight slacks stood facing them. She held a pair of cutical scissors; evidently she had been trimming and improving her nails, which Eric saw were long and luminous.

"I'm Dr. Sweetscent. I've joined Gino Molinari's staff." He almost said *your father's* staff; he caught the words barely in time.

"I know," Mary Reineke said. "And he wants me; he's feeling lousy. Just a minute." She turned to look for a coat, disappearing momentarily.

"A high school girl," the Secret Service man on Eric's left said. He shook his head. "For any ordinary guy it'd be a felony."

"Shut up," his companion snapped, as Mary Reineke returned wearing a heavy, blue-black, large-button, navy-style jacket.

"Couple of smart guys," Mary said to the Secret Service men. "You two take off; I want to talk to Dr. Sweetscent without you sticking your big fat ears into it."

"Okay, Mary." Grinning, the Secret Service men departed. Eric was alone in the corridor with the girl in the heavy jacket, pants and slippers.

They walked in silence and then Mary said, "How is he?"

Cautiously, Eric said, "In many ways exceptionally healthy. Almost unbelievably so. But—"

"But he's dying. All the time. Sick, but it just goes on and on—I wish it would end; I wish he'd—" She paused thoughtfully. "No, I don't wish that. If Gino died I'd be booted out. Along with all the cousins and uncles and bambinos. There'd be a general housecleaning of all the debris that clutters up this place." Her tongue was amazingly bitter and fierce; Eric glanced sharply at her, taken aback. "Are you here to cure him?" Mary asked.

"Well, I can try. I can at least—"

"Or are you here to administer the—what do they call it? The final blow. You know. Coup something."

"Coup de grace," Eric said.

"Yes." Mary Reineke nodded. "Well? Which did you come for? Or don't you know? Are you as confused as he is, is that it?"

"I'm not confused," Eric said, after a pause.

"Then you know your duty. You're the artiforg man, aren't you? The top org-trans surgeon . . . I read about you in *Time,* I think. Don't you think *Time* is a highly informative magazine in all fields? I read it from cover to cover every week, especially the medical and scientific sections."

Eric said, "Do—you go to school?"

"I graduated. High school, not college; I've got no interest in what they call 'higher learning.' "

"What did you want to be?"

"What do you mean?" She eyed him suspiciously.

"I mean what career did you intend to enter?"

"I don't need a career."

"But you didn't know that; you had no way of telling you'd wind up—" He gestured. "Be here at the White House."

"Sure I did. I always knew, all my life. Since I was three."

"How?"

"I was—I am—one of those precogs. I could tell the future." Her tone was calm.

"Can you still do it?"

"Sure."

"Then you don't need to ask me why I'm here; you can look ahead and see what I do."

"What you do," Mary said, "isn't that important; it doesn't register." She smiled then, showing beautiful, regular, white teeth.

"I can't believe that," he said, nettled.

"Then be your own precog; don't ask me what I know if you're not interested in the results. Or not able to accept them. This is a cutthroat environment, here at the White House; a hundred people are clamoring to get Gino's attention all the time, twenty-four hours a day. You have to fight your way through the throngs. That's why Gino gets sick—or rather pretends to be sick."

" 'Pretends,' " Eric said.

"He's a hysteric; you know, where they think they have illnesses but really don't. It's his way of keeping people off his back; he's just too sick to deal with them." She laughed merrily. "You know that—you've examined him. He doesn't actually have anything."

"Have you read the file?"

"Sure."

"Then you know that Gino Molinari has had cancer at three separate occasions."

"So what?" She gestured. "Hysterical cancer."

"In the medical profession no such—"

"Which are you going to believe, your textbooks or what you see with your own eyes?" She studied him intently. "If you expect to survive here you better become a realist; you better learn to detect facts when you meet up with them. You think Teagarden is glad you're here? You're a menace to his status; he's already begun trying to find ways to discredit you—or haven't you noticed?"

"No," he said. "I haven't noticed."

"Then you haven't got a chance. Teagarden will have you out of here so fast—" She broke off. Ahead lay the sick man's door and the two rows of Secret Service men. "You know why Gino has those pains actually? So he can be pampered. So people will wait on him as if he's a baby; he wants to be a baby again so he won't have grownup responsibilities. See?"

"Theories like that" Eric said, "sound so perfect, they're so glib, so easy to say—"

"But true," Mary said. "In this case." She pushed past the Secret Service men, opened the door, and entered. Going up to Gino's bed, she gazed down at him and said, "Get on your feet, you big lazy bastard."

Opening his eyes, Gino stirred leadenly. "Oh, it's you. Sorry, but I—"

"Sorry nothing," Mary said in a sharp voice. "You're not sick. Get up! I'm ashamed of you; everybody's ashamed of you. You're just scared and acting like a baby—how do you expect me to respect you when you act like this?"

After a time Gino said, "Maybe I don't expect you to." He seemed depressed more than anything else by the girl's tirade. Now he made out Eric. "You hear her, doctor?" he said gloomily. "Nobody can stop her; she comes in here when I'm dying and talks to me like that—maybe that's the reason I'm dying." He rubbed his stomach gingerly. "I don't feel them right now. I think that shot you gave me did it; what was in that?"

Not the shot, Eric thought, but the surgery downstairs on McNeil. Your complaint is gone because an assistant cook on the White House staff now has an artiforg heart. I was right.

"If you're okay—" Mary began.

"Okay," Molinari sighed. "I'll get up; just leave me alone, will you, for chrissake?" He stirred about, struggling to get up from the bed. "Okay—I'll get up; will that satisfy you?" His voice rose to a shout of anger.

Turning to Eric, Mary Reineke said, "You see? I can get him out of bed; I can put him back on his feet like a man."

"Congratulations," Gino murmured sourly as he shakily rose to a standing position. "I don't need a medical staff; all I need is you. But I notice it was Dr. Sweetscent here who got rid of my pains, not you. What did you ever do but bawl me out? If I'm back up it's because of him." He passed by her, to the closet for his robe.

"He resents me," Mary said to Eric. "But underneath he knows I'm right." She seemed perfectly placid and sure of herself; she stood with her arms folded, watching the Secretary as he tied the sash of his blue robe and got on his deerskin slippers.

"Big-time," Molinari muttered to Eric, jerking his head at Mary. "She runs things—according to her."

"Do you have to do what she says?" Eric inquired.

Molinari laughed. "Sure. Don't I?"

"What happens if you don't? Does she make the heavens fall?"

"Yes, she pulls down everything." Molinari nodded. "It's

a psionic talent she has . . . it's called *being a woman.* Like your wife Kathy. I'm glad to have her around; I like her. I don't care if she bawls me out—after all, I did get out of bed and it didn't hurt me; she was right."

"I always know when you're malingering," Mary said.

"Come with me, doctor," Molinari said to Eric. "There's something they've set up for me to watch; I want you to see it too."

Trailed by Secret Service men, they crossed the corridor and entered a guarded, locked room which Eric realized was a projection chamber; the far wall consisted of a permanent vidscreen installation on a grand scale.

"Me making a speech," Molinari explained to Eric as they seated themselves. He signaled and a video tape began to roll, projected on the large screen. "It'll be delivered tomorrow night, over all the TV networks. I want your opinion on it in advance, in case there's anything I should change." He glanced slyly at Eric, as if there was more he was not saying.

Why would he want my opinion? Eric wondered as he watched the image of the UN Secretary fill the screen. The Mole in full military regalia as C-in-C of Terra's armed forces: medals and arm bands and ribbons and, above all, the stiff marshal's hat with its visor partly shielding the round, heavy-jowled face so that only the lower part, the grimy chin, was visible with its disconcertingly harsh scowl.

And the jowls, unaccountably, were not flabby; they had become, for no reason which Eric could conjure up, firm and determined. It was a rocklike, severe face which showed on the screen, stern and strengthened by an inner authority that Eric had not seen before in the Mole . . . or had he?

Yes, he thought. But it had been years ago, when the Mole had first taken office, when he had been younger and there had not been the crushing responsibility. And now, on the screen, the Mole spoke. And his voice—*it was the old original voice from past times;* it was exactly as it had all been, a decade ago, before this terrible, losing war.

Chuckling, Molinari said from the deep, foam-rubber chair in which he lounged beside Eric, "I look pretty good, don't I?"

"You do." The speech rolled on, sonorous, even containing, now and then, a trace of the awesome, the majestic. And it was precisely this which Molinari had lost: he had become pitiable. On the screen the mature, dignified man in military garb expressed himself clearly in a voice that snapped out its sentences without hesitancy; the UN Secretary, in the video tape, demanded and informed, did not beg, did not turn to the electorate of Terra for help . . . he *told* them what to do in this period of crisis. And that was as it should be. But how had it been done? How did the pleading, hypochondriacal invalid, suffering from his eternal half-killing complaints, rise up and do this? Eric was mystified.

Beside him Molinari said, "It's a fake. That's not me." He grinned with delight as Eric stared first at him and then at the screen.

"Then who is it?"

"It's nobody. It's a robant. General Robant Servant Enterprises made it up for me—this speech is its first appearance. Pretty good, like my old self, makes me feel young again just to watch it." And, Eric saw, the UN Secretary did seem more his old self; he had genuinely perked up as he sat watching the simulacrum on the screen. The Mole, above and beyond everyone else, was taken in by the ersatz spectacle; he was its first convert. "Want to see the thing? It's top secret, of course—only three or four people know about it, besides Dawson Cutter of GRS Enterprises, of course. But they'll keep it confidential; they're used to handling classified material in the process of war-contract letting." He thumped Eric on the back. "You're getting let in on one of the secrets of state—how does that feel? This is the way the modern state is run; there's things the electorate doesn't know, shouldn't know for their own good. All governments have functioned this way, not just mine. You imagine it's just mine? If you do you've got a lot to learn. I'm using a robant

to make my speeches for me because at this point I don't—"
he gestured—"present quite the proper visual image, despite
the make-up technicians who work me over. It's just an impossible job." Now he had become dour, no longer joking.
"So I gave up. I'm being realistic." He settled back in his
chair, moodily.

"Who wrote the speech?"

"I did. I can still put together a political manifesto, depicting the situation, telling them how we stand and where
we're going and what we've got to do. My mind is still there."
The Mole tapped his big bulging forehead. "However, I naturally had help."

" 'Help,' " Eric echoed.

"A man I want you to meet—a brilliant new young lawyer
who acts as confidential adviser to me, without pay. Don
Festenburg, a whiz; you'll be as impressed as I was. He has
a knack of remolding, condensing, extracting the substance
and presenting it in a few distilled sentences . . . I always
had a tendency to run on at excessive length; everybody
knows that. But not anymore, not with Festenburg around.
He programmed this simulacrum—he's really saved my life."

On the screen his synthetic image was saying command-
ingly, "—and gathering up the collective éclat of our several
national societies, we as Terrans present a formidable association, more than just a planet but admittedly less, at the
moment, than an interplanetary empire on the order of Lilistar . . . although perhaps—"

"I—would prefer not to have a look at the simulacrum,"
Eric decided.

Molinari shrugged. "It's an opportunity, but if you're not
interested or if it distresses you—" He eyed Eric. "You'd
rather retain your idealistic image of me; rather imagine that
the thing talking up there on the screen is real." He laughed.
"I thought a doctor, like a lawyer and a priest, could with-
stand the shock of seeing life as it is; I thought truth was
your daily bread." He leaned toward Eric earnestly; under
him his chair squeaked in protest, giving under his excessive

weight. "I'm too old. I can't talk brilliantly anymore. God knows I'd like to. But this is a solution; would it be better just to give up?"

"No," Eric admitted. That wouldn't solve their problems.

"So I use a robant substitute, speaking lines that Don Festenburg programmed. The point is: we'll go on. And that's what matters. So learn to live with it, doctor; grow up." His face was cold now, unyielding.

"Okay," Eric said after a moment.

Molinari tapped him on the shoulder and said in a low voice, "The 'Starmen don't know about this simulacrum and Don Festenburg's work; I don't want them to find out, doctor, because I'd like to impress them, too. You understand? In fact I'm sending a print of this video tape to Lilistar; it's already on the way. You want to know the truth, doctor? Frankly, I'm more interested in impressing them than I am our own population. How does that strike you? Tell me honestly?"

"It strikes me," Eric said, "as an acute commentary on our plight."

The Mole regarded him somberly. "Perhaps so. But what you don't realize is that this is nothing; if you had any idea of—"

"Don't tell me any more. Not right now."

On the screen the imitation of Gino Molinari boomed and expostulated, gesticulated to the unseen TV audience.

"Sure, sure," Molinari agreed, mollified. "Sorry to have bothered you with my troubles in the first place." Downcast, his face more lined and weary than before, he turned his attention back to the screen, to the healthy, vigorous, completely synthetic image of his earlier self.

In the kitchen of her conapt Kathy Sweetscent lifted a small paring knife with difficulty, attempted to cut a purple onion, but found to her incredulity that she had somehow slashed her finger; she stood mutely holding the knife, watching the crimson drops slide from her finger to merge with the water sprinkled across her wrist. She would no longer handle even the most commonplace object. The damn drug! she thought with embittered fury. Every minute it's making me more powerless. Now everything defeats me. So how the hell am I going to fix dinner?

Standing behind her, Jonas Ackerman said with concern, "Something has to be done for you, Kathy." He watched her as she went to the bathroom for a Band-Aid. "Now you're spilling the Band-Aids everywhere; you can't even handle that." He complained, "If you'd tell me what it is, what—"

"Put the Band-Aid on for me, will you?" She stood silently as Jonas wrapped her cut finger. "It is JJ-180," she blurted suddenly, without premeditation. "I'm on it, Jonas. The 'Starmen did it. Please help me, get me off it. Okay?"

Shaken, Jonas said, "I—don't know exactly what I can do, because it's such a new drug. Of course we'll get in touch with our subsidiary right away. And the whole company will back you up, including Virgil."

"Go talk to Virgil right now."

"*Now?* Your time sense, Kathy; you feel this urgency because of the drug. I can see him tomorrow."

"Damn it, I'm not going to die because of this drug. So you better see him tonight, Jonas; do you understand?"

After a pause Jonas said, "I'll call him."

"The vidlines are tapped. By the 'Starmen."

"That's a paranoid idea. From the drug."

"I'm afraid of them." She was trembling. "They can do anything. You go and see Virgil face to face, Jonas; calling isn't enough. Or don't you care what happens to me?"

"Of course I care! Okay, I'll go and see the old man. But will you be all right alone?"

"Yes," Kathy said. "I'll just sit in the living room and do nothing. I'll just wait for you to come back with some kind of help. What could happen to me if I don't try to do anything, if I just sit there?"

"You might get yourself into a state of morbid agitation. You might be swamped with panic . . . start to run. If it's true you're on JJ-180—"

"It's true!" she said loudly. "Do you think I'm kidding?"

"Okay," Jonas said, giving in. He led her to the couch in the living room, sat her down. "God, I hope you'll be all right—I hope I'm not making a mistake." He was sweating and pale, his face wizened with worry. "See you in about half an hour, Kathy. Christ, if something goes wrong, Eric'll never forgive me and I won't blame him." The apartment door shut after him. He did not even say goodbye.

She was alone.

At once she went to the vidphone and dialed. "A cab." She gave her address and hung up.

A moment later, her coat over her shoulders, she hurried from the building and out onto the nocturnal sidewalk.

When the autonomic cab had picked her up she instructed it by means of the card which Corning had given her.

If I can get more of the drug, she thought, my mind will clear and I can reason out what I have to do; as I am now I can't think. Anything I decide now, in this state, would be spurious. I owe it to myself to restore the normal functioning—or rather the desired functioning—of my faculties; without that I can't plan or survive and I'm doomed. I know, she thought fiercely, that the only way out for me would be suicide; it's just a matter of a few hours at the most. And Jonas couldn't help me in that short a time.

The only way I could have gotten rid of him, she realized, is the way I chose: by telling him of my addiction. Otherwise he would have hung around me forever and I never would have had a chance to get to Corning for more. I gained the opportunity I need, but now the Ackermans understand what's wrong with me and they'll try even harder to keep me from going to Cheyenne and joining Eric. Maybe I should go there tonight, not even return to my apartment. Just take off as soon as I have the capsules. Leave everything I own behind, abandoned.

How demented can you get? she asked herself. And it required only one exposure to JJ-180 to do this; what'll I be like when I've taken it repeatedly . . . or even just *twice*?

The future, to her, was mercifully obscure. She frankly did not know.

"Your destination, miss." The cab settled onto the roof-top landing field of a building. "That will be one dollar and twenty cents US plus a twenty-five-cent tip."

"Screw you and the tip," Kathy said, opening her purse; her hands shook and she could barely get out the money.

"Yes, miss," the autonomic cab said obediently.

She paid and then stepped out. A dull guide-light showed her the descent. What a rundown building for 'Starmen to inhabit, she thought. It surely isn't good enough for them; they must be pretending to be Terrans. The only consolation was a bitter one: the 'Starmen, like Terra, were losing the war, would ultimately be defeated. Relishing that thought, she increased her pace, felt more confidence; she did not simply hate the 'Starmen: she could, for a moment, despise them.

In this fortified frame of mind she reached the conapt held by the 'Starmen, rang the bell, and waited.

It was Corning himself who answered, she saw, behind him, other 'Starmen, evidently in conference. *In camera,* she said to herself; I'm disturbing them. Too bad; he said to come.

"Mrs. Sweetscent." Corning turned to the people behind him. "Isn't that a superb name? Come in, Kathy." He held the door wide.

"Give it to me out here." She remained in the hall. "I'm on my way to Cheyenne; you'll be glad to hear that. So don't waste my time." She held out her hand.

An expression of pity—incredibly—passed over Corning's face; he masterfully suppressed it. But she had seen it, and this, more than anything else that had happened, even the addiction itself or her suffering when the drug had worn off— nothing shocked her so much as Corning's pity. If it could move a 'Starman . . . she cringed. Oh God, she thought; I really am in trouble. I must be on my way to death.

"Look," she said reasonably. "My addiction may not last forever. I've found out that you lied; the drug comes from Terra, not from the enemy, and sooner or later our subsidiary will be able to free me. So I'm not afraid." She waited while Corning went to get the drug; at least she presumed that this was what he had gone for. He certainly had vanished somewhere.

One of the other 'Starmen, observing her leisurely, said, "You could float that drug around Lilistar for a decade and never find anyone unstable enough to succumb."

"Right," Kathy agreed. "That's the difference between you and us; we look alike but inside you're tough and we're weak. Gosh, I envy you. How long is it going to take Mr. Corning?"

"He'll be back in a moment," the 'Starman said. To a companion he said, "She's pretty."

"Yes, pretty as an animal," the other 'Starman answered. "So you like pretty animals? Is that why you were assigned to this?"

Corning returned. "Kathy, I'm giving you three caps. Don't take more than one at a time. Otherwise its toxicity would probably be fatal to your heart action."

"Okay." She accepted the capsules. "Do you have a cup or glass of water so I can take one right now?"

He brought her a glass, stood watching sympathetically as she swallowed the capsule. "I'm doing this," she explained, "to clear my mind so I can plan what to do. I've got friends helping me. But I will go to Cheyenne because a deal is a deal, even with you. Can you give me the name of someone there—you know, who can give me further supplies when I need them? *If* I need them, I mean."

"We have no one in Cheyenne who can help you. I'm very much afraid you'll have to travel back here when your three caps are gone."

"Your infiltration of Cheyenne doesn't consist of much, then."

"I guess not." Corning did not appear perturbed, however.

"Goodbye," Kathy said, starting away from the door. "Look at you," she said, addressing the group of 'Starmen within the apartment. "God but you're detestable. So confident. What kind of victory is it to—" She broke off; what was the use? "Virgil Ackerman knows about me. I'll bet he can do something; he's not afraid of you, he's too big a man."

"All right," Corning said, nodding. "You cherish that comforting delusion, Kathy. Meanwhile be sure you don't tell anyone else, because if you do, then no more caps. You shouldn't have told the Ackermans but I'll let that pass; after all, you were dazed when the drug wore off—we expected that. You did it in a state of panic. Good luck, Kathy. And we'll hear from you shortly."

"Can't you give her further instructions now?" a 'Starman said from behind Corning, sleepy-eyed and toadlike, drawling his question.

"She wouldn't be able to retain anything more," Corning said. "It's asking a lot of her already; can't you see how overtaxed she is?"

"Kiss her goodbye," the 'Starman behind him suggested. He strolled forward. "Or if that doesn't cheer her up—"

The apartment door shut in Kathy's face.

She stood a moment and then started back down the hall, toward the ascent ramp. Dizzy, she thought; I'm beginning to become disoriented—I hope I can make it to a cab. Once I'm in the cab I'll be okay. Jesus, she thought, they treated me badly; I should care but I really don't. Not as long as I have these two remaining capsules of JJ-180. And can get more.

The capsules were like a contracted form of life itself and yet at the same time everything they contained was fabricated from absolute delusion. What a mess, she thought drably as she emerged on the roof field and glanced about for the red, winking light of an autonomic cab. A——mess.

She had found a cab, was seated in it and on her way to Cheyenne, when she experienced the drug beginning to take effect.

Its initial manifestation was baffling. She wondered if perhaps a clue to its true action could be inferred from this; it seemed to her terribly important and she tried with every bit of mental energy she had to comprehend it. So simple and yet so meaningful.

The cut on her finger had disappeared.

She sat examining the spot, touching the smooth, perfect

skin. No break. No scar. Her finger, exactly as before . . . as if time had been rolled back. The Band-Aid, too, was gone, and that seemed to clinch it, make it thoroughly comprehensible, even to her swiftly deteriorating faculties.

"Look at my hand," she instructed the cab, holding her hand up. "Do you see any sign of an injury? Would you believe that I slashed myself badly, just half an hour ago?"

"No, miss," the cab said as it passed out over the flat desert of Arizona, heading north toward Utah. "You appear uninjured."

Now I understand what the drug does, she thought. Why it causes objects and people to become insubstantial. It's not so magical, and it's not merely hallucinogenic; my cut is really gone—*this is no illusion.* Will I remember this later on? Maybe, because of the drug, I'll forget; there never will have been a cut, after a little while longer, as the action of the drug spreads out, engulfs more and more of me.

"Do you have a pencil?" she asked the cab.

"Here, miss." From a slot in the seat-back ahead of her a tablet of paper with attached writing stylus appeared.

Carefully Kathy wrote: *JJ-180 took me back to before I had severe cut on finger.* "What day is this?" she asked the cab.

"May 18, miss."

She tried to recall if that was correct, but now she felt muddled; was it already slipping away from her? Good thing she had written the note. Or had she written the note? On her lap the tablet lay with its stylus.

The note read: *JJ-180 took me*

And that was all; the remainder dwindled into mere labored convolutions without meaning.

And yet she knew that she had completed the sentence, whatever it had been; now she could not recall it. As if by reflex she examined her hand. But how was her hand involved? "Cab," she said hurriedly, as she felt the balance of her personality ebbing away, "what did I ask you just a moment ago?"

"The date."

"Before that."

"You requested a writing implement and paper, miss."

"Anything before that?"

The cab seemed to hesitate. But perhaps that was her imagination. "No, miss; nothing before that."

"Nothing about *my hand?*"

Now there was no doubt about it; the circuits of the cab did stall. At last it said creakily, "No, miss."

"Thank you," Kathy said, and sat back against the seat, rubbing her forehead and thinking, So it's confused, too. Then this is not merely subjective; there's been a genuine snarl in time, involving both me and my surroundings.

The cab said, as if in apology for its inability to assist her, "Since the trip will be several hours, miss, would you enjoy to watch TV? It, the screen, is placed directly before you; only touch the pedal."

Reflexively she lit the screen with the tip of her toe; it came to life at once and Kathy found herself facing a familiar image, that of their leader, Gino Molinari, in the middle of a speech.

"Is that channel satisfactory?" the cab asked, still apologetic.

"Oh sure," she said. "Anyhow when he gets up and rants it's on all channels." That was the law.

And yet here, too, in this familiar spectacle, something strange absorbed her; peering at the screen, she thought, He looks younger. The way I remember him when I was a child. Ebullient, full of animation and shouting excitement, his eyes alive with that old intensity: his original self that no one has forgotten, although long since gone. However, obviously it was *not* long since gone; she witnessed it now with her own eyes, and was more bewildered than ever.

Is JJ-180 doing this to me? she asked herself, and got no answer.

"You enjoy to watch Mr. Molinari?" the cab inquired.

"Yes," Kathy said, "I enjoy to watch."

"May I hazard," the cab said, "that he will obtain the office for which he is running, that of UN Secretary?"

"You stupid autonomic robant machine," Kathy said witheringly. "He's been in office years now." Running? she thought. Yes, the Mole had looked like this during his campaign, decades ago . . . perhaps that was what had confused the circuits of the cab. "I apologize," she said. "But where the hell have you been? Parked in an autofac repair garage for twenty-two years?"

"No, miss. In active service. Your own wits, if I may say so, seem scrambled. Do you request medical assistance? We are at this moment over desert land but soon we will pass St. George, Utah."

She felt violently irritable. "Of course I don't need medical assistance; I'm healthy." But the cab was right. The influence of the drug was upon her full force now. She felt sick and she shut her eyes, pressing her fingers against her forehead as if to push back the expanding zone of her psychological reality, her private, subjective self. I'm scared, she realized. I feel as if my womb is about to fall out; this time it's hitting me much harder than before, it's not the same, maybe because I'm alone instead of with a group. But I'll just have to endure it. If I can.

"Miss," the cab said suddenly, "would you repeat my destination? I have forgotten it." Its circuits clicked in rapid succession as if it were in mechanical distress. "Assist me, please."

"I don't know where you're going," she said. "That's your business; you figure it out. Just fly around, if you can't remember." What did she care where it went? What did it have to do with her?

"It began with a C," the cab said hopefully.

"Chicago."

"I feel otherwise. However, if you're sure—" Its mechanism throbbed as it altered course.

You and I are both in this, Kathy realized. This drug-induced fugue. You made a mistake, Mr. Corning, to give me the drug without supervision. Corning? Who was Corning?

"I know where we were going," she said aloud. "To Corning."

"There is no such place," the cab said flatly.

"There must be." She felt panic. "Check your data again."

"Honestly, there isn't!"

"Then we're lost," Kathy said, and felt resigned. "God, this is awful. I have to be in Corning tonight, and there's no such place; what'll I do? Suggest something. I depend on you; please don't leave me to founder like this—I feel as if I'm losing my mind."

"I'll request administrative assistance," the cab said. "From top-level dispatching service at New York. Just a moment." It was silent for a time. "Miss, there *is* no top-level dispatching service at New York, or if there is, I can't raise them."

"Is there anything at New York?"

"Radio stations, lots of them. But no TV transmissions or anything on the FM band or ultra-high frequency; nothing on the band we use. Currently I am picking up a radio station which is broadcasting something entitled 'Mary Marlin.' A piano piece by Debussy is being played as theme."

She knew her history; after all she was an antique collector and it was her job. "Put it on your audio system so I can hear it," she instructed.

A moment later she heard a female voice, detailing a wretched tale of suffering to some other female, a dreary account at best. And yet it filled Kathy with frantic excitement.

They're wrong, she thought, her mind working at its peak pitch. This won't destroy me. They forgot this era is my specialty—I know it as well as the present. There's nothing threatening or disintegrative about this experience for me; in fact it's an opportunity.

"Leave the radio on," she told the cab. "And just keep flying." Attentively, she listened to the soap opera as the cab continued on.

8

It had—against nature and reason—become daytime. And the autonomic cab knew the impossibility of this; its voice was screechy with pain as it exclaimed to Kathy, "On the highway below, miss! An ancient car that can't possibly exist!" It sank lower. "See for yourself! *Look!*"

Gazing down, Kathy agreed, "Yes. A 1932 Model A Ford. And I agree with you; there haven't been any Model A Fords for generations." Rapidly and with precision she reflected, then said, "I want you to land."

"Where?" Decidedly, the autonomic cab did not like the idea.

"That village ahead. Land on a rooftop there." She felt calm. But in her mind one realization dominated: it was the drug. And only the drug. This would last only so long as the drug operated within her cycle of brain metabolism; JJ-180 had brought her here without warning and JJ-180 would, eventually, return her to her own time—also without warning. "I am going to find a bank," Kathy said aloud. "And set up a savings account. By doing so—" And then she realized that she possessed no currency of this period; hence there existed no way by which she could transact business. So what could she do? Nothing? Call President Roosevelt and caution him about Pearl Harbor, she decided caustically.

Change history. Suggest that years from now they not develop the atom bomb.

She felt impotent—and yet overwhelmed with her potential power; she experienced both sensations at once, finding the mixture radically unpleasant. Bring some artifact back to the present for Wash-35? Or check on some research quibble, settle some historical dispute? Snare the actual authentic Babe Ruth, bring him back to inhabit our Martian enterprise? It would certainly impart verisimilitude.

"Virgil Ackerman," she said slowly, "is alive in this period as a small boy. Does that suggest anything?"

"No," the cab said.

"It gives me enormous power over him." She opened her purse. "I'll give him something. The coins I have, bills." Whisper to him the date the United States enters the war, she thought. He can use that knowledge later on, somehow . . . he'll find a way; he's always been smart, much smarter than I. God, she thought, if only I could put my finger on it! Tell him to invest in what? General Dynamics? Bet on Joe Louis in every fight? Buy real estate in Los Angeles? What do you tell an eight- or nine-year-old boy when you have exact and complete knowledge of the next hundred and twenty years?

"Miss," the cab said plaintively, "we've been in the air so long that I'm running short of fuel."

Chilled, she said, "But you ought to be good for fifteen hours."

"I was low." It admitted this reluctantly. "It's my fault; I'm sorry. I was on my way to a service station when you contacted me."

"You damn fool mechanism," she said with fury. But that was that; they couldn't reach Washington, D.C.; they were at least a thousand miles from it. And this period, of course, lacked the high-grade super-refined protonex which the cab required. And then all at once she knew what she had to do. The cab had given her the idea, unintentionally. Protonex was the finest fuel ever developed—and it was derived from sea water. All she had to do was mail a container of protonex to Virgil Ackerman's father, instruct him to procure an analysis of it and then a patent on it.

But there was no way she could mail anything, not without money to buy stamps. In her purse she had a small wad of dog-eared postage stamps, but of course all from her own era, from 2055. ——, she said furiously to herself, overwhelmed. Here I have it right before me, the solution as to what I should do—and I *can't* do it.

"How," she asked the cab, "can I send a letter in this time period with no contemporary stamps? Tell me that."

"Send the letter unstamped, with no return address, miss. The post office will deliver it with a postage due stamp attached."

"Yes," she said, "of course." But she could not get protonex into a first-class envelope; it would have to go parcel post, and in that class, lacking franking power, it would not be delivered. "Listen," she said. "Do you have any transistors in your circuits?"

"A few. But transistors became obsolete when—"

"Give me one. I don't care what it does to you; yank it out and let me have it, and the smaller it is the better."

Presently, from the slot in the back of the seat before her, a transistor rolled; she caught it as it fell.

"That puts my radio transmitter out of service," the cab complained. "I'll have to bill you for it; it'll be expensive because of—"

"Shut up," Kathy said. "And land in that town; get down as soon as you can." She wrote hurriedly on the tablet of paper: "This is a radio part from the future, Virgil Ackerman. Show it to no one but save it until the early 1940s. Then take it to Westinghouse Corp. or to General Electric or any electronics (radio) firm. It will make you rich. I am Katherine Sweetscent. Remember me for this, later on."

The cab landed gingerly on the roof of an office building in the center of the small town. Below on the sidewalk the rustic, archaic-looking passersby gaped.

"Land on the street," Kathy reinstructed the cab. "I have to put this in the mail." She found an envelope in her purse, hurriedly wrote out Virgil's address in Wash-35, put the transistor and note into the envelope and sealed it. Below them the street with its obsolete old cars rose slowly.

A moment later she was racing to a mailbox; she deposited the letter and then stood gasping for breath.

She had done it. Insured Virgil's economic future and therefore her own. This would make his career and hers forever.

The hell with you, Eric Sweetscent, she said to herself. I don't ever have to marry you now; I've left you behind.

And then she realized with dismay, I've still got to marry you in order to acquire the name. So that Virgil can identify me, later on in the future, in our own time. What she had done, then, came to exactly nothing.

Slowly, she returned to the parked cab.

"Miss," the cab said, "can you help me find fuel, please?"

"You won't find any fuel here," Kathy said. Its obstinate refusal—or inability—to grasp the situation maddened her. "Unless you can run on sixty octane gasoline, which I very much doubt."

A passerby, a middle-aged man wearing a straw hat, frozen in his tracks by the sight of the autonomic cab, called to her, "Hey lady, what's that, anyhow? A US Marine Corps secret weapon for war games?"

"Yes," Kathy answered. "And in addition later on it'll stop the Nazis." As she boarded the cab she said to the group of people who had cautiously formed around the cab at a safe distance, "Keep the date December 7, 1941, in mind; it'll be a day to remember." She closed the cab door. "Let's go. I could tell those people so much . . . but it seems hardly worth it. A bunch of Middle Western hicks." This town, she decided, lay either in Kansas or Missouri, from the looks of it. Frankly, it repelled her.

The cab dutifully ascended.

The 'Starmen should see Kansas in 1935, she said to herself. If they did they might not care to take over Terra; it might not seem worth it.

To the cab she said, "Land in a pasture. We'll sit it out

until we're back in our own time period." It probably would not be long now; she had an impression of a devouring in-substantiality here in this era—the reality outside the cab had gained a gaseous quality which she recognized from her previous encounter with the drug.

"Are you joking?" the cab said. "Is it actually possible that we—"

"The problem," she said tartly, "is not in returning to our own time; the problem is finding a way to stay under the drug's influence until something of worth can be accomplished." The time was just not long enough.

"What drug, miss?"

"None of your goddam business," Kathy said. "You nosy autonomic nonentity with your big prying circuits all opened up and flapping." She lit a cigarette and leaned back against the seat, feeling weary. It had been a tough day and she knew, with acuity, that more lay ahead.

The sallow-faced young man, who oddly enough already possessed a conspicuous paunch, as if physically yielding to the more lush pleasures at this, the planet's financial and political capital, shook Eric Sweetscent's hand damply and said, "I'm Don Festenburg, doctor. It's good to hear you're joining us. How about an old-fashioned?"

"No thanks," Eric said. There was something about Festenburg which he did not care for but he could not put his finger on it. Despite his obesity and bad complexion Festenburg seemed friendly enough, and certainly he was competent; the latter alone counted, after all. But—Eric pondered as he watched Festenburg mix himself his drink. Perhaps it's because I don't think anyone should speak for the Secretary, he decided. I'd resent anyone who holds the job Festenburg does.

"Since we're alone," Festenburg said, glancing around the room, "I'd like to suggest something that may make me more palatable to you." He grinned knowingly. "I can tell what your feelings are; I'm sensitive, doctor, even if I'm the pyknic body-type. Suppose I suggested that an elaborate ruse has been carried off successfully, convincing even you. The flabby, aging, utterly discouraged and hypochondriacal Gino Molinari whom you've met and accepted as the authentic UN Secretary—" Festenburg lazily stirred his drink, eyeing Eric. *"That's the robant simulacrum.* And the robust, energetic figure you witnessed on video tape a short while ago is the living man. And this ruse must necessarily be maintained, of course, to sidetrack no one else but our beloved ally, the 'Starmen."

"What?" Startled, he gaped. "Why would—"

"The 'Starmen consider us harmless, unworthy of their military attention, only so long as our leader is palpably feeble. Quite visibly unable to discharge his responsibilities— in other words, in no sense a rival to them, a threat."

After a pause Eric said, "I don't believe this."

"Well," Festenburg said, shrugging, "it's an interesting idea from the ivory tower, intellectual standpoint. Don't you agree?" He walked toward Eric, swirling the contents of his glass. Standing very close to him, Festenburg breathed his noxious breath into Eric's face and said, "It *could* be. And until you actually subject Gino to an intensive physical examination you won't know, because everything in that file you read—it could all be faked. Designed to validate a gross, well-worked-out swindle." His eyes twinkled with merciless amusement. "You think I'm out of my mind? I'm just playing, like a schizoid, with ideas for the fun of it, without regard to their actual consequences? Maybe so. But you can't prove what I just now told you is untrue, and as long as this remains the case—" He took a massive swallow of his drink, then made a face. "Don't deplore what you saw on that Ampex video tape. Okay?"

"But as you say," Eric said, "I'll know as soon as I have a chance to examine him." And, he thought, that will come soon. "So if you'll excuse me I'd like to end this conversation. I haven't yet had time to set up my conapt here satisfactorily."

"Your wife—what's her name? Kathy?—isn't coming, is she?" Don Festenburg winked. "You can enjoy yourself. I'm in a position to give you a hand. That's my department, the land of the illicit, the feral, and the—let's just call it the peculiar. Instead of the unnatural. But you come from Tijuana; I probably can't teach you a thing."

Eric said, "You can teach me to deplore not only what I saw on the video tape but—" He broke off. Festenburg's personal life was, after all, his own business.

"But its creator as well," Festenburg finished for him. "Doctor, did you know that in the Middle Ages the ruling courts had people who lived in bottles, spent their entire lives . . . all shrunken, of course, put in while babies, allowed to grow—to some extent, anyhow—within the bottle. We don't have that now. However—Cheyenne is the contemporary ranking seat of kings; there are a few sights that could be shown you, if you're interested. Perhaps from the purely medical standpoint—a sort of professional, disinterested—"

"I think whatever it is you want to show me would only make me less pleased with my decision to come to Cheyenne," Eric said. "So frankly I don't see what profit it would serve."

"Wait," Festenburg said, holding up his hand. "One item. Just this particular exhibit, all properly sealed hermetically, bathed in a solution that maintains the thing ad infinitum, or, as you probably will prefer, ad nauseam. May I take you there? It's in what we at the White House call room 3-C." Festenburg walked to the door, held it open for Eric.

After a pause Eric followed.

Hands in the pockets of his rumpled, unpressed trousers, Festenburg led the way down one corridor after another until at last they stood on a subsurface level, facing two high-ranking Secret Service men stationed at a metal reinforced door marked TOP SECRET. NO UNAUTHORIZED PERSONNEL PERMITTED.

"I'm authorized," Festenburg said genially. "Gino's given me the run of the warren; he has great trust in me, and because of this you're going to see a state secret which you normally would never in a thousand years be allowed to view." As he passed by the uniformed Secret Service men and pushed open the door he added, "However, there will be one disappointing aspect of this; I'm going to show it to you but not explain it. I'd *like* to explain it but—very simply I can't."

In the center of the murky, cold room Eric saw a casket. As Festenburg had said, it was hermetically sealed; a pump throbbed dully, at its task of maintaining at extreme low temperatures whatever lay within the casket.

"Look at it," Festenburg said sharply.

Deliberately pausing, Eric lit a cigarette, then walked over.

In the casket, supine, lay Gino Molinari, his face locked in agony. He was dead. Blood could be seen, dried drops on his neck. His uniform was torn, stained with mud. Both hands were lifted, the fingers writhing, as if trying even now to fight back at whatever—whoever—it was that had murdered him. Yes, Eric thought. I'm seeing the results of an assassination; this is the leader's corpse, flailed with bullets emanating from a weapon with notably high muzzle velocity; the man's body had been twisted, almost torn apart. It had been a savage assault. And—successful.

"Well," Festenburg said, after a time, taking in a deep rush of breath, "there are several ways this item—which I like to think of as Exhibit One of the Cheyenne Freak Show— can be explained. Let's assume it's a robant. Waiting here in the wings for the moment that Gino needs it. Built by GRS Enterprises, the inventive Dawson Cutter, whom you must meet someday."

"Why would Molinari need this?"

Festenburg, scratching his nose, said, "Several reasons. In case of an attempted assassination—one which failed—this could be exhibited, taking the heat off Gino while he hid out. Or—it could be for the benefit of our sanguine ally; Gino may have it in the back of his mind that some incredibly complex, baroque plan will be necessary, something involving his retirement from office under the pressure they're exerting on him."

"You're sure this is a robant?" To Eric the thing in the casket looked real.

"I don't even *think* it is, let alone know." Festenburg jerked his head and Eric saw that the two Secret Service men had entered the room; obviously it would not be possible to inspect the corpse.

"How long has it been here?"

"Only Gino knows and he won't say; he just smiles slyly. 'You wait, Don,' he says in his secretive fashion. 'I got a big use for it.' "

"And if it's not a robant—"

"Then it's Gino Molinari lying there ripped apart by machine-gun slugs. A primitive, outmoded weapon but it certainly can kill its victim beyond the possibility of even org-trans repair; you can see that the brain case has been punctured—the brain is destroyed. If it is Gino, *then where's it from?* The future? There is a theory, having to do with your firm, TF&D. A subsidiary has developed a drug which permits its user to move freely in time. You know about that?" He studied Eric intently.

"No," Eric admitted. The rumor was more or less new to him.

"Anyhow, here's this corpse," Festenburg said. "Lying here day after day, driving me nuts. Perhaps it's from an alternate present in which Gino has been assassinated, driven out of office the hard way by a splinter political group of Terrans backed by Lilistar. But there's a further ramification of this theory, one which really haunts me." Festenburg's tone now was somber; he was no longer in a joking mood. "That would imply something about the virile, strutting Gino Molinari who made that video tape; that's not a robant either and GRS Enterprises did not manufacture it because it too is an authentic Gino Molinari from an alternate present. One in which war didn't come about, one perhaps in which Terra didn't even get mixed up with Lilistar. Gino Molinari has gone into a more reassuring world and plucked his healthy counterpart over here to assist him. What do you think, doctor? Could that be it?"

Baffled, Eric said, "If I knew something about that drug—"

"I assumed you would. I'm disappointed; that was my reason for bringing you here. Anyhow—there's one other possibility . . . logically. Suggested by this assassinated corpse here." Festenburg hesitated. "I hate to mention it because it's so bizarre that it makes my other conjectures look tainted by association."

"Go ahead," Eric said tightly.

"There is no Gino Molinari."

Eric grunted. Good grief, he thought.

"*All* of them are robants. The healthy one who's on the video tape, the tired, sick one you've met, this dead one here in the casket—that somebody, possibly GRS Enterprises, engineered this to keep the 'Starmen from taking over our planet. So far they've made use of the ill one." Festenburg gestured. "And now they've hauled out the healthy one, made the first tape of him. *And there may be more.* Logically why not? I've even tried to imagine what other alternatives might be like. You tell me. In addition to the three we know, *what's left?*"

Eric said, "Obviously it leaves the possibility of building one with powers above the norm. Beyond the merely healthy." He thought, then, of Molinari's recovery from one terminal illness after another. "But maybe we have that already. Have you read the medical file?"

"Yes." Festenburg nodded. "And there's one very interesting quality about it. None of the tests were conducted by any persons now on his medical staff. Teagarden didn't authorize any of them; the tests predate him, and as far as I know, Teagarden, like yourself, has never managed to subject Gino to even a cursory physical exam. Nor do I think he ever will. Nor do I think *you* ever will, doctor. Even if you're kept around here for years."

"Your mind," Eric said, "is certainly hyperactive."

"Am I a glandular case?"

"That has no bearing on the matter. But you certainly have spun a lot of ad hoc ideas out of your own head."

"Based on facts," Festenburg pointed out. "I want to know what Gino is up to. I think he's one hell of a smart man. I think he can outthink the 'Starmen any day of the week, and if he had the economic resources and the population behind him that they have, he'd be in the driver's seat, no contest.

As it is, he's in charge of one dinky planet and they have a system-wide empire of twelve planets and eight moons. It's frankly a wonder he's been able to accomplish all he has. You know, doctor, you're here to find out what's making Gino sick. I say that's not the issue. It's obvious what's making him sick: the whole darn situation. The real question is: *What's keeping him alive?* That's the real mystery. The miracle."

"I guess you're right." Grudgingly, he had to admit that despite his repellent qualities Festenburg was intelligent and original; he had managed to see the problem properly. No wonder Molinari had hired him.

"You've met the schoolgirl shrew?"

"Mary Reineke?" Eric nodded.

"Christ, here's this tragic, complicated mess, this sick man barely making it through the day with the weight of the world, of Terra itself, on his back, knowing he's losing the war, knowing the reegs are going to get us if by some miracle Lilistar doesn't—and in addition he's got Mary on his back. And the final blistering irony is that Mary, by being a shrew and simple-minded, selfish, demanding, and anything else you want to articulate as a basic character defect—she does have him on his feet; you've seen her get him out of bed and back into uniform, functioning again. Do you know anything about Zen, doctor? This is a Zen paradox, because from a logical standpoint Mary ought to have been the final straw that utterly destroyed Gino. It makes you rethink the entire role of adversity in human life. To tell you the truth, I detest her. She detests me, too, naturally. Our only working connection is through Gino; we both want him to make it."

"Has she been shown the video tape of the healthy Molinari?"

Festenburg glanced up swiftly. "A wise thought. Has Mary seen the tape? Yes, maybe or no—check one. Not to my knowledge. But if you suppose my alternate-present theory, and that it's *not* a robant on that tape, if it's a human being, that magnetic, fire-eating, striving demigod, and if Mary catches sight of it—you can assume the following: the other

Molinaris will disappear. Because what you saw on that tape is exactly what Mary Reineke wants—insists—that Gino be."

It was an extraordinary thought. Eric wondered if Gino was aware of this aspect of the situation; if so, it might explain why he had waited so long to employ this tactic.

"I wonder," he said to Festenburg, "how the sick Gino, whom we know, could be a robant, in view of Mary Reineke's existence."

"How so? Why not?"

"To put it in delicate terms . . . wouldn't Mary be somewhat peeved by being the mistress of a product of GRS Enterprises?"

"I'm getting tired, doctor," Festenburg said. "Let's write finis to this discussion—you go and fix up your swinkly new conapt which they've donated to you for your loyal services here at Cheyenne." He moved toward the door; the two top-position Secret Service men stepped aside.

Eric said, "I'll give you one opinion of my own. Having met Gino Molinari I refuse to believe GRS could construct something so human and—"

"But you haven't met the one they filmed," Festenburg said quietly. "It's interesting, doctor. By drawing on himself from the alternates contained in the mishmash of time Gino may have collected an ensemble capable of facing the ally. Three or four Gino Molinaris, forming a committee, would be rather formidable . . . don't you agree? Think of the combined ingenuity; think of the harebrained, clever, wild schemes they could hatch up working collectively." As he opened the door he added, "You've met the sick one and glimpsed the well one—weren't *you* impressed?"

"Yes," Eric admitted.

"Would you now vote with those who want to see him sacked? And yet when you try to pin down what he's actually done that's so impressive—it isn't there. If we were winning the war, or forcing back Lilistar's investment of our planet . . . but we're not. So what is it specifically, doctor, that Gino's done that so impresses you? Tell me." He waited.

"I—guess I can't say specifically. But—"

A White House employee, a uniformed robant, appeared and confronted Eric Sweetscent. "Secretary Molinari has been looking for you, doctor. He's waiting to see you in his office; I'll lead the way."

"Oops," Festenburg said, chagrined and all at once quite nervous. "Evidently I kept you too long."

Without a further exchange Eric followed the robant up the corridor to the elevator. This was probably important; he had that intuition.

In his office Molinari sat in a wheelchair, a blanket over his lap, his face gray and sunken. "Where were you?" he said, as Eric came into sight. "Well, it doesn't matter; listen, doctor—the 'Starmen have called a conference and I want you to be with me while I attend. I want you to be on hand constantly, just in case. I'm not feeling well and I wish this damn get-together could be avoided or at least postponed for a few weeks. But they insist." He began to wheel himself from the office. "Come on. It's going to start anytime."

"I met Don Festenburg."

"Brilliant rat, isn't he? I put complete faith in our eventual success in him. What did he show you?"

It seemed unreasonable to tell Molinari that he had been viewing his corpse, especially in view of the fact that the man had just now said he did not feel well. So Eric merely said, "He took me around the building."

"Festenburg has the run of the place—because of the trust I put in him." At a bend in the corridor a gang of stenographers, translators, State Department officials, and armed guards met Molinari; his wheelchair disappeared into the corporate body and did not reappear. Eric, however, could still hear him talking away, explaining what lay ahead. "Freneksy is here. So this is going to be rough. I have an idea what they want, but we'll have to wait and see. Better not to anticipate; that way you do their work for them, you sort of turn on yourself and do yourself in."

Freneksy, Eric thought with a sensation of dread. Lilistar's Prime Minister, here personally on Terra.

No wonder Molinari felt sick.

9

The members of Terra's delegation to the hastily called conference occupied seats on one side of the long oak table, and now, on the far side, the personages from Lilistar began to emerge from side corridors and find chairs. As a whole they did not look sinister; they looked, in fact, overworked and harried, caught up, as was Terra, by the strain of conducting the war. Obviously they had no time to spare. They were clearly mortal.

"Translation," a 'Starman said in English, "will be done by human agency not by machine, as any machine might make a permanent record, which is contrary to our desires here."

Molinari grunted, nodded.

Now Freneksy appeared; the 'Star delegation and several members of the Terran rose in a show of respect; the 'Starmen clapped their hands as the bald, lean, oddly round-skulled man took a chair at the center of the delegation and began without preliminaries to open a briefcase of documents.

But his eyes. Eric noticed that, as Freneksy glanced briefly up at Molinari and smiled in greeting, Freneksy had what Eric thought of—and recognized in his practice as—paranoid eyes. Once he had learned to spot this, future identification generally came easy. This was not the glittering, restless stare of ordinary suspicion; this was a motionless gaze, a gathering of the totality of faculties within to comprise a single undisturbed psychomotor concentration. Freneksy did not decide to do this; in fact he was helpless, compelled to confront his compatriots and adversaries alike in this fashion, with this unending ensnaring fixity. It was an attentiveness which made empathic understanding impossible; the eyes did not reflect any inner reality; they gave back to the viewer exactly what he himself was. The eyes stopped communication dead; they were a barrier that could not be penetrated this side of the tomb.

Freneksy was not a bureaucrat and he did not—could not even if he tried—subordinate himself to his office. Freneksy remained a man—in the bad sense; he retained, in the midst of the busy activity of official conduct, the essence of the purely personal, as if to him everything was deliberate and intentional—a contest between people, not one between abstract or ideal issues.

What Minister Freneksy does, Eric realized, is to deprive all the others of the sanctity of their office. Of the security-producing reality of their titled position. Facing Freneksy, they became as they were born; isolated and individual, unsupported by the institutions which they were supposed to represent.

Take Molinari. Customarily, the Mole was the UN Secretary; he as an individual had—and properly so—dissolved into his function. But facing Minister Freneksy, the naked, hapless, lonely man reemerged—and was required to stand up to the Minister in this unhappy infinitude. The normal *relativeness* of existence, lived with others in a fluctuating state of more or less adequate security, had vanished.

Poor Gino Molinari, Eric thought. Because facing Freneksy the Mole might as well not have become UN Secretary. And meanwhile Minister Freneksy became even more cold, more lifeless; he did not burn with the desire to destroy or dominate: he merely took away what his antagonist possessed—and left him nothing and nowhere, literally.

It was perfectly clear to Eric, at this point, why Molinari's procession of lethal illnesses had not proved fatal. The illnesses were not merely a symptom of the stress under which he lay; *they were simultaneously a solution to that stress.*

He could not as yet make out quite precisely how the illnesses behaved in order to function as a response to Freneksy. But he had the deep and acute intution that he would very soon; the confrontation between Freneksy and Molinari lay only moments away, and everything which the Mole had would have to be trotted out, if the Mole wished to survive.

Beside Eric a minor State Department official muttered, "Oppressive in here, isn't it? Wish they'd open a window or turn on the vent system."

Eric thought, No mechanical vent system will clear this air. Because the oppression emanates from those seated across from us and it will not depart until they depart—and perhaps not even then.

Leaning toward Eric, Molinari said, "Sit here beside me." He drew the chair back. "Listen, doctor, do you have your bag of instruments with you?"

"It's in my conapt."

Molinari at once dispatched a robant runner. "I want you to have the bag at all times." He cleared his throat, then turned toward those seated on the far side of the table. "Minister Freneksy, I have a, uh, statement. I'd like to read it; the statement summarizes Earth's present position as regards—"

"Secretary," Freneksy said suddenly in English, "before you read any statement I would like to describe the status of the war effort on Front A." Freneksy rose; an aide at once unrolled a map projection which took effect on the far wall. The room sank into shadow.

Grunting, Molinari placed his written statement back inside the jacket of his uniform; he would not get his opportunity to read it. In an obvious manner he had been preempted. And, for a political strategist, this was a grave defeat. The initiative, if it had ever been his, was gone now.

"Our combined armies," Freneksy stated, "are shortening their lines for strategic purposes. The reegs are expending inordinate amounts of men and material in this area." He indicated a sector on the map; it lay halfway between two planets of the Alpha System. "They will not be able to continue this long; I predict a bankruptcy of their strength no later than a month—Terran count—from now. The reegs do not understand yet that this is to be a long war. Victory, for them, must come soon or not at all. We, however—" Freneksy indicated the entire map with a sweep of the pointer. "We are maturely aware of the overall strategic meaning of this struggle, and how long it must remain with us in terms of time as well as space. Also, the reegs are spread too thinly. If a major battle were to break out here—" Freneksy indicated the spot "—they could not support their forces already committed. Further, we will have twenty more first-line divisions in action by the end of the Terran year; this is a promise, Secretary. We have yet to call up several classes here on Terra, whereas the reegs have scraped the barrel." He paused.

Molinari murmured, "Is your bag here yet, doctor?"

"Not yet," Eric said, looking for the robant runner; it had not returned.

Leaning close to Eric, the Mole whispered, "Listen. You know what I've been experiencing lately? Head noises. Rushing sounds—you know, in my ears. Swoop, zwoop. Does that sound like anything?"

Minister Freneksy had continued. "We have new weapons, also emanating from Planet Four of the Empire; you will be astonished, Secretary, when you see video clips of them in tactical operation. They are devastating in their accuracy. I will not attempt to describe them in detail now; I prefer to wait until the tapes are available. I personally supervised their engineering and construction."

His head almost touching Eric's, Molinari whispered, "And when I turn my head from side to side I get a distinct cracking sound from the base of my neck. Can you hear it?" He turned his head from side to side, nodding in a slow, stiff manner. "What is that? It resounds unpleasantly as hell in my ears."

Eric said nothing; he was watching Freneksy, barely paying attention to the whispering from the man beside him.

"Secretary," Freneksy said, pausing, "consider this aspect of our joint effort; the reegs' space-drive output has been severely restricted due to the success by our W-bombs. Those which have come off their assembly lines recently—we are informed by MCI—are unreliable, and a number of highly destructive contaminations have occurred in deep space aboard their line ships."

The robant runner entered the room now, with Eric's instrument case.

Ignoring this, Freneksy continued, his voice harsh and insistent. "I also point out, Secretary, that on Front Blue the Terran brigades have not performed well, no doubt due to a lack of proper equipment. Victory is of course inevitable for us—eventually. But right now we must see to it that our troops who hold the line against the reegs are not put in the position of facing the enemy deprived of adequate material. It is criminal to allow men to fight under those circumstances; don't you agree, Secretary?" Without pausing, Freneksy continued, "Therefore you can see the urgency of increasing Terra's output of strategic war goods and weapons of all sort."

Molinari saw Eric's instrument case and nodded with relief. "You have it," he said. "Good. Keep it ready, just in case. You know what I think these head noises are from? Hypertension."

Cautiously, Eric said, "Could be."

Now Minister Freneksy had ceased; his expressionless face seemed to become more severe, more withdrawn into the vacuum of his own intensity, the nonBeing which seemed to be his major quality. Irritated by Molinari's lack of attention, Freneksy was drawing from this well of his own antiexistence, Eric decided. Casting his principle over the conference room and the people in it, as if forcing everyone away from each other step by step.

"Secretary," Freneksy said, "this now is most crucial. My generals in the field tell me that the new reeg offensive weapon, their—"

"Wait," Molinari croaked. "I wish to confer with my colleague, here beside me." Bending so close to Eric that his soft, perspiration-dampened cheek pressed against his neck, Molinari whispered to him, "And you know what else? I seem to be having trouble with my eyes. As if I'm going completely blind. Here's what I want you to do, doctor; give me a pressure reading right now. Just to be sure it's not dangerously high. I feel it is, frankly."

Eric opened his instrument case.

At the wall map Minister Freneksy said, "Secretary, we must attend to this decisive detail before we can continue. Terran troops do not stand up well against the reegs' new homeostatic bomb, hence I would like to relieve a million and a half of my own factory workers and put them into uniform, replacing them in Empire factories with Terrans. This is an advantage for you, Secretary, in that Terrans will not be fighting and dying in the lines but will be safe inside Empire factories. However, this must be done soon or not at all." He added, "This explains my desire for an immediate conference at a superior level."

Eric read, from the testing disc, a pressure of 290 for Molinari, an elevation unnaturally high and ominous.

"Bad, isn't it?" Molinari said, resting his head on his arms. "Get Teagarden in here," he instructed a robant. "I want him to confer with Dr. Sweetscent; tell him to be prepared to make a diagnosis on the spot."

"Secretary," Freneksy said, "we cannot continue unless you turn your attention to what I'm saying. My request for a million and a half Terran males and females for work in Empire factories—did you hear that? This crucial requisition must be honored at once; transport of these entities must begin no later than the end of this week, your time."

"Um," Molinari murmured. "Yes, Minister, I heard; I'm pondering this request."

"There is nothing to ponder," Freneksy said. "It must be achieved if we are to hold the line on Front C, where reeg pressure is now greatest. A breakthrough is imminent, and Terran brigades have not—"

"I'll have to consult with my Labor Secretary," Molinari said, after a long pause. "Get his approval."

"We *must* have the one and a half million of your people!"

Reaching into his jacket, Molinari fished out his folded sheets of paper. "Minister, this statement which I—"

"Do I have your promise?" Freneksy demanded. "So that we can go on to other matters, now?"

"I'm sick," Molinari said.

There was silence.

At last Freneksy said thoughtfully, "I am aware, Secretary, that your health has not been good for years now. Therefore I took the liberty of bringing an Empire physician with me to this conference. This is Dr. Gornel." On the far side of the table a lank-faced 'Starman nodded curtly to the Mole. "I would like him to examine you, with a view toward making a permanent correction of your physical problems."

"Thank you, Minister," Molinari said. "Your kindness in bringing Dr. Gornel is deeply appreciated. However, I have my own staff physician here, Dr. Sweetscent. He and Dr. Teagarden are about to perform an exploratory examination to determine the cause of my hypertension."

"Now?" Freneksy said, and showed, for the first time, a trace of genuine emotion. Amazed anger.

"My blood pressure is dangerously high," Molinari explained. "If it continues I'll lose my eyesight. In fact already I'm suffering impaired vision." In a low voice he said to Eric, "Doctor, everything around me has become dim; I think I'm already blind. Where the hell's Teagarden?"

Eric said, "I can seek for the source of the hypertension, Secretary; I have the necessary diagnostic instruments with me." He reached into his case once more. "Initially I'll give you an injection of radioactive salts which will carry through your bloodstream—"

"I know," Molinari said. "And collect at the source of the vasoconstriction. Go ahead." He rolled up his sleeve and held out his furry arm; Eric pressed the self-cleansing head of the injecting tube against a vein near the elbow and pressed the tab.

Severely, Minister Freneksy said, "What is taking place, Secretary? Can't we continue with the conference?"

"Yes, go ahead," Molinari said, nodding. "Dr. Sweetscent is merely making an exploration to—"

"Medical matters bore me," Freneksy interrupted. "Secretary, there is a further proposal I wish to make to you now. First, I would like to have my physician, Dr. Gornel, placed permanently on your staff to supervise your medical care. Secondly, I have been informed by the Empire counterintelligence agency operating here on Terra that a group of malcontents, desiring an end to Terra's participation in the war, are planning your assassination; hence I wish, for your safety, to provide you with a perpetual armed guard of 'Starmen commando troops who will, by their extreme courage and determination and efficiency, protect your person at all times. They number twenty-five, an adequate number, given their unique quality."

"What?" Molinari said. He shuddered. "What do you find, doctor?" He seemed confused now, unable to keep his attention fixed on both Eric and the progress of the conference. "Wait, Minister." To Eric he murmured, "What the hell do you find, doctor? Or did you just tell me? Sorry." He rubbed his forehead. "I'm blind!" His voice was filled with panic. "Do something, doctor!"

Eric, examining the sighting graph which traced the movement of the radioactive salts in Molinari's circulatory system said, "There appears to be a stricture of the renal artery which passes through your right kidney. A ring which—"

"I know," Molinari said, nodding. "I knew the stricture was in my right kidney; I've had it before. You'll have to operate, doctor, and cut the ring or it'll kill me." He seemed too weak now to raise his head; he sat slumped over, face in his hands. "God, I feel terrible," he mumbled. Then he raised his head and said to Freneksy, "Minister, I must undergo an immediate corrective operation to relieve this arterial stricture. We'll have to postpone this discussion." He rose to his feet, swayed, and then fell noisily back; Eric and the man from State caught him, helped him back into his chair. The Mole seemed incredibly heavy and inert; Eric could hardly support him, even with assistance.

Freneksy declared, "The conference must continue."

"All right," Molinari gasped. "I'll have the operation while you talk." He nodded weakly to Eric. "Don't wait for Teagarden; get started."

"Here?" Eric said.

"It'll have to be," Molinari whimpered. "Cut the ring, doctor, or I'm dead. I'm dying—I know it." He slumped, then, against the table. And this time he did not draw himself back up to a sitting position; he remained as he was. Like some great discarded, tossed sack.

At the far end of the table UN Vice Secretary Rick Prindle said to Eric, "Begin, doctor. As he said, it's urgent; you know that." Obviously he—and the others present—had been through this before.

Freneksy said, "Secretary, will you empower Mr. Prindle to take your official place in Terra-Lilistar negotiations?"

There was no answer from Molinari; he had passed into unconsciousness.

From his case Eric lifted a small surgical homeostatic unit; it would suffice—he hoped—for the delicate operation. Drilling its own path, and closing the passage behind it, the tool would penetrate the dermal layer and then the omentum until it reached the renal stricture, whereupon, if it was behaving properly, it would begin construction of a plastic bypass for the arterial section; this would be safer, at the moment, than attempting to remove the ring.

The door opened and Dr. Teagarden entered; he hurried up to Eric, saw Molinari lying unconscious with his head on the table, and said, "Are you prepared to operate?"

"I have the equipment; yes, I'm ready."

"No artiforg, of course?"

"It isn't necessary."

Teagarden took hold of Molinari by the wrist, measured his pulse; then he whipped out a stethoscope, unbuttoned the Secretary's jacket and shirt, listened to his heart. "Weak and irregular. We'd better cool him off."

"Yes," Eric agreed, and brought a cold-pak assembly from his case.

Freneksy, coming over to see, said, "You're going to lower his body temperature during the operation?"

"Yes, we'll put him out," Eric said. "The metabolic processes—"

"I don't care to hear," Freneksy said. "Biological matters do not interest me; all I am concerned with is the evident fact that the Secretary is unable to continue at present with this discussion. A discussion for which we have traveled a number of light-years." His face displayed a dull, baffled anger which he could not suppress.

Eric said, "We have no choice, Minister. Molinari is dying."

"I realize that," Freneksy said, and walked away, his fists clenched.

"He's technically dead," Teagarden said, still listening to Molinari's heart action. "Put the freeze into effect at once, doctor."

Eric swiftly attached the cold-pak to Moinari's neck, started its self-contained compression-circuit up. The cold radiated out from it; he let go and turned his attention to the surgical tool.

Minister Freneksy conferred, speaking in his own tongue, with the Empire doctor; he lifted his head all at once and said crisply, "I would like Dr. Gornel to assist in this operation."

Vice Secretary Prindle spoke up. "It can't be permitted. Molinari has given strict orders that only his own staff doctors, chosen by himself personally, are to touch his person." He nodded to Tom Johannson and his corps of Secret Service men; they moved closer to Molinari.

"Why?" Freneksy asked.

"They're familiar with his case history," Prindle said woodenly.

Freneksy shrugged, walked away; he seemed even more baffled now, even bewildered. "It's inconceivable to me," he said aloud, his back to the table, "that this could be permitted to happen, that Secretary Molinari could let his physical condition deteriorate to such a point."

To Teagarden, Eric said, "Has this happened before?"

"You mean has Molinari died during a conference with the 'Starmen?" Teagarden smiled reflexively. "Four times. Right here in this room, even in the same chair. You may start your borer, now."

Placing the homeostatic surgical tool against Molinari's lower right side, Eric activated it; the device, the size of a shot glass, at once flung itself into activity, delivering first a strong local anesthetic and then beginning its task of cutting its way to the renal artery and the kidney.

The only sound in the room now was the whirring caused by the action of the tool; everyone, including Minister Freneksy, watched it disappear from sight, burrowing into Molinari's heavy, motionless, slumped body.

"Teagarden," Eric said, "I suggest that we keep—" He stood back and lit a cigarette. "Watch for a case of hypertension occurring somewhere here in the White House, another partially blocked renal artery or—"

"It's come up already. A maid on the third floor. Hereditary malformation, as it has to be of course. But coming to a crisis in this woman during the last twenty-four hours because of an overdose of amphetamines; she began to lose her sight and we decided to go ahead and operate—that's where I was when I was summoned here. I was just finishing up."

"Then you know," Eric said.

"Know what?" Teagarden's voice was low, concealed from those across the table. "We'll discuss it later. But I can assure you that I know nothing. *Nor do you.*"

Coming over to them, Minister Freneksy said, "How soon will Molinari be capable of resuming this discussion?"

Eric and Teagarden glanced at each other. Caught each other's eye.

"Hard to say," Teagarden said presently.

"Hours? Days? *Weeks?* Last time it was ten days." Freneksy's face writhed with impotence. "I am simply unable to remain here on Terra that long; the conference will have to be rescheduled for later in the year if it's to be a wait of more than seventy-two hours." Behind him his consulting staff, his military and industrial and protocol advisers, were already putting their notes away in their briefcases, closing up shop.

Eric said, "Probably he won't be strong enough within the two-day period generally allowed in cases like this; his overall condition is too—"

Turning to Prindle, Minister Freneksy said, "And you decline any authority as Vice Secretary to speak in his place? What an abominable situation! It's obvious why Terra—" He broke off. "Secretary Molinari is a personal friend of mine," he said, then. "I'm keenly concerned as to his welfare. But why must Lilistar bear the major burden in this war? Why can Terra go on dragging her feet indefinitely?"

Neither Prindle nor the two doctors answered.

In his own language Freneksy spoke to his delegation; they rose en masse, obviously prepared to depart.

The conference, because of Molinari's sudden near-fatal illness, had been called off. At least for now. Eric felt overwhelming relief.

Through his illness Molinari had escaped. But only temporarily.

Nevertheless, that was something. *That was enough.* The million and a half Terrans, demanded by Lilistar for its factories, would not be rounded up . . . Eric glanced at Teagarden, exchanged a brief flash of agreement and comprehension. Meanwhile, the borer went about its task, unaided, whining on.

A psychosomatic, hypochondriacal illness had protected the lives of a great many people and it made Eric rethink, already, the value of medicine, the effect of bringing about a "cure" for Molinari's condition.

It seemed to him as he listened to the borer at work that he was now beginning to understand the situation—and what was really required of him by the ailing UN Secretary who lay against the conference table, neither seeing nor hearing, in a state where the problems of the discussion with Minister Freneksy did not exist.

Later, in his well-guarded bedroom, Gino Molinari sat propped up on pillows, weakly contemplating the homeopape the *New York Times,* which had been placed at his disposal.

"It's okay to read, isn't it, doctor?" he murmured faintly.

"I think so," Eric said. The operation had been totally successful; the elevated blood pressure had been restored to a normal plateau, commensurate with the patient's age and general condition.

"Look at what the damn papers are able to get wind of." Molinari passed the first section to Eric.

> POLICY MEET CALLED OFF ABRUPTLY
> DUE TO SECRETARY'S ILLNESS. 'STAR
> DELEGATION HEADED BY FRENEKSY IN
> SECLUSION.

"How do they find those things out?" Molinari complained peevishly. "God, it makes me look bad; makes it obvious I finked out at a crucial time." He glared at Eric. "If I had any guts I'd have stood up to Freneksy on that labor-force conscription demand." He shut his eyes wearily. "I knew the demand was coming. Knew it last week, even."

"Don't blame yourself," Eric said. How much of the physiological fugal dynamism was comprehensible to Molinari? None of it, evidently; Molinari not only did not grasp the purpose of his illness—he did not even approve of it. And so it continued to function at an unconscious level.

But how long can this go on? Eric wondered. With such a powerful dichotomy between conscious aspiration and unconscious will to escape . . . perhaps, finally, an illness would be produced from which the Secretary would never emerge; it would not only be fatal, *it would be final.*

The door to the room opened; there stood Mary Reineke.

Taking her by the arm, Eric led her back out into the hall, shutting the door after them. "Can't I see him?" she demanded indignantly.

"In a minute." He studied her, still unable to determine just how well she understood the situation. "I want to ask you something. Has Molinari undergone any psychiatric therapy or analysis that you know of?" No mention existed in the file but he had a hunch.

"Why should he?" Mary toyed with the zipper of her shirt. "He's not crazy."

That certainly was true; he nodded. "But his physical—"

"Gino has bad luck. That's why he's always getting sick. You know no psychiatrist is going to change his luck." Mary Reineke added with reluctance, "Yes, he did consult an analyst once, last year, a few times. But that's top secret; if the homeopapes got hold of it—"

"Give me the analyst's name."

"The hell I will." Her black eyes snapped with hostile triumph; she glared at him unwinkingly. "I won't even tell Dr. Teagarden, and him I like."

"After watching Gino's illness in action I feel I—"

"The analyst," Mary broke in, "is dead. Gino had him killed."

Eric stared at her.

"Guess why." She smiled with the random malice of a teenage girl, the purposeless, delicious cruelty which took him back in a flash to his own boyhood. To the agonies such girls had caused him before. "It was something the analyst said. About Gino's illness. I don't know what it was but I assume he was on the right track . . . as you think you are. So do you really want to be so clever?"

"You remind me," he said, "of Minister Freneksy."

She pushed by him, toward Gino's door. "I want to go on in; goodbye."

"Did you know that Gino died there in that conference room today?"

"Yes, he had to. Just for a few moments, of course; not long enough to muddle his brain cells. And of course you and Teagarden cooled him right down; I know about that, too. Why do I remind you of Freneksy, *that* crulp!" She came back toward him, studying him intently. "I'm not like him at all. You're just trying to make me sore so I'll tell you something."

Eric said, "What do you think I want you to tell me?"

"About Gino's suicide impulses." She spoke matter-of-factly. "He has them; everybody knows that. That's why I was brought here by his relatives, to make sure somebody spent every night with him, snuggled right up against him in bed every hour or watching him while he paces around when he can't sleep. He can't be alone at night; he's got to have me to talk to. And I can talk sense to him—you know, restore his perspective at four o'clock in the morning. That's hard to do, but I do it." She smiled. "See? Do you have somebody to do that for *you,* doctor? At your four a.m. moments?"

Presently he shook his head no.

"A shame. You need it. Too bad I can't do it for you, too, but one's enough. Anyhow you're not my type. But good luck—maybe someday you'll find someone like me." Opening the door, she disappeared. He stood alone in the corridor, feeling futile. And, all at once, extremely lonely.

I wonder what became of the analyst's files? he thought mechanically, turning his mind back to his job. No doubt Gino had them destroyed, so as not to fall into 'Star hands.

That's right, he thought. It is about four a.m. when it hits the hardest. But there's no one else like you, he thought. So that's that.

"Dr. Sweetscent?"

He glanced up. A Secret Service man had approached him. "Yes."

"Doctor, there's a woman outside who says she's your wife; she wants to be admitted to the building."

"It can't be," Eric said, with fear.

"You want to come with me and see if you can identify her, please?"

Automatically he fell in beside the Secret Service man. "Tell her to go away," he said. No, he thought, that won't do; you don't handle your problems like that, like a child waving a wand. "I have no doubt it's Kathy," he said. "Followed me here after all. In the name of God—what dreadful luck. Did you ever feel this way?" he asked the Secret Service man. "Did you ever find yourself unable to live with someone you had to live with?"

"Nope," the Secret Service man said unfeelingly, leading the way.

10

His wife stood in a corner of the outside compound which was the White House receiving room, reading a homeopape, the *New York Times;* she wore a dark coat and a good deal of make-up. Her skin, however, looked pale and her eyes seemed enormous, filled with anguish.

As he entered the compound she glanced up and said, "I'm reading about you; it seems you operated on Molinari and saved his life. Congratulations." She smiled at him but it was a bleak, trembling smile. "Take me somewhere and buy me a cup of coffee; I have a lot to tell you."

"You've got nothing to tell me," he said, unable to keep his stunned dismay out of his voice.

"I had a major insight after you left," Kathy said.

"So did I. It was that we'd done the right thing by splitting up."

"That's strange, because my insight was just the opposite," she said.

"I see that. Obviously. You're here. Listen: by law I don't have to live with you. All I'm required to do—"

"You ought to listen to what I have to say," Kathy said steadily. "It wouldn't be morally right for you just to walk off; that's too easy."

He sighed. Useful philosophy by which to achieve one's

goals. But nevertheless he was snared. "Okay," he agreed. "I can't do that, just as I couldn't honestly deny you're my wife. So let's have the coffee." He felt fatalistic. Perhaps it was an attenuated form of his self-destructive instinct. In any case he had given in; taking her arm, he guided her along the passage, past the White House guards, toward the nearest cafeteria. "You look bad," he said. "Your color. And you're so tense."

"I've had a bad time," she admitted, "since you left. I guess I'm really dependent on you."

"Symbiosis," he said. "Unhealthy."

"It's not that!"

"Sure it is. This proves it. No, I'm not going to go back with you on the old basis." He felt—at least for the moment—determined; he was prepared to fight it out, here and now. Eyeing her, he said, "Kathy, you look quite sick."

"That's because you've been hanging around the Mole; you're getting used to a sick environment. I'm perfectly well, just a little tired."

But she looked—smaller. As if something in her had dwindled away, as if she had dried up. It was almost—age. Yet not quite. Could their separation have done this much damage? He doubted it. His wife, since he had seen her last, had become frail, and he did not like this; despite his animosity he felt concern.

"You better get a multiphasic," he said. "A complete checkup."

"Christ," Kathy said, "I'm okay. I mean, I'll be okay, if you and I can iron out our misunderstanding and—"

"The termination of a relationship," he said, "is not a misunderstanding. It's a reorganization of life." He got his coffee cup and hers, filled both from the dispenser, paid the robant cashier.

When they had seated themselves at a table, Kathy lit a cigarette and said, "All right, suppose I admit it; without you I'm completely falling apart. Do you care?"

"I care, but that doesn't mean—"

"You'd just let me fade away and perish."

"I have one sick man who occupies all my time and attention. I can't heal you too." Especially, he thought, when I don't genuinely want to.

"But all you have to do is—" She sighed, sipped her coffee glumly; her hand trembled, he noticed, in an almost pseudo Parkinsonism. "Nothing. Just accept me back. Then I'll be well."

"No," he said. "I frankly don't believe it. You're sicker than that; there's some other cause." I'm not in the medical profession by mistake, he thought. I can spot a thoroughgoing illness pattern when I see it. But he could not diagnose it beyond that. "I think you know what ails you," he said bluntly. "You could tell me if you cared to. This makes me more wary than ever; you're not telling me all that you should, you're not being honest or responsible, and that's a hell of a basis on which to—"

"Okay!" She stared at him. "I'm sick; I admit it! But let's just say it's my business; you don't have to worry."

"I'd say," he said, "that there's been neurological damage."

Her head jerked; what color she had now drained from her face.

"I think," he said suddenly, "that I'm going to do something I genuinely think may be premature and overly drastic, but I'll try it and see what comes of it. I'm going to have you arrested."

"Good God *why*?" Panic stricken, she gazed at him, now speechless; her hands lifted in defense, then fell back.

He rose, walked over to a cafeteria employee. "Miss," he said, "would you have a Secret Service man come to my table?" He pointed to his table.

"Yes sir," the woman said, blinking but unperturbed. She turned to a busboy, who, without further discussion, scampered off into the kitchen.

Eric returned to his table, reseated himself opposite Kathy. He resumed sipping his coffee, trying to keep himself calm and at the same time bracing himself for the scene that lay ahead. "My rationale," he said, "is that it's for your own good. Of course I don't know yet. But I think it'll turn out that way. And I think you know it."

Blanched, wizened with fright, Kathy implored, "I'll leave, Eric; I'll go back to San Diego—okay?"

"No," he said. "You got yourself into this by coming here; you made it my business. So you'll have to suffer the consequences. As they say." He felt completely rational and in control; it was a bad situation but he sensed the possibilities of something imminent which was far worse.

Kathy said huskily, "Okay, Eric. I'll tell you what it is. I've got myself addicted to JJ-180. That's the drug I told you about, the drug we all, including Marm Hastings, took. Now you know. I have nothing more to say; that covers it. And I've taken it once since. And just one exposure is addicting. As you no doubt realize; after all, you are a doctor."

"Who else knows?"

"Jonas Ackerman."

"You got it through Tijuana Fur & Dye? From our subsidiary?"

"Y-yes." She did not meet his gaze. Presently she added, "That's why Jonas knows; he got it for me—but don't tell anybody that. Please."

Eric said, "I won't." His mind had begun to function properly again, thank God. Was this the drug which Don Festenburg had obliquely referred to? The term JJ-180 roused dormant memories; he tried to straighten them out. "You made a hell of a mistake," he said, "from what I remember hearing about Frohedadrine, as it's also called. Yes, Hazeltine makes it."

At the table a Secret Service man appeared. "Yes, doctor?"

"I just wanted to inform you that this woman is my wife, as she says. And I'd like to have her cleared to remain here with me."

"All right, doctor. We'll run a routine security probe on her. But I'm certain it's okay." The Secret Service man nodded and departed.

"Thanks," Kathy said presently.

"I consider addiction to such a toxic drug a major illness," Eric said. "In this day and age worse than cancer or a massive cardiac arrest. It's obvious I can't dump you. You'll probably have to enter a hospital; you're probably aware of that already. I'll contact Hazeltine, find out all they know . . . but you understand it may be hopeless."

"Yes." She ducked her head in a spasmodic nod.

"Anyhow, you seem to have a great deal of courage." He reached out, took hold of her hand; it was dry and cold. Lifeless. He let it go. "That has always been one thing I've admired in you—you're not a coward. Of course that's how you got yourself into this in the first place, by having the guts to try some new substance. Well, so now we're back together." Glued fast to each other by your possibly fatal drug habit, he thought with morose despair. What a reason to resume our marriage. It was just a little too much for him.

"You're a good egg, too," Kathy said.

"Do you have any more of the stuff?"

She hesitated. "N-no."

"You're lying."

"I won't give it up. I'd rather leave you and try to make it on my own." Her fear had become, momentarily, obstinate defiance. "Look, if I'm hooked on JJ-180 I *can't* give you the supply I possess—that's what it means to be hooked! I don't want to take any more; I have to take it. Anyhow, there's not much." She shuddered. "It makes me wish I were dead; that goes without saying. God, I don't know how I got myself into this."

"What's the experience like? I understand it involves time."

"Yes, you lose your fixed point of reference; you pass easily back and forth. What I'd like to do is put myself at the service of someone or something, find a use for the period that I'm in the hands of. Could the Secretary use me? Eric, maybe I could get us out of the war; I could warn Molinari before he signs the Pact of Peace." Her eyes glowed with hope. "Isn't it worth trying?"

"Maybe so." However, he recalled Festenburg's statements

on the subject; perhaps Molinari had use of JJ-180 already. But the Mole clearly had not tried—or been able—to find a route back to pre-pact days. Perhaps the drug affected each person uniquely. Many stimulant, hallucinogenic drugs did.

"Can I get access to him through you?" Kathy asked.

"I—suppose so." But something sprang to life inside him and made him wary. "It would take time. Right now he's recovering from the kidney operation, as you seem to know."

She shook her head then, nodding with pain. "Jesus, I feel awful, Eric. Like I'm not going to survive. You know . . . impending disaster. Give me a bunch of tranquilizers; it might help a little." She held out her hand and again he saw how badly it shook. Even worse, it seemed, than before.

"I'll put you in the building's infirmary," he decided, rising to his feet. "For the time being. While I figure out what to do. I'd prefer not to give you any medication, though; it might further potentiate the drug. With a new substance you never—"

Kathy broke in, "Want to know what I did, Eric, while you were off getting the Secret Service? I dropped a cap of JJ-180 into your coffee cup. Don't laugh; I'm serious. It's true, and you've drunk it. So you're addicted now. The effects should begin anytime; you'd better get out of this cafeteria and to your own conapt, because they're enormous." Her voice was flat and drab. "I did it because I thought you were going to have me arrested; you said you were and I believed you. So it's your own fault. I'm sorry . . . I wish I hadn't, but anyhow now you have a motive for curing me; you've *got* to find a solution. I just couldn't depend on your sheer good-will; we've had too much trouble between us. Isn't that so?"

He managed to say, "I've heard that about addicts in general; they like to hook other people."

"Do you forgive me?" Kathy asked, also rising.

"No," he said. He felt wrathful and dizzy. Not only do I not forgive you, he thought, but I'll do everything I can to deny you a cure; nothing means anything to me now except getting back at you. Even my own cure. He felt pure, absolute hate for her. Yes, this was what she would do; this was his wife. This was precisely why he had tried to get away.

"We're in this together," Kathy said.

As steadily as possible he walked toward the exit of the cafeteria, step by step, past the tables, people. Leaving her.

He almost made it. He almost.

Everything returned. But totally different. New. Changed.

Across from him Don Festenburg leaned back, said, "You're lucky. But I'd better explain this. Here. The calendar." He pushed a brass object; across the desk Eric saw. "You've moved slightly over one year ahead." Eric stared. Sightlessly. Ornate inscriptions. "This is June 17, 2056. You're one of the happy few the drug affects this way. Most of them wander off into the past and get bogged down in manufacturing alternate universes; you know, playing God until at last the nerve destruction is too great and they degenerate to random twitches."

Eric tried to think of something useful to say. Could not.

"Save yourself the effort," Festenburg said, seeing him struggle. "I can do the talking; you'll only be here a few minutes so let me get it said. A year ago, when you were given JJ-180 in the building cafeteria, I was fortunate enough to get in on the flurry; your wife became hysterical and you of course—disappeared. She was taken in tow by the Secret Service and she admitted her addiction and what she had done."

"Oh." The room dropped and rose as he reflexively nodded.

"So that—you're feeling better? So anyhow, but now Kathy is cured, but we won't go into that; it hardly matters."

"What about—"

"Yes, your problem. Your addiction. There was no cure then, a year ago. However, you'll be gratified to hear that there is now. It came into being a couple of months ago, and I've been waiting for you to show up—so much more is known about JJ-180 now that I was privileged to compute almost to the minute when and where you'd appear." Reaching into his rumpled coat pocket, Festenburg brought out a small glass bottle. "This is the antidote which TF&D's subsidiary now manufactures. Would you like it? If you took it now, twenty milligrams, you'd be free of your addiction even after you return to your own time." He smiled, his sallow face wrinkling unnaturally. "But—there are problems."

Eric said, "How is the war going?"

Deprecatingly, Festenburg said, "What do you care? Good God, Sweetscent; your life depends on this bottle—you don't know what addiction to that stuff is like!"

"Is Molinari still alive?"

Festenburg shook his head. "Minutes he's got and he wants to know about the Mole's state of health. Listen." He leaned toward Eric, his mouth turned down poutingly, his face puffy with agitation. *"I want to make a deal, doctor.* I'm asking astonishingly little in return for these medication tablets. *Please* do business with me; the next time you take the drug— if you're not cured—you'll go ten years into the future and that'll be too late, too far."

Eric said, "Too late for you, but not for me. The cure will still exist."

"You won't even ask what I want in return?"

"No."

"Why not?"

Eric shrugged. "I don't feel comfortable; I'm being subjected to pressure and I don't care for that—I'll take my chances with the drug without you." It was sufficient merely to know that a cure existed. Such knowledge obliterated his anxiety and left him free to do as he liked. "Obviously, my best bet is to use the drug as often as physiologically possible, two or three times, going farther into the future each time, and then when its destructive effects become too great—"

"Even one use," Festenburg said between his clenched teeth, "causes irreversible brain damage. You damn fool— *you've already used it too much.* You saw your wife; you want that damage for yourself?"

After a moment, considering deeply, Eric said, "For what

I'll get out of it, yes. By the time I've used it twice I'll know the outcome of the war and if the outcome is unfavorable possibly I'll be in a position to advise Molinari how it could be avoided. What's my health compared to that?" He was silent then; it seemed perfectly clear to him. There was nothing to discuss; he sat waiting for the effects of the drug to wear off. He waited to return to his own time.

Opening the glass bottle, Festenburg poured out the white tablets; he dropped them to the floor and ground them to dust under his heel.

"Did it occur to you," Festenburg said, "that within the next ten years Terra may be so destroyed in the war that TF&D's subsidiary may no longer be in a position to supply this antidote?"

It had not occurred to him; although jolted, he managed not to show it. "We'll see," he murmured.

"Frankly I have no knowledge of the future. However, I have knowledge of the past—of *your* future, this last year." He produced a homeopape, which he turned toward Eric and spread out on the desk. "Six months following your experience in the White House cafeteria. It'll interest you."

Eric scanned the lead article and its headline.

SWEETSCENT IMPLICATED AS PRIME MOVER IN
DOCTOR'S PLOT AGAINST ACTING UN SECRETARY
DONALD FESTENBURG, HELD BY SECRET SERVICE

Abruptly Festenburg whipped the newspaper away, crumpling it and tossing it behind him. "I'm not saying what became of Molinari—find that out for yourself, since you're uninterested in reaching a rational agreement with me."

After a pause Eric said, "You've had a year to print up a fake of the *Times,* I seem to recall that such has been done before in political history . . . Joseph Stalin did it to Lenin during Lenin's last year. Had a completely phony edition of *Pravda* printed, given to Lenin, who—"

"My uniform," Festenburg said wildly, his face dark red

and quivering as if it were about to burst. "Look at my shoulder patches!"

"Why couldn't that be faked, too? I'm not saying it is, or that the homeopape was faked." After all, he was not in a position to know one way or another. "I'm merely saying it could be, and that's enough to cause me to suspend my judgment."

With enormous effort Festenburg managed to gain partial control of himself. "All right; you're playing it cautious. This entire experience is disorienting to you—I understand. But doctor, be realistic for a moment; you've seen the pape, you know that in a way which I'm not specifying I succeeded Molinari as UN Secretary. Plus the fact that six months from your own time period you were caught red-handed conspiring against me. And—"

"Acting UN Secretary," Eric amended.

"What?" Festenburg stared at him.

"A pro tem situation is implied. Transitional. And I wasn't—or won't be—caught 'red-handed.' The pape merely relates an accusation; there's been no trial, no conviction. I could be innocent. I could be about to be framed, and by you. Again, recall Stalin during his last year, the so-called—"

"Don't lecture me in my own field! Yes, I know of the situation you related; I know how completely Stalin fooled the dying Lenin. And I know about the doctor's plot, paranoically engineered by Stalin during his final illness. Okay—" Festenburg's voice was steady. "I admit it. That homeopape which I showed you just now—it was faked."

Eric smiled.

"And I'm not Acting UN Secretary," Festenburg continued. "But as to what actually has happened—*I'll leave it to you to guess*. And you're not going to be able to; you're going to return to your own time a few moments from now knowing nothing, not a damn thing, about the world of the future—whereas if you had made a few deals with me you could know everything." He glowered at Eric.

"I guess," Eric said, "I'm a fool."

"More than that: polymorphic perverse. You could be going back armed with incredible weapons—in the figurative sense, of course—to save yourself, your wife, Molinari. And for one year you'll stew . . . assuming that you survive your drug addiction that long. We'll see."

For the first time Eric felt a wavering doubt. Was he making an error? After all, he had not even heard what he would need to pony up in order to consummate the deal. But now the antidote had been destroyed; it was too late. This was just talk.

Rising, Eric took a quick look out of the window at the city of Cheyenne.

The city was in ruins.

While he stood staring at that he felt the reality of the room, the substantiality of what he saw, ebb; it eased away from him and he clutched at it, trying to retain it.

"Much luck, doctor," Festenburg said hollowly, and then he, too, became a streak of foglike wispiness that eddied gray and indistinct around him, blending with the disintegrated remnants of the desk, the walls of the room, the objects that a moment before had been utterly stable.

He lurched—and struggled to catch himself. Losing his balance, he pitched into the sickening experience of no weight . . . and then, with pain banging at his head, he looked up, saw around him the tables and people of the White House cafeteria.

A group had formed around him. Concerned but hesitant. Unwilling to actually touch him; they remained spectators.

"Thanks for the help," he grated, and got unsteadily to his feet.

The spectators melted guiltily off to their tables, leaving him alone. Alone—except for Kathy.

"You were out about three minutes," she said.

He said nothing; he had no desire to speak to her, to have anything to do with her. He felt nauseated and his legs shook under him; his head felt splintered and broken and he thought, This must be how it feels to experience carbon monoxide poisoning. As described in the old textbooks. A sense of having imbibed of death itself.

"Can I help you?" Kathy asked. "I remember how I felt the first time."

Eric said, "I'll take you to the infirmary now." He grabbed her by the arm; her purse bobbed against him. "You must have your supply in your purse," he said, and yanked it away from her.

A moment later he held two elongated spansules in his hand. Dropping them into his pocket, he returned her purse to her.

"Thanks," she said with massive irony.

"Thank you, too, dear. We've each got a lot of love for one another. In this new phase of our marital relationship." He led her from the cafeteria then; she accompanied him without resistance.

I'm glad I didn't make a deal with Festenburg, he thought. But Festenburg would be after him again; this was not the end. However, he possessed an advantage over Festenburg, one which the sallow-faced speech writer did not—at this date—know of.

From his encounter a year hence he knew that Festenburg had political ambitions. That in some fashion he would attempt a coup and would try to buy support. The UN Secretary uniform had turned out to be ersatz, but Festenburg's aspirations had not.

And it was entirely possible that Festenburg had not yet begun this phase of his career.

Festenburg, in this time period, could not take Eric Sweetscent by surprise because one year in the future, unknown to his present self, he had tipped his hand. And, in doing so, had not grasped the implications of what he had done.

It was a major political error and one which could not be retrieved. Especially in view of the fact that other political strategists, some with immense capabilities, were on the scene.

One of these was Gino Molinari.

After he had gotten his wife admitted to the White House infirmary, he placed a vidphone call to Jonas Ackerman at TF&D in Tijuana.

"So you know about Kathy," Jonas said. He did not look happy.

"I'm not going to ask you why you did it," Eric said. "I'm calling in order to—"

"Did what?" Jonas' face convulsed. "She told you I put her on the stuff, did she? Not true, Eric. Why should I do that? Ask yourself."

"We won't discuss that now." There was no time. "I want to find out, first, if Virgil knows anything about JJ-180."

"Yes, but no more than I do. There's not much—"

"Let me talk to Virgil."

Reluctantly, Jonas switched the call to Virgil's office. Eric after a moment faced the old man, who leered with guileless abandon when he saw who was calling. "Eric! I read in the pape—you've already saved his life once. I knew you'd make out. Now, if you can do that every day—" Virgil chuckled delightedly.

"Kathy is addicted to JJ-180. I need help; I have to get her off it."

The pleased emotions left Virgil's face. "That's horrible! But what can I do, Eric? I'd like to, of course. We all love Kathy around here. You're a doctor, Eric; you ought to be able to do something for her." He tried to babble on but Eric interrupted.

"Tell me who to contact at the subsidiary. Where JJ-180 is made."

"Oh yes. Hazeltine Corporation in Detroit. Let's see . . . who should you talk to there? Maybe Bert Hazeltine himself. Just a minute; Jonas is up here in my office. He's saying something."

Jonas appeared on the vidscreen. "I was trying to tell you, Eric. When I found out about Kathy's situation I contacted Hazeltine Corporation immediately. They've already sent someone out; he's on his way to Cheyenne; I figured Kathy would show up there after she disappeared. Keep Virgil and me posted as to what progress he can make. Good luck." He disappeared from the screen, evidently relieved to have contributed his share.

Thanking Virgil, Eric rang off. Rising, he at once went to the White House receiving room to see if the representative of Hazeltine Corporation had shown up yet.

"Oh yes, Dr. Sweetscent," the girl said, checking her book. "Two persons arrived just a moment ago; you're being paged in the halls and in the cafeterias." She read the names from the book. "A Mr. Bert Hazeltine and a woman, Miss Bachis . . . I'm trying to read her writing; I think that's it. They were sent upstairs to your conapt."

When he reached his conapt he found the door ajar; in the small living room sat two individuals, a middle-aged man, well dressed in a long overcoat, and a blonde-haired woman, in her late thirties; she wore glasses and her features were heavy and professionally competent.

"Mr. Hazeltine?" Eric said, entering with his hand out.

Both the man and woman rose. "Hello, Dr. Sweetscent." Bert Hazeltine shook hands with him. "This is Hilda Bachis; she's with the UN Narcotics Control Bureau. They had to be informed of your wife's situation, doctor; it's the law. However—"

Miss Bachis spoke up crisply, "We're not interested in arresting or punishing your wife, doctor; we want to help her, as you do. We've already arranged to see her but we thought we'd talk with you first and then go down to the infirmary."

In a quiet voice Hazeltine said, "Your wife has how large a supply of the drug with her?"

"None," Eric said.

"Let me explain to you, then," Hazeltine said, "the difference between habituation and addiction. In addiction—"

"I'm a doctor," Eric reminded him. "You don't have to spell it out for me." He seated himself, still feeling the effects of his bout with the drug; his head still ached and his chest hurt when he breathed.

"Then you realize that the drug has entered her liver metabolism and now is required for that metabolism to continue. If she's denied the drug she'll die in—" Hazeltine calculated. "How much has she taken?"

"Two or three capsules."

"Without it she'll die very possibly within twenty-four hours."

"And with it?"

"She'll live roughly four months. By that time, doctor, we may have an antidote; don't think we're not trying. We've even tried artiforg transplant, removing the liver and substituting—"

"Then she's got to have more of the drug," Eric said, and he thought about himself. His own situation. "Suppose she had only taken it once. Would that—"

"Doctor," Hazeltine said, "don't you understand? JJ-180 was not designed as a medicine; *it's a weapon of war*. It was *intended* to be capable of creating an absolute addiction by a single dose; it was *intended* to bring about extensive nerve and brain damage. It's odorless and tasteless; you can't tell when it's being administered to you in, say, food or drink. From the start we faced the problem of our own people becoming accidentally addicted; we were waiting until we had the cure and then we would use JJ-180 against the enemy. But—" He eyed Eric. "Your wife was not accidentally addicted, doctor. It was done with deliberate intent. We know where she got it." He glanced at Miss Bachis.

"Your wife couldn't have obtained it from Tijuana Fur & Dye," Miss Bachis said, "because no quantity of the drug whatsoever has been released by Hazeltine to its parent company."

"Our ally," Bert Hazeltine said. "It was a protocol of the Pact of Peace; we had to deliver to them a sample of every new weapon of war produced on Terra. The UN compelled me to ship a quantity of JJ-180 to Lilistar." His face had become slack with what for him was now a stale, flat resentment.

Miss Bachis said, "The quantity of JJ-180, for security

purposes, was shipped to Lilistar in five separate containers on five separate transports. Four reached Lilistar. One did not; the reegs destroyed it with an automine. And, since then, we've heard persistent rumors through our intelligence service operating within the Empire that 'Star agents have carried the drug back here to Terra, to use against our people."

Eric nodded. "All right; she didn't get it at Tijuana Fur & Dye." But what did it matter where Kathy had gotten it?

"So your wife," Miss Bachis said, "has been approached by 'Star intelligence agents and therefore can't be kept here in Cheyenne; we've already talked to the Secret Service and she's to be transferred back to Tijuana or San Diego. There's no alternative; she hasn't admitted it, of course, but she's being supplied in exchange for acting as a 'Star recruit. That could be why she followed you here."

"But," Eric said, "if you cut off her supply of the drug—"

"We don't intend that," Hazeltine said. "In fact just the opposite; the most thoroughgoing method of detaching her from the 'Star agents is to supply her directly from our stock. That's policy in cases such as this . . . and your wife is not the first, doctor; we've seen this before and, take my word for it, we know what to do. That is, within the limited number of possibilities open to us. First, she needs the drug merely to stay alive; that alone makes it essential to keep her supplied. But there's one more fact you should know. The shipment that was sent to Lilistar but was destroyed by a reeg mine . . . we understand now that the reegs were able to salvage portions of that ship. They obtained a minute but nonetheless real quantity of JJ-180." He paused. "They're working on a cure, too."

The room was silent.

"*We* don't have a cure anywhere on Terra," Hazeltine continued, after a pause. "Lilistar, of course, isn't even trying, despite what they may have told your wife; they're simply cranking out their own supply of the drug, no doubt to use against us as well as the enemy. That's a fact of life. But—a cure may already exist among the reegs; it would be unfair and morally wrong not to tell you this. I'm not suggesting that you defect to the enemy; I'm not suggesting anything— I'm just being honest with you. In four months we may have it or we may not; I have no way of knowing the future."

"The drug," Eric said, "permits some of its users to pass into the future."

Hazeltine and Miss Bachis exchanged glances.

"True," Hazeltine said, nodding. "That's highly classified information, as you no doubt know. I suppose you learned that from your wife. Is that the direction she moves when she's under the influence of the drug? It's relatively rare; withdrawal into the past seems to be the rule."

Guardedly Eric said, "Kathy and I have talked about it."

"Well," Hazeltine said, "it's a possibility, logically at least. To go into the future, obtain the cure—perhaps not a quantity of it but anyhow the formula; memorize it and then return to the present, turn the formula over to our chemists at H. Corporation. And that would be that. It seems almost *too* easy, doesn't it? The drug's effects contain the method of procuring the nullifying agent, the source of a new, unknown molecule to enter the liver metabolism in place of JJ-180. . . . The first objection that occurs to me is that there may never be such an antidote, in which case going into the future is useless. After all, there is not yet any sure cure for addiction to opium derivatives; heroin is still illegal and dangerous, as much so as a century ago. But another objection, a deeper one, occurs to me. Frankly—and I've supervised all phases of testing JJ-180—I feel that the time period entered by the subject under its influence is phony. I don't believe it's the real future or the real past."

"Then what is it?" Eric asked.

"What we at Hazeltine Corporation have maintained from the start; we claim that JJ-180 is a hallucinogenic drug and we mean just that. Just because the hallucinations seem real, that's no criterion to go by; *most* hallucinations seem real whatever the cause, whether from a drug, a psychosis, brain damage, or electrical stimulation given directly to specific areas of the brain. You must know that, doctor; a person experiencing hallucinosis doesn't merely think he sees, say, a tree of oranges—he really does see it. For him it's an authentic experience, as much so as our presence here in your living room. No one who's taken JJ-180 and gone into the past has returned with any artifact; he doesn't disappear or—"

Miss Bachis interrupted, "I disagree, Mr. Hazeltine. I've talked to a number of JJ-180 addicts and they've given details about the past which I'm positive they wouldn't know except by having gone there. I can't prove it but I do believe it. Excuse me for interrupting."

"Buried memories," Hazeltine said irritably. "Or Christ, possibly past lives; maybe there is reincarnation."

Eric said, "If JJ-180 did induce authentic time travel it might not constitute a good weapon to use against the reegs. It might give them more than it took. So you must believe it's hallucinosis, Mr. Hazeltine. As long as you have plans of selling it to the government."

"An *ad hominem* argument," Hazeltine said. "Attack my motives, not my argument; I'm surprised, doctor." He looked glum. "But maybe you're right. How do I know? I've never taken it, and we've given it to no one once we discovered its addictive properties; we're limited to animal experiments, our first—and unfortunate—human subjects, and more recent ones such as your wife whom the 'Starmen have made into addicts. And—" He hesitated, then shrugged and continued. "And, obviously, we've given it to captured reegs in POW camps; otherwise we would have no way of determining its effects on them."

"How have they responded?" Eric asked.

"More or less as our own people. Complete addiction, neurological decay, hallucinations of an overpowering order which made them apathetic to their actual situation." He added, half to himself, "The things you have to do in wartime. And they talk about the Nazis."

Miss Bachis said, "We must win the war, Mr. Hazeltine."

"Yes," Hazeltine said lifelessly. "Oh, you're so goddam

right, Miss Bachis; how truly right you are." He stared sight-lessly down at the floor.

"Give Dr. Sweetscent the supply of the drug," Miss Bachis said.

Nodding, Hazeltine reached into his coat. "Here." He held out a flat metal tin. "JJ-180. Legally we can't give it to your wife; we can't supply a known addict. So you take it—this is a formality, obviously—and what you do with it is your own business. Anyhow, there's enough in that tin to keep her alive for as long as she'll live." He did not meet Eric's gaze; he continued to stare at the floor.

Eric, as he accepted the tin, said, "You're not very happy about this invention of your company's."

"Happy?" Hazeltine echoed. "Oh sure; can't you see? Doesn't it show? You know, oddly enough, the worst has been watching the reeg POWs after they've taken it. They just plain fold up, wilt; there's no remission at all for them . . . they live JJ-180, once they've touched it. They're *glad* to be on it; the hallucinations are that—what should I say?—entertaining for them . . . no, not entertaining. En-grossing? I don't know, but they act as if they've looked into the ultimate. But it's one which, clinically speaking, phys-iologically speaking, constitutes as insidious hell."

"Life is short," Eric pointed out.

"And brutish and nasty," Hazeltine added, vaguely quot-ing, as if responding unconsciously. "I can't be fatalistic, doctor. Maybe you're lucky or smart, some such thing."

"No," Eric said. "Hardly that." To be a depressive was certainly not desirable; fatalism was not a talent but a pro-tracted illness. "How soon after taking JJ-180 do the with-drawal symptoms appear? In other words must—"

"You can go from twelve to twenty-four hours between dosages," Miss Bachis said. "Then the physiological require-ments, the collapse of adequate liver metabolism, sets in. It's—unpleasant. So to speak."

Hazeltine said hoarsely, "Unpleasant—God in heaven, be realistic; it's unendurable. It's a death agony, literally. And the person knows it. *Feels* it without being able to label it.

After all, how many of us have gone into our death agonies?"

"Gino Molinari has," Eric said. "But he's unique." Placing the tin of JJ-180 in his coat pocket, he thought, So I have up to twenty-four hours before I'll be forced to take my second dose of the drug. But it could come as soon as this evening.

So the reegs may have a cure, he thought. Would I go over to them to save my life? Kathy's life? I wonder. He did not really know.

Perhaps, he thought, I'll know after I undergo my first bout with the withdrawal symptoms. And, if not that, after I detect the first signs of neurological deterioration in my body.

It still dazed him that his wife had, just like that, addicted him. What hatred that showed. What enormous contempt for the value of life. But didn't he feel the same way? He remembered his initial discussion with Gino Molinari; his sentiments had emerged then and he had faced them. In the final analysis he felt as Kathy did. This was one great effect of war; the survival of one individual seemed trivial. So perhaps he could blame it on the war. That would make it easier.

But he knew better.

11

On his way to the infirmary to turn over to Kathy her supply of the drug, he found himself facing, unbelievably, the slumped, ill figure of Gino Molinari. In his wheelchair the UN Secretary sat with his heavy wool rug over his knees, his eyes writhing like separate living things, pinning Eric into immobility.

"Your conapt was bugged," Molinari said. "Your conversation with Hazeltine and Bachis was picked up, recorded, and delivered in transcript form to me."

"So quickly?" Eric managed to say. Thank God he had made no reference to his own addiction.

"Get her out of here," Molinari moaned. "She's a 'Star fink; she'll do anything—I know. This has happened before." He was shaking. "As a matter of fact she's already out of here; my Secret Service men grabbed her and took her to the field, to a 'copter. So I don't know why I'm getting myself upset like this . . . intellectually I know the situation's in hand."

"If you have a transcript you know that Miss Bachis already arranged for Kathy to—"

"I know! All right." Molinari panted for breath, his face unhealthy and raw; his skin hung in folds, dark, wrinkled wattles of loose flesh. "See how Lilistar operates? Using our own drug against us; it's just like the bastards, something they'd get a kick out of. We ought to drop it in their reservoirs. I let you in here and then you let your wife in; to obtain that crap, that miserable drug, she'd be willing to do anything—assassinate me if they asked her to. I know everything there is to know about Frohedadrine; I'm the one who thought up the name. From the German *Froh,* meaning joy, and the Latin *heda-,* the root for pleasure. *Drine,* of course—" He broke off, his swollen lips twitching. "I'm too sick to get agitated like this; I'm supposed to be recovering from that operation. *Are you trying to heal me or kill me, doctor? Or do you know?"*

Eric said, "I don't know." He felt confused, numbed; this was just too much.

"You look bad. This is tough on you, even though according to your security file and your own statements you detest your wife—and she you. I guess you figure if you'd stayed with her she wouldn't have become an addict. Listen: everyone has to live his own life; she has to take the responsibility. You didn't make her do it. She *decided* to do it. Does that help you? Feel any better?" He scanned Eric's face for his reaction.

"I'll—be okay," Eric said briefly.

"In a pig's ass. You look as bad as she does; I went down there to have a look at her, I couldn't resist. The poor goddam dame; you already can make out the destruction caused by that stuff. And giving her a new liver and all new blood won't help; that's been tried before, as they told you."

"Did you talk to Kathy at all?"

"Me? Talk to a 'Star fink?" Molinari glared at him. "Yes, I talked to her a little. While they were wheeling her out. I was curious to see what sort of woman you'd get mixed up with; you've got a masochistic streak eight yards wide and she proves it; she's a harpy, Sweetscent, a monster. Like you told me. You know what she said?" He grinned. "She told me *you're* an addict. Anything to cause trouble, right?"

"Right," Eric said stiffly.

"Why are you looking at me that way?" Molinari regarded

him, his black, fat eyes showing his regained control. "It upsets you to hear that, doesn't it? To know she'd do everything possible to destroy your career here. Eric, if I thought you'd dabbled with that stuff I wouldn't have you kicked out of here; *I'd have you killed*. During wartime I kill people; it's my job. Just as you know and I know, because we discussed it, there may come a time not far from now when it'll be necessary for you to—" He hesitated. "What we said. Kill even me. Right, doctor?"

Eric said, "I have to give her the drug supply. May I go, Secretary? Before they take off."

"No," Molinari said. "You can't go because there's something I want to ask you. Minister Freneksy is here still; you're aware of that. With his party, in the East Wing, in seclusion." He held out his hand. "I want one capsule of JJ-180, doctor. Give it to me and then forget we had this talk."

To himself Eric thought, I know what you're going to do. Or rather try to do. But you don't have a chance; this isn't the Renaissance.

"I'm going to hand it to him personally," Molinari said. "To see that it actually gets there and isn't drunk by some pimp along the way."

"No," Eric said. "I absolutely refuse."

"Why?" Molinari cocked his head on one side.

"It's suicidal. For everyone on Terra."

"You know how the Russians got rid of Beria? Beria carried a pistol into the Kremlin, which was against the law; he had it in his briefcase and they stole his briefcase and shot him with his own pistol. You think matters at the top have to be complex? There're simple solutions average people always overlook; that's the main defect of the mass man—" Molinari broke off, put his hand suddenly to his chest. "My heart. I think it stopped. It's going now, but for a second there, nothing." He had blanched and his voice now ebbed to a whisper.

"I'll wheel you to your room." Eric stepped behind Molinari's wheelchair and began to push it; the Mole did not protest but sat slumped forward, massaging his fleshy chest, exploring and touching himself, with the tentativeness of disintegrating, overwhelming fear. Everything else was forgotten; he perceived nothing more than his sick, failing body. It had become his universe.

With the assistance of two nurses he managed to get Molinari back into bed.

"Listen, Sweetscent," Molinari whispered as he lay back against the pillow. "I don't have to get that stuff through you; I can put pressure on Hazeltine and he'll deliver it right to me. Virgil Ackerman is a friend of mine; Virgil will see to it that Hazeltine complies. And don't try to tell me my job; you do yours and I'll do mine." He shut his eyes and groaned. "God, I know an artery near my heart just burst; I can feel the blood leaking out. Get Teagarden in here." Again he groaned and then turned his face to the wall. "What a day. But I'll get that Freneksy yet." All at once he opened his eyes and said, "I knew it was a stupid idea. But that's the kind of ideas I've been having lately, dumb ideas like that. And what else can I do but that? Can you think of something else?" He waited. "No. Because there isn't anything else, that's why." Again he shut his eyes. "I feel terrible. I think I really am dying this time and you won't be able to save me."

"I'll get Dr. Teagarden," Eric said, and started toward the door.

Molinari said, "I know you're an addict, doctor." He drew himself up slightly. "I can almost invariably tell when someone is lying, and your wife wasn't. As soon as I saw you I spotted it; you don't know how much you've changed."

After a pause Eric said, "What are you going to do?"

"We'll see, doctor," Molinari said, and again turned his face to the wall.

As soon as he had completed the task of delivering the supply of JJ-180 to Kathy he boarded an express ship for Detroit.

Forty-five minutes later he had reached the Detroit field and was on his way to Hazeltine Corporation by taxi. Gino

Molinari, not the drug, had forced him to move this swiftly; he could not even wait until evening.

"Here we are, sir," the autonomic circuit of the cab said respectfully. It slid open its door so that he could emerge. "That gray one-story building with the hedge of rose-colored calyx with the whorl of green bracts at the base . . . that is Hazeltine Corporation." Looking out, Eric saw the building, the lawn and heather hedge. It wasn't a large structure as industrial installations went. So this was the point at which JJ-180 had entered the world.

"Wait," he instructed the cab. "Do you have a glass of water?"

"Certainly." From the slot facing Eric a paper cup of water slid forward, teetered on the lip of the slot, and then halted.

Seated in the cab Eric swallowed the capsule of JJ-180 which he had brought with him. Purloined from Kathy's stock.

Several minutes passed.

"Why aren't you getting out, sir?" the cab inquired. "Have I done something wrong?"

Eric waited. When he felt the drug begin to reach him he paid the cab, got out and walked slowly up the redwood-round path toward the office of Hazeltine Corporation.

The building flashed as if caught by a whip of lightning. And, overhead, the sky twisted laterally. He saw, gazing up, the clear blue of day dawdle as if attempting to remain and then collapse; he shut his eyes because the dizziness was too great, the reference point of outside objects had become too tenuous, and he walked, step by step, feeling his way ahead, bent down, for some reason motivated to continue in motion, however slow.

It hurt. This, unlike the initial exposure, was a major readjustment of the reality structure impinging on him. His steps made no sound, he noticed; he had strayed onto the lawn, but he still kept his eyes shut. Hallucination, he thought, of another world. Is Hazeltine right? By a paradox perhaps I can answer that within the hallucination itself . . . if that is what it is. He did not think so; Hazeltine was wrong.

When a heather branch brushed his arm he let his eyes open. One of his feet had penetrated the soft black soil of a flower bed; he rested on a half-crushed tuberous begonia. Past the heather hedge the gray side of Hazeltine Corporation rose, exactly as before, and above it the sky was a washed-out blue with irregular clouds sweeping toward the north, the same sky, as nearly as he could tell. What had changed? He returned to the redwood-round path. Shall I go in? he asked himself. He looked back toward the street. The cab had gone. Detroit, the buildings and ramps of the city, seemed somehow elaborate. But he did not know this area.

When he reached the porch the door flew open automatically for him and he looked in on a neat office, with relaxing, leather-covered chairs, magazines, a deep-pile carpet whose design changed continuously . . . he saw, through an open doorway, a business area: accounting machines and a computer of some ordinary kind, and at the same time he heard the buzz of activity beyond that, from the labs themselves.

As he started to sit down, a four-armed reeg walked into the office, its blue, chitinous face inexpressive, its embryonic wings pressed tightly to its sloping, bullet-shiny back. It whistled a greeting to him—he had not heard that about them— and passed on out through the doorway. Another reeg, manipulating its extensive network of double-jointed arms vigorously, made its appearance, traveled up to Eric Sweet-scent, halted, and produced a small square box.

Scudding across the side of the box, words in English took shape and departed; he woke to the fact that he had to pay attention to them. The reeg was communicating with him.

WELCOME TO HAZELTINE CORPORATION

He read the words but did not know what to do with them. This was a receptionist; he saw that the reeg was a female. How did he reply? The reeg waited, buzzing; its structure was so convoluted that it seemed unable to remain entirely still; its multilensed eyes shrank and grew as they were partially absorbed back into the skull, then pushed out like flattened corks. If he hadn't known better he would have said it was blind. And then he realized that these were its false eyes; the genuine ones, compound, were at its top-arm elbows.

He said, "May I speak to one of your chemists?" And he thought, So we did lose the war. To these things. And now terra is occupied. And its industries are run by these. But, he thought, human beings still exist, because this reeg was not dumbfounded to see me; it has accepted my presence as natural. So we can't be mere slaves, either.

REGARDING WHAT MATTER?

Hesitating, he said, "A drug. Produced here in the past. Called either Frohedadrine or JJ-180; both names refer to the same product."

JUST A MOMENT PLEASE

The female reeg scuttled through the inner doorway to the business office, then disappeared entirely. He stood waiting, thinking to himself that if this was a hallucination it certainly was not a voluntary one.

A larger reeg, a male, appeared; its joints seemed stiff and Eric realized that it was old. They had a short life span, measured in terms of months, not years. This one had almost come to the end of his.

Utilizing the translating box, the elderly male reeg said:

WHAT IS YOUR INQUIRY ABOUT JJ-180? PLEASE BE BRIEF

Eric bent, picked up a magazine that lay on a table nearby. It was not in English; the cover bore a picture of two reegs and the writing consisted of the crabbed, pictorial reegian script. Startled, he stared at it. The magazine was *Life*. Somehow it shocked him more than the actual sight of the enemy itself.

PLEASE

The elderly reeg rattled with impatience.

Eric said, "I want to purchase an antidote to the addictive drug JJ-180. In order to break my addiction."

YOU DID NOT NEED ME FOR THAT; THE
RECEPTIONIST COULD HAVE TAKEN
CARE OF YOU

Turning, the elderly reeg scrabbled haltingly off, eager to return to his work. Eric was left alone.

The receptionist returned with a small brown paper bag; she held it out to him, not with a jointed arm but with a mandible. Eric accepted it, opened it, and looked inside. A bottle of pills. This was it; there was nothing more to be done.

THAT WILL BE FOUR THIRTY-FIVE SIR

The receptionist watched as he got out his wallet; he took a five-dollar-bill from it and passed it to her.

I AM SORRY SIR; THIS IS OUTDATED WARTIME
CURRENCY NO LONGER IN USE

"You can't take it?" he said.

WE HAVE A RULE FORBIDDING US TO

"I see," he said numbly, and wondered what to do. He could gulp down the contents of the bottle before she could stop him. But then he would probably be arrested, and the rest he could visualize in an instant; once their police had examined his identification they would know that he came from the past. And they would be aware that he might carry back information affecting the outcome—which had obviously been favorable for them—of the war. And they couldn't afford that. They would have to murder him. Even if the two races now lived in concert.

"My watch," he said. He unfastened it from his wrist, passed it to the female reeg. "Seventeen jewel, seventy-year battery." On inspiration he added, "An antique, perfectly preserved. From prewar days."

JUST A MOMENT SIR

Accepting the watch, the receptionist made her way on her long yielding legs to the business office, conferred with someone invisible to Eric; he waited, making no attempt to devour the pills—he felt trapped in a membrane of crushing density, unable to act or escape from action, caught in a halfway land between.

From the business office something emerged. He looked up.

It was a human. A man, young, with close-cropped hair, wearing a work smock that was stained and rumpled. "What's the trouble, buddy?" the man asked. Behind him the reeg receptionist followed, her joints clacking.

Eric said, "Sorry to bother you. Could you and I talk in private?"

The man shrugged. "Sure." He led Eric from the room and into what appeared to be a storage chamber; shutting the door, the man turned to him placidly and said, "That watch is worth three hundred dollars; she doesn't know what to do with it—she's only got a 600-type brain; you know how the D-class is." He lit a cigarette, offered the pack—Camels—to Eric.

"I'm a time traveler," Eric said as he took a cigarette.

"Sure you are." The man laughed. He extended his match to Eric.

"Don't you know the action of JJ-180? It was made right here."

After a thoughtful pause the man said, "But not for years. Because of its addictive qualities and its toxicity. In fact there hasn't been any since the war."

"They won the war?"

" 'They'? Who's that?"

"The reegs," Eric said.

"The reegs," the man said, "is us. Not they. *They* was Lilistar. If you're a time traveler you ought to know that even better than I."

"The Pact of Peace—"

"There was no 'Pact of Peace.' Listen, buddy, I minored in world history in college; I was going to teach. I know all about the last war; it was my specialty. Gino Molinari—he was UN Secretary then, just before hostilities broke out—signed the Era of Common Understanding Protocols with the reegs and then the reegs and the 'Starmen started fighting and Molinari brought us in, on the reeg side, because of the protocols, and we won." He smiled. "And this stuff you say you're hooked on, it was a weapon that Hazeltine Corp. developed in 2055, during the war, for use against Lilistar, and it didn't work out because the Freneksytes were advanced even over us in pharmacology and quickly worked out an antidote—which antidote you're attempting to buy. God, they *had* to develop it; we got the snunk into their drinking water; that was the Mole's idea himself." He explained, "That was Molinari's nickname."

"All right," Eric said. "Let's just leave it at this. I want to buy the antidote. I want to trade that watch. It is satisfactory?" He still held the brown paper bag; reaching into it, he lifted out the bottle. "Get me some water and let me take it and then let me get out of here; I don't know how long it'll be before I go back to my own time. Is there any objection to that?" He had difficulty controlling his voice; it tried to rise and escape. And he was shaking, but he did not know with what. Anger, possibly fear—more likely bewilderment. At this point he did not even know if he were bewildered.

"Calm down." Cigarette jutting from his lips, the man walked off, evidently in search of water. "Can you take them with a Coke?"

"Yes," Eric said.

The man returned with a half-empty bottle of Coca-Cola and watched as Eric struggled to get the pills down one after another.

At the door the female reeg receptionist appeared.

IS HE ALL RIGHT?

"Yes," the man said, as Eric managed to wash down the last pill.

WILL YOU TAKE CHARGE OF THE WATCH?

Accepting it from her, the man said, "Of course it's company property; that goes without saying." He started out of the storeroom.

"Was there ever a UN Secretary near the end of the war named Donald Festenburg?" Eric said.

"No," the man said.

HE SHOULD RECEIVE SOME CASH SETTLEMENT FOR THE
WATCH IN ADDITION TO THE MEDICATION

The flashing box, declaring its message was extended by the female reeg toward the man; he halted, frowning, then shrugged. "One hundred in cash," he said to Eric. "Take it or leave it; it's all the same to me."

"I'll take it," Eric said, and followed him to the business office. As the man counted out the money—in odd, unfamiliar bills which Eric had never seen the like of—he thought of another question. "How did Gino Molinari end his term in office?"

The man glanced up. "Assassinated."

"Shot?"

"Yes, by old-fashioned lead slugs. A fanatic got him. Because of his lenient immigration policy, his letting the reegs settle here on Terra. There was a racist faction, scared about polluting the blood . . . as if reegs and humans could interbreed." He laughed.

This, then, Eric thought, may be the world from which Molinari got that bullet-riddled corpse which Festenburg showed me. The dead Gino Molinari lying mangled and blood-spattered in his helium-filled casket.

From behind him a dry, matter-of-fact voice said, "Are you not going to make the attempt, Dr. Sweetscent, to take the antidote for JJ-180 back to your wife?"

It was an organism without eyes entirely, and he thought, seeing it, of fruit he had come onto as a child, overripe pears lying in the weedy grass, covered by a crawling layer of yellow jackets attracted by the sweet odor of rot. The creature was vaguely spherical. It had fitted itself into a harness, however, which had squeezed its soft body tortuously; no doubt it needed this in order to get around in the Terran environment. But he wondered why it was worth it to the thing.

"Is he really a time traveler?" the man at the cash register asked, jerking his head at Eric.

The spherical organism, wedged within its plastic harness, said by means of its mechanical audio system, "Yes, Mr. Taubman, he is." It floated toward Eric, then halted, a foot above the ground, making an indistinct sucking noise, as if pulling fluids through its artificial tubes.

"This guy," Taubman said to Eric, indicating the spherical organism, "is from Betelgeuse. His name is Willy K. He's one of our best chemists." He shut the register. "He's a telepath; they all are. They get a kick out of prying into our minds and the reegs' but they're harmless. We like them." He walked over to Willy K, bent toward him, and said, "Listen, if he's a time traveler—I mean, we can't let him just walk out of here; isn't he dangerous or worth something? Shouldn't we at least call in the city police? I thought he was nuts or kidding me."

Willy K floated a little closer to Eric, then withdrew. "There is no way we can keep him here, Mr. Taubman. When the drug wears off he will go back to his own period. However, I would like to interrogate him to a certain extent while he's here." To Eric he said, "Unless you object, sir."

"I don't know," Eric said, rubbing his forehead. It had been too much of the unexpected, hearing Willy K ask about Kathy; it had disoriented him entirely and all he wanted to do now was leave—he had no curiosity, no interest in the situation.

"I sympathize with your situation," Willy K said. "In any case to question you formally is sham; I am getting everything I want from you as it is. What I had hoped to do was answer, if I could, some of your questions by the way I phrased mine. Your wife, for example. You have great conflicting emotions about her, fear for the most part, then hatred, and also a good deal of undistorted love."

Taubman said, "God, how the Betels love to be psychologists. It must come natural to telepaths; I don't think they can even help it." He loitered nearby, evidently interested in Willy K's probing.

"*Can* I take the antidote back to Kathy?"

"No, but you can memorize the formula," Willy K said. "So that Hazeltine Corporation, in your time, can reproduce it. But I don't think you want to. I'm not going to urge you to . . . and I can't force you to."

"You mean his wife's hooked on JJ-180, too," Taubman said, "and he isn't going to try to help her?"

"You're not married," Willy K said. "In marriage the greatest hatred that is possible between human beings can be generated, perhaps because of the constant proximity, perhaps because once there was love. The intimacy is still there, even though the love element has disappeared. So a will to power, a struggle for domination, comes into being." To Taubman he explained, "It was his wife Kathy who addicted him in the first place, so it is easy to understand his sentiments."

"I hope I never get in a fix like that," Taubman said. "Hating someone I once loved."

The female reeg had clacked up to listen, watching the conversation as it was reproduced on the surface of her translating box. Now she added her own comment.

HATE AND LOVE ARE CLOSELY LINKED, MUCH
MORE SO THAN MOST TERRANS REALIZE

"Do you have another cigarette?" Eric asked Taubman.

"Sure." Taubman passed him the pack.

"What I find most interesting of all," Willy K said, "is that Dr. Sweetscent comes from a universe in which a pact exists between Terra and Lilistar. And that in his year, 2055, a war is being fought in which they are slowly but steadily losing. Clearly this is not our past but another past entirely. And, in his mind, I find the excruciatingly interesting thought that Terra's quondam warlord, Gino Molinari, has already discovered this rank of parallel universes and has made use of it for his immediate political advantage." Willy K was silent a moment and then declared, "No, Dr. Sweetscent, after having visualized your memory of the Molinari corpse I am fairly certain that it was not obtained from our world; true, Molinari died by assassination, but I recall pics of his corpse and there is a small but crucial difference. In our world the Secretary was hit repeatedly in the facial area; his features were destroyed. The corpse you saw was not so damaged and I would assume it comes from *another* world in which he was assassinated, similar to ours but not identical."

"This must be why so few time travelers have shown up here," Taubman said. "They're scattered through all the different possible futures."

"As to the virile Molinari," Willy K said thoughtfully, "I suppose that, too, is an alternate configuration. You realize of course, doctor, that all this indicates that your Secretary *has taken JJ-180 himself;* there is therefore an element of cruel hypocrisy in his threatening you with death if you became addicted. But I would guess, by several clues in your mind, that he also possesses the 'Star-manufactured antidote which you just now took. So he has no fears and can move freely about among the worlds."

The Mole, Eric realized, could have given me and Kathy the antidote any time.

It was hard for him to accept that about Gino Molinari;

he had seemed more humane than this. He was just playing with us, Eric realized. As Willy K said, with an element of cruel hypocrisy.

"But wait," Willy K cautioned. "We don't know what he intended to do; he had just found out about your addiction, and he was as usual suffering from a spasm of his chronic illness pattern. He might have given it to you in time. Before it ceased to matter."

COULD YOU EXPLAIN THIS DISCUSSION?

The reeg receptionist, and also Taubman, had lost the thread of the discourse.

"Would you care to begin the laborious process of memorizing the formula?" Willy K said to Eric. "It will take all the time you have left."

"All right," Eric said, and listened intently.

WAIT

Willy K ceased, rotated his supporting mechanism inquiringly.

THE DOCTOR HAS LEARNED SOMETHING
MORE IMPORTANT THAN ANY CHEMICAL
FORMULA

"What is it?" Eric asked her.

IN YOUR UNIVERSE WE ARE YOUR ENEMY BUT HERE YOU
HAVE SEEN TERRANS AND OURSELVES LIVE TOGETHER. YOU
KNOW THAT WAR AGAINST US IS UNNECESSARY. AND WHAT
IS MORE IMPORTANT, SO DOES YOUR LEADER.

That was so. No wonder Molinari had no heart for the war; it was not merely a suspicion on his part that this was the wrong war with the wrong enemy and the wrong ally; it was a fact which he had experienced for himself, perhaps many times. And all due to JJ-180.

But not only that. There was something more, something so ominous that he wondered why the inhibition barriers of his mind had permitted the thought to rise from his unconscious. JJ-180 had reached Lilistar—and in quantity. 'Starmen had certainly been experimenting with it. So they, too, knew the alternate possibility, knew that Terra's better hope lay in cooperation with the reegs. Had witnessed it for themselves.

In both branches of possibility Lilistar had lost the war. With or without Terra on her side. Or—

Was there a third alternative, one in which Lilistar and the reegs joined against Terra?

"A pact between Lilistar and the reegs is unlikely," Willy K said. "They have been antagonists for too many years. I feel that it is only your planet, on which we now stand, that hangs in the balance; Lilistar will be defeated by the reeg power in any eventuality."

"But that means," Eric said, "that the 'Starmen have nothing to lose; if they know they can't win—" He could imagine Freneksy's reaction to this information. The nihilism, the destructive violence of the 'Starmen, would be inconceivable.

"True," Willy K agreed. "So your Secretary is wise to walk softly. Now perhaps you can comprehend why his illness pattern must be so vast, why he must push himself actually over the brink, into repeated death, to serve his people. And why he would hesitate to provide you with the antidote to JJ-180; if 'Star intelligence agents—and your wife may be one—learned that he possessed it, they might—" Willy K was silent. "It is hard, as you yourself might observe, to predict the behavior of psychotics. But this much is clear: they would not ignore the situation."

"They'd find a way to get it away from him," Eric said.

"You've missed the point. Their attitude would be punitive; they would know that Molinari possesses too much power, that by having unhindered use of JJ-180, without the possibility of addiction, of neural deterioration, *he can't be con-*

trolled by them. This is why, on a deep, psychosomatic basis, Molinari can defy Minister Freneksy. He is not entirely helpless."

"This is all over my head," Taubman said. "Excuse me." He walked off.

The reeg receptionist remained.

URGE YOUR SECRETARY TO CONTACT THE
REEG AUTHORITY. WE WOULD ASSIST IN
PROTECTING TERRA FROM STAR VENGEANCE, I AM SURE.

It was, Eric thought, a rather wistful message which the multi-armed creature had flashed at him with her translation box. The reegs might *want* to assist, but 'Starmen were already on Terra, holding key positions. At the first hint that Terra was negotiating with the reegs the 'Starmen would move in prearranged order; they would seize the planet overnight.

A tiny Terran-controlled state might function for a limited time in the Cheyenne vicinity, shelled and bombed day and night by the 'Starmen. But then it, too, would capitulate. Its shield of Jupiter-obtained rexeroid compounds would not protect it forever—and Molinari knew that. Terra would become a conquered state, supplying war material and slave labor to Lilistar. And the war would go on.

And the irony was this: as a slave planet Terra would be able to contribute more to the war effort than she did now as a quasi-independent entity. And no one recognized this more than did the Mole. Hence his entire foreign policy; this explained everything that he did.

"By the way," Willy K said, and there was a trace of amusement in his voice. "Your former employer, Virgil Ackerman, is still alive; he still governs Tijuana Fur & Dye. He is two hundred and thirty years old and retains twenty org-trans surgeons within call. I believe I have read that he has gone through four matched sets of kidneys, five livers, spleens, and undetermined numbers of hearts—"

"I feel sick," Eric said, and rocked back and forth.

"The drug is wearing off." Willy K floated toward a chair. "Miss Ceeg, assist him, please!"

"I'm okay," Eric said thickly. His head ached and nausea staggered him. All the lines, the surfaces around him, had become astigmatic; under him the chair felt unreal and then, abruptly, he fell, lay on his side.

"The transition is difficult," Willy K said. "Apparently we can't help him, Miss Ceeg. Good luck to your Secretary, doctor. I can appreciate what a great service he performed for your people. Perhaps I will write a letter to the *New York Times,* conveying this knowledge."

A prism of primal colors tapped at Eric like an illuminated wind; it was, he thought, the wind of life blowing over him, sweeping him where it desired without regard for his small wishes. And then the winds became black; they were no longer the winds of life but the opaque smoke of death.

He saw, projected as a pseudo environment around him, a travesty of his injured nervous system; the multitudes of conduits were visibly corrupted, had turned inky as the drug's damage spread throughout him and established its grim self. A voiceless bird, some carrion eater of the storm, sat on his chest, croaking in the silence left behind as the winds receded from him. The bird remained and he felt its dunglike claws penetrate his lungs, his chest cavity, and then his abdominal cavity. Nothing within him remained untouched; it had all been disfigured and even the antidote had not stopped this. As long as he lived he would never regain the purity of the original organism.

This was the price exacted from him by the deciding forces.

Dragging himself to a crouched position, he saw that he inhabited an empty waiting room. No one had seen him and he was free to get up and go. He rose to his feet, steadied himself by means of a chrome and leather chair.

The magazines, in the nearby rack, were in English. And their covers, laughing Terrans. Not reegs.

"Did you want something?" A male voice, lisping slightly. A Hazeltine employee wearing florid, fashionable robes.

"No," Eric said. This was his own time; he recognized the trappings of 2055. "Thanks just the same."

A moment later he had made his way painfully outdoors in the direction of the sidewalk, down the path of redwood rounds.

What he wanted was a cab, a place to sit down and rest, as he made his trip back to Cheyenne. He had gotten what he wanted; presumably he was no longer an addict and if he cared to he could also free his wife. And in addition he had viewed a world over which the shadow of Lilistar did not obtain.

"Ferry you somewhere, sir?" An autonomic cab drifted toward him.

"Yes," he said, and walked toward it.

Suppose an entire planet took the drug, he thought as he boarded. A mass fugue away from our dismal, ever-narrowing world of reality. Suppose Tijuana Fur & Dye gave the order to produce it in enormous quantity, distributed it, through the government's help, to everyone. Would that be a moral solution? Are we entitled to that?

Anyhow it couldn't be done. The 'Starmen would move in first.

"Where to, sir?" the cab's circuit inquired.

He decided to use it for the entire trip; it would take only a few minutes longer. "To Cheyenne."

"I can't, sir. Not *there*." It sounded nervous. "Request another—"

"Why not?" He came awake instantly.

"Because as is well known all Cheyenne belongs to *them*. To the enemy." It added, "And traffic into enemy areas is illegal, as you know."

"What enemy?"

"The traitor Gino Molinari," the cab answered. "Who sought to betray the war effort; you know, sir. The former UN Secretary who conspired with reeg agents to—"

"What is the date?" Eric demanded.

"June 15, 2056."

He had—possibly through the action of the antidote—failed to make it to his own time; it was one year later and there was nothing he could do about it. And he had saved out no more of the drug; the rest had been given to Kathy at the airfield, and so he was stuck here in what obviously was 'Star-dominated territory. Like most of Terra.

And yet Gino Molinari was alive! He still hung on; Cheyenne had not fallen in a day or a week—perhaps the reegs had been able to bring in reinforcements to assist the Secret Service.

He could find out from the cab. As they flew along.

And Don Festenburg could have told me this, he realized, because this is precisely the time period at which I encountered him there in his office with the phony homeopape and mock-up UN Secretary uniform.

"Just head west," he told the cab. I've got to get back to Cheyenne, he realized. Somehow, by some route.

"Yes sir," the cab said. "And by the way sir, you failed to show me your travel permit. May I see it now? Just a formality, of course."

"What travel permit?" But he knew; it would be an issue of the governing 'Star occupation agency, and without their permission Terrans could not come and go. This was a conquered planet and very much still at war.

"Please, sir," the cab said. It had begun to descend once more. "Otherwise I am required to carry you to the nearest 'Star military police barracks; that is one mile east. A short trip from here."

"I'll bet it is," Eric agreed. "From any point, not just from here. I'll bet they're all over."

The cab dropped lower and lower. "Right you are, sir. They're very convenient." It clicked off its engine and coasted.

12

"I'll tell you what," Eric said as the cab's wheels touched the ground; it slid to a gradual halt at the curb and he saw, just ahead, an ominous structure with armed guards at the entrance. The guards wore the gray of Lilistar. "I'll make a deal with you."

"What deal?" the cab said, with suspicion.

"My travel permit is back at Hazeltine Corporation—remember, where you picked me up? Along with my wallet. All my money's there, too. If you turn me over to the 'Star military police my money won't be worth anything to me; you know what they'll do."

"Yes sir," the cab agreed. "You'll be put to death. It's the new law, passed by decree on the tenth of May. Unauthorized travel by—"

"So why not give my money to you? As a tip. You take me back to Hazeltine Corporation, I'll pick up my wallet, I'll show you my travel permit so you won't have to bring me here again. And you can have the money. You can see how I'd benefit by the deal and how you would, too."

"We'd both gain," the cab agreed. Its autonomic circuit clicked rapidly as it calculated. "How much money do you have, sir?"

"I'm a courier for Hazeltine. In my wallet there's about twenty-five thousand dollars."

"I see! In occupation script or in pre-occupation UN bank notes?"

"The latter of course."

"I'll comply!" the cab decided eagerly. And took off once more. "In the strict sense you can't be said to have traveled, inasmuch as the destination you gave me is enemy territory and hence I did not turn even for a moment in that direction. No law has been broken." It turned in the direction of Detroit, greedy for its loot.

When it set down at the parking lot of Hazeltine Corporation Eric got out hurriedly. "I'll be right back." He loped across the pavement toward a doorway of the building; a moment later he was inside. An immense testing lab lay extended before him.

When he found a Hazeltine employee he said, "My name is Eric Sweetscent; I'm on the personal staff of Virgil Ackerman and there's been an accident. Will you get in touch with Mr. Ackerman at TF&D for me, please?"

The employee, a male clerk, hesitated. "I understood—" He lowered his voice fearfully. "Isn't Mr. Virgil Ackerman at Wash-35 on Mars? Mr. Jonas Ackerman is in charge at Tijuana Fur & Dye now and I know Mr. Virgil Ackerman is listed in the Weekly Security Bulletins as a war criminal because he fled when the occupation began."

"Can you contact Wash-35 for me?"

"Enemy territory?"

"Get me Jonas on the vidphone, then." There was not much else he could do. He followed the clerk into the business office, feeling futile.

Presently the call had been put through. Jonas' features formed on the screen; when he saw Eric he blinked and stammered, "But—they got *you*, too?" He blurted, "Why'd you leave Wash-35? My God, you were safe there with Virgil. I'm ringing off; this is some kind of a trap—the MPs will—" The screen died. Jonas had hurriedly cut the circuit.

So his other self, his normally phased, one-year-later self, had made it to Wash-35 with Virgil; that was terribly reassuring—almost unthinkably so. No doubt the reegs had managed to—

His one-year-later self.

That meant that somehow he had gotten back to 2055. Otherwise there couldn't be a self of 2056 to have fled with Virgil. And the only way he could reach 2055 would be by means of JJ-180.

And the only source of the drug was here. He was standing in the one right spot on the entire planet, by accident, due to the trick he had managed to pull off at the expense of the idiotic autonomic cab.

Relocating the clerk, Eric said, "I'm supposed to requisition a supply of the drug Frohedadrine. One hundred milligrams. And I'm in a hurry. You want to see my identification? I can prove I work for TF&D." And then it came to him. "Call Bert Hazeltine; he'll identify me." Undoubtedly Hazeltine would remember him from the encounter at Cheyenne.

The clerk muttered, "But they shot Mr. Hazeltine. You must remember that; how come you don't? When they took over this place in January."

The expression on Eric's face must have conveyed his shock. Because all at once the clerk's manner changed.

"You were a friend of his, I guess," the clerk said.

"Yes." Eric nodded; that could be said.

"Bert was a good man to work for. Nothing like these 'Star bastards." The clerk made up his mind. "I don't know why you're here or what's wrong with you but I'll get the hundred milligrams of JJ-180; I know where it's kept."

"Thanks."

The clerk hurried off. Time passed. Eric wondered about the cab; was it still waiting outside on the lot? Would it, if pressed too hard, attempt to come into the building after him? An absurd and yet nerve-wracking thought, the autonomic cab forcing its way into Hazeltine, bursting—or trying to burst—through the cement wall.

The clerk returned and held out a handful of capsules to Eric.

From a nearby water cooler Eric got a cup, filled it, mouthed a capsule, and raised the Dixie cup.

"That's the recently altered JJ-180 formula," the clerk said, watching him keenly. "I better tell you, now that I see it's for yourself." He was all at once pale.

Lowering the cup of water, Eric said, "Altered how?"

"Retains the addictive and liver-toxic properties but the time-freeing hallucinations are gone." The clerk explained, "When the 'Starmen came in here they ordered our chemists to reconstruct the drug; it was their idea, not ours."

"Why?" In the name of God, what good was a drug consisting of nothing but addictive and toxic properties?

"For a weapon of war against the reegs. And—" The clerk hestiated. "Also it's used to addict rebel Terrans who've gone over to the enemy." He did not look very happy about that part of it.

Tossing the capsules of JJ-180 onto a nearby lab bench, Eric said, "I give up." And then he had one more—meager— idea. "If I can get approval from Jonas will you supply me a company ship? I'll call him again; Jonas is an old friend of mine." He walked toward the vidphone, the clerk trailing after him. If he could get Jonas to listen—

Two Lilistar MPs entered the lab; behind them, in the parking lot, Eric saw a 'Star patrol ship parked beside his autonomic cab.

"You're under arrest," one of the MPs said to him, pointing an oddly shaped stick in Eric's direction. "For travel without authorization and felony fraud. Your cab got tired of waiting and called in a complaint."

"What fraud?" Eric said. The clerk, now, had wisely vanished. "I'm a staff member of Tijuana Fur & Dye; I'm here on business."

The oddly shaped stick glowed and Eric felt as if his brain had been touched; without hesitation he moved toward the lab door, his right hand pawing in a ticlike, useless gesture at his forehead. Okay, he thought. I'm coming. He had lost any idea of resisting the Lilistar MPs now, or even of arguing with them; he was glad to get into their patrol ship.

A moment later they had taken off; the ship glided above the rooftops of Detroit, heading toward the barracks two miles away.

"Kill him now," one of the MPs said to his companion. "And drop his body out; why take him to the barracks?"

"Hell, we can just push him out," the other MP said. "The fall will kill him." He touched a button at the control panel of the ship and a vertical hatch slipped open; Eric saw the buildings below, the streets and conapts of the city. "Think happy thoughts," the MP said to Eric, "on the way down." Grabbing Eric by the arm, he slung him into a helpless, crippled posture and shoved him toward the hatch. It was all expert and entirely professional; he found himself teetering at the lip of the hatch and then the MP released him in order to escape falling himself.

From beneath the patrol ship a second ship, larger, pitted and scarred, an interplan military vessel with cannon bristling as spines, floated on its back as it ascended like some raptorial water creature. With care it fired a microbolt into the open hatch, picking off the MP who stood by Eric and then one of its larger cannon opened up and the front portion of the MP patrol ship burst and flew outward, spattering Eric and the remaining MP with molten debris.

The MP patrol ship dropped like a stone toward the city below.

Awakening from his stricken trance, the remaining MP ran to the wall of the ship and threw on the emergency manually-operated guidance system. The ship ceased to fall; it glided, wind-swept, in a spiral pattern until at last it crashed and bumped and skidded along a street, missing wheels and cabs, nosed into the curb, lifted its tail into the air and came to rest.

The remaining MP staggered up, grabbed his pistol, and somehow got to the hatch; he crouched sideways and began firing. After the third shot he snapped backward; his pistol dropped from his hand and skidded against the hull of the ship and he tumbled into a ball that rolled helplessly like an animal that had been run over until at last it collided with a portion of the hull. There it stopped, gradually unwinding into man shape once more.

The pitted, grimy military ship had parked on the street close by and now its forward side-hatch opened and a man hopped out. As Eric stepped from the MP patrol ship the man sprinted up to him.

"Hey," the man panted. "It's me."

"Who are you?" Eric said; the man who had tackled the MP ship with his own was certainly familiar—Eric confronted a face which he had seen many times and yet it was distorted now, witnessed from a weird angle, as if inside out, pulled through infinity. The man's hair was parted on the wrong side so that his head seemed lopsided, wrong in all its lines. What amazed him was the physical unattractiveness of the man. He was too fat and a little too old. Unpleasantly gray. It was a shock to see himself like this, without preparation; do I really look like that? he asked himself morosely. What had become of the clean-cut youth whose image he still, evidently, superimposed onto his shaving mirror each morning . . . who had substituted this man bordering on middle age?

"So I've gotten fat; so what?" his self of 2056 said. "Christ, I saved your life; they were going to pitch you out."

"I know that," Eric said irritably. He hurried along beside the man who was himself; they entered the interplan ship and his 2056 self at once slammed the hatch shut and sent the ship hurtling into the sky, out of reach of any possibility of containment by the Lilistar military police. This was obviously an advanced ship of the line; this was no barge.

"Without intending to insult your intelligence," his 2056 self said, "which I personally consider very high, I'd like to review for your benefit a few of the moronic aspects of what you had in mind. First, if you had been able to obtain the original type of JJ-180 it would have carried you to the future, not back to 2055, and you would have been readdicted. What you need—and you seemed for a time to have worked this out—is not more JJ-180 but something to balance the effects of the antidote." His 2056 self nodded his head. "Over there in my coat." His coat hung by magnetic spot on the wall of the ship. "Hazeltine has had a year to develop it. In exchange for your bringing them the formula for the antidote—you couldn't give them the formula if you couldn't get back to 2055. And you know you do. Or will, rather."

"Whose ship is this?" It impressed him. It could pass freely through Lilistar lines, penetrate Terra's defenses with ease.

"It's reeg. Made available to Virgil at Wash-35. In case something goes wrong. We're going to bring Molinari to Wash-35 when Cheyenne falls, which it eventually will, probably in another month."

"How's his health?"

"Much better. He's doing what he wants now, what he knows he should be doing. And there's more . . . but you'll find out. Go get the antidote to Lilistar's antidote."

Eric fumbled in the pockets of the coat, found the tablets, took them without benefit of water. "Listen," he said, "what's the story on Kathy? We ought to confer." It was good having someone he could talk to about his most wasting, obsessive problem, even if it was only himself; at least the illusion of collaboration was achieved.

"Well, you got—will get—her off JJ-180. But not before she's suffered major physical damage. She'll never be pretty again, even with reconstructive surgery, which she'll try several times before she gives up. There's more but I'd rather not tell you; it'll just make your difficulties worse. I'll say only this. Have you ever heard of Korsakow's syndrome?"

"No," Eric said. But of course he had. It was his job.

"Traditionally it's a psychosis occurring in alcoholics; it consists of actual pathological destruction of cortical brain tissue due to long periods of intoxication. But it also can occur from the steady use of narcotic drugs."

"Are you saying that Kathy has it?"

"Remember those periods when she wouldn't eat for three days at a time? And her violent, destructive rages—and ideas of reference, that everyone was being mean to her. Korsakow's syndrome, and not from JJ-180, but from all the drugs she took prior to that. The doctors at Cheyenne, while getting her ready to be returned to San Diego, ran an EEG on her and picked it up. They'll tell you very soon after your return to 2055. So prepare yourself." He added, "It's irreversible. Needless to say. Removal of the toxic agents is not enough."

Both of them were silent then.

"It's rough," his 2056 self said finally, "to be married to a woman with psychotic traits. As well as showing her physical deterioration. She's still my wife. Our wife. Under phenothiazine sedation she's quiet, anyhow. You know, it's interesting that I—we—didn't pick it up, weren't able to diagnose a case we're living with day in, day out. A commentary on the blinding aspects of subjectivity and over-familiarity. It unfolded slowly, of course; that tended to conceal its identity. I think eventually she'll have to be institutionalized, but I'm putting that off. Possibly until after the war's won. Which it will be."

"You have proof? Through JJ-180?"

"Nobody's using JJ-180 anymore except for Lilistar, and that as you know is only for the toxic and addictive properties. So many alternate futures have been disclosed that the task of relating them to our world had to be put aside for after the war. It takes literally years to test out a new drug thoroughly; we both know that. But of course we'll win the war; the reegs have invested half of Lilistar's Empire. Now listen to me. I have instructions for you and you must fulfill them; otherwise another alternate future will split off and it may cancel my stand with you against the 'Star MPs.'"

"I understand," Eric said.

"In Arizona, at POW Camp 29, there's a reeg major from the reegian intelligence service. Deg Dal Il is his code name; you can contact him through that, since it's Terra's code, not theirs. The camp authorities have got him studying insurance claims filed against the government in order to detect frauds, if you can believe that. So he's still busy at work piping data back to his superiors, even though our POW. It's he who'll be the link between Molinari and the reegs."

"What do I do with him? Take him to Cheyenne?"

"To Tijuana. To TF&D's central offices. You buy him from the camp authorities; it's slave labor. You didn't know that, did you, that large Terran industrial constellations could acquire free labor from the POW camps. Well, when you show up at Camp 29 and tell them you're from TF&D and you want a clever reeg, they'll understand."

"You learn something new every day of the week," Eric said.

"But your main problem lies with Molinari. It's up to you to persuade him to visit Tijuana to confer with Deg Dal Il and hence establish the first link in the chain of circumstances that's going to get Terra pried loose from Lilistar and over to the reegs without everyone being killed in the process. I'll tell you why it'll be difficult. Molinari has a scheme. He's been involved in a personal struggle, man to man, against Freneksy; it's his masculinity that he feels is at stake. For him it's not abstract, it's immediate and physical. And you saw the virile Molinari strutting on the video tape. That's his secret weapon, his V-2. He's starting to throw in the healthy duplicates of himself from the rank of parallel worlds, and as he knows he's got quite a supply of them to draw on. *His whole psychology, his point of orientation, is to dabble with death and yet somehow surmount it.* In the confrontation with Minister Freneksy—whom he fears—he can die a thousand times and still spring back. The deteriorating process, the encroachment of his psychosomatic illness process, will cease as soon as he throws the first healthy Molinari in. And when you get back to Cheyenne you'll just be in time to witness it; the video tapes go on all the TV networks that night. At prime viewing time."

Eric said musingly, "So he's as sick right now as it will be necessary for him ever to be."

"And that's exceedingly sick, doctor."

"Yes, doctor." Eric eyed his 2056 self. "We agree in our diagnoses."

"Late tonight, by your time, not mine, Minister Freneksy will demand—and get—another face-to-face conference with Molinari. And the healthy, virile substitute will be the one there in that room . . . while the sick one, our one, recovers in his upstairs private quarters, guarded by his Secret Service, watching the video tapes on TV and thinking grand thoughts to himself as to how easily he has found a way of evading Minister Freneksy and his burgeoning, excessive demands."

"I assume the virile Molinari from the other Terra has involved himself willingly."

"Delighted to. All of them are. All of them see the penultimate in life as a successful grudge-battle waged above and below the belt against Freneksy. Molinari is a politician and he lives for this—lives for it while at the same time it kills him. The healthy one, after his conference with Freneksy, will suffer his first attack of pyloric spasms; the attrition will start to eat away at him, too. And so on down the rank, until at last Freneksy is dead, as someday he has to be, and hopefully before Molinari."

"Beating Molinari to it will take some doing," Eric said.

"But this isn't morbid; this is straight out of the Middle Ages, the clash of armed knights. Molinari is Arthur with the spear wound in his side; guess who Freneksy is. And the interesting thing, to me, is that since Lilistar has no period of chivalry, Freneksy has no comprehension of this. He simply sees it in terms of a struggle for economic domination; who runs whose factories and can sequester whose labor force."

"No romance," Eric said. "How about the reegs? Will they understand the Mole? Have they a period of knighthood in their past?"

"With four arms and a chitinous shell," his 2056 counterpart said, "it would have been something to see one of them in action. I don't know, because neither you nor I nor any other Terran that I ever met bothered to learn as much about reeg civilization as we should have. You have the name of the reeg intelligence major?"

"Deg something."

"Deg. Dal. Il. Think to yourself; the dog dallied and it made him ill."

"Christ," Eric said.

"I nauseate you, don't I? Well, you nauseate me, too; you strike me as flabby and blubbery and your posture is terrible. No wonder you're stuck with a wife like Kathy; you got what you deserved. During the next year why don't you show some guts? Why don't you pull yourself together and go find another woman so by the time it gets to me, in 2056, things aren't quite so goddam fouled up? You owe it to me; I saved your life, got you away from Lilistar's police." His 2056 self glowered at him.

"What woman do you suggest?" Eric said guardedly.

"Mary Reineke."

"You're out of your mind."

"Listen; Mary and Molinari have a quarrel about a month from now, your time. You could exploit it. I didn't but that can be changed; you can set up a slightly different future, everything the same except for the marital situation. Divorce Kathy and marry Mary Reineke or *someone*—anyone." There was desperation, all at once, in his counterpart's voice. "My God, I see this ahead, this having to institutionalize her, and for the rest of her life—*I don't want to do that; I want out.*"

"With or without us—"

"I know. She'll wind up there anyhow. But do I have to be the one? Together you and I ought to be able to reinforce ourselves. It'll be hard; Kathy'll fight a divorce action like a crazed thing. But bring the action in Tijuana; Mexican divorce law is looser than in the States. Get a good lawyer. I've picked one; he's in Ensenada. Jesus Guadarala. Can you remember that? I couldn't quite make it there to start litigation through him, but dammit, you can." He eyed Eric hopefully.

"I'll try," Eric said presently.

"Now I have to let you out. The medication you took will start to work on you in a few minutes and I don't care to have you drop five miles to the surface of the planet." The ship began to descend. "I'll let you off in Salt Lake City; it's a big place, you won't be noticed. And when you're back in 2055 you can catch a cab to Arizona."

"I don't have any 2055 money," Eric remembered. "Or do I?" He was confused; too much had happened. He groped for his wallet. "I got into a panic after that attempt on my part to buy the antidote from Hazeltine with wartime—"

"Don't ruminate over the details. I know them already."

They completed the flight to Earth's surface in silence, each inhibited by his gloomy contempt for the other. It was, Eric decided, a graphic demonstration of the necessity for having respect for one's own self. And this gave him for the first time an insight into his fatalistic quasi-suicidal inclinations . . . they were undoubtedly based on this same flaw. To survive he would have to learn to view himself and his accomplishments differently.

"You're wasting your time," his counterpart said after the ship had landed in an irrigated pasture outside Salt Lake City. "You're not going to change."

As he stepped from the ship onto the spongy, moist alfalfa Eric said, "According to you, anyhow. But we'll see."

Without a further word his 2056 self slammed the hatch and took off; the ship shot up into the sky and disappeared.

Eric trudged toward the nearby paved road.

In Salt Lake City proper he snared a cab. It did not ask for his travel permit and he realized that imperceptibly, probably as he was walking toward town along the road, he had slipped a year back and was now in his own time. Nevertheless he decided to make sure.

"Give me the date," he instructed the cab.

"June 15, sir," the cab said as it buzzed south over green mountains and valleys.

"What year?"

The cab said, "Are you a Mr. Rip Van Winkle or something, sir? It's 2055. And I hope it satisfies you." The cab was old and somewhat seedy, needing repairs; its irritability showed in the activity of its autonomic circuitry.

"It does," Eric said.

By use of the cab's vidphone he learned from the information center at Phoenix the location of the prisoner of war camp; this was not classified information. Presently the cab flew above flat desert lands and monotonous hills of rock and empty basins which in former times had been lakes. And then, in the midst of this barren, unexploited wilderness, the cab set him down; he had arrived at POW Camp 29, and it was just where he had expected it to be; in the most uninhabitable spot conceivable. To him the great desert lands of Nevada and Arizona were like a dismal alien planet, not Earth at all; frankly he preferred the parts of Mars which he had seen near Wash-35.

"Lots of luck, sir," the cab said. He paid it and it zoomed noisily off, its plate shuddering.

"Thanks," Eric said. He walked to the guardhouse at the entrance of the camp; to the soldier within he explained that he had been sent by Tijuana Fur & Dye to buy a POW for clerical work that had to be processed with absolute accuracy.

"Just one?" the soldier asked him as he led the way to his superior's office. "We can give you fifty reegs. Two hundred. We're overrun with them right now. From that last battle we nailed six of their transports."

In the colonel's office he filled out forms, signed for TF&D. Payment, he explained, would be forwarded through normal channels at the end of the month in response to presentation of a formal statement.

"Take your pick," the colonel, bored to death, told him. "Look all around; you can have any one of them—they're all alike, though."

Eric said, "I see a reeg filing forms there in the next room. He—or it—looks efficient."

"That's old Deg," the colonel said. "Deg's a fixture around here; captured in the first week of the war. Even built himself one of those translating boxes so he could be of more use to us. I wish all of them were as cooperative as Deg."

"I'll take him," Eric said.

"We'll have to affix a considerable additional fee," the colonel said slyly. "Because of the amount of training he's received here from us." He made a note of that. "And a service charge for the translating box."

"You said he built it."

"We supplied the materials."

At last they agreed on a price and then Eric walked into the next room and up to the reeg, busy with his four multijointed arms at the insurance claim files. "You belong to TF&D now," Eric informed him. "So come along." To the colonel he said, "Will he try to escape or fight me?"

"They never do," the colonel said, lighting a cigar and leaning against the wall of his office with dreary ennui, "They don't have the mentality for it; they're just bugs. Huge, shiny bugs."

Presently he was back outside in the hot sun, waiting for a cab from nearby Phoenix. If I had known it would take such a short time, he said to himself, I would have held onto the cranky, elderly cab. He felt uncomfortable, standing with the silent reeg; this was, after all, their formal enemy. Reegs battled with and killed Terrans, and this one had been and still was a commissioned officer.

Like a fly the reeg cleaned himself, combing his wings, his sensory antennae, then his lower set of extremities. He carried his translating box under one brittle arm, never letting go of it.

"Are you glad to get out of that POW camp?" Eric asked.

Words, pale in the strong desert sun, appeared on the box.

NOT PARTICULARLY

The cab arrived and Eric, along with Deg Dal Il, entered it. Soon they were in the air, turning in the direction of Tijuana.

Eric said, "I know you're an officer in reeg intelligence. That's why I bought you."

The box remained blank. But the reeg trembled. His

opaque, compound eyes became even more filmed-over and the false ones gaped emptily.

"I'll take the risk of telling you this right now," Eric said. "I'm an intermediary acting to bring you together with someone high in UN circles. It's in your interest, yours and your people's, to co-operate with me. You will be dropped off at my firm—"

The box came to life.

RETURN ME TO THE CAMP

"All right," Eric said. "I know you have to act out the pose you've maintained for so long now. Even though it's no longer necessary. I'm aware that you're still in contact with your government. That's why you can be useful to the personage you're to meet in Tijuana. Through you he can establish relations with your government—" He hesitated, then plunged in. "Without the 'Starmen knowing." That was saying a lot; he had mightily presumed on what, for his part, was a very small role.

After a pause the box relit.

I HAVE ALWAYS COOPERATED

"But this is different." And he dropped the subject then and there. For the remainder of the trip he did not try to communicate with Deg Dal Il; it was obviously the wrong thing to do. Deg Dal Il knew it and he knew it. The rest was up to someone else, not him.

When they reached Tijuana Eric rented a room at the Caesar Hotel on the main street of town; the desk clerk, a Mexican, stared at the reeg but asked no questions. This was Tijuana, Eric reflected as he and Deg ascended to their floor. Everyone minded his own business; it had always been like this here, and even now, in wartime, Tijuana remained unchanged. You could obtain anything, do anything, you wanted. As long as it was not done blatantly on the public

street. And most expecially if it was consummated at night.
Because at night Tijuana became a transformed city in which
everything, even unimaginable things, was possible. Once it
had been abortions, narcotics, women, and gambling. Now
it was concourse with the enemy.

In the hotel room he handed over a copy of the ownership
papers to Deg Dal Il; in case trouble arose during his absence
the papers would prove that the reeg had not escaped from
a POW camp, nor was he a spy. In addition Eric provided
him with money. And instructed him to contact TF&D if any
difficulty—especially the appearance of 'Star intelligence
agents—supervened. The reeg was to remain in the hotel
room at all times, eating his meals there, watching the TV
if he wished, admitting NO one if he could avoid it, and if
somehow 'Star agents got through to him, he was to reveal
nothing. Even if this brought about his death.

"I think it's my place to tell you that," Eric said, "not
because I lack respect for reeg life or because I believe Terrans ought to tell a reeg when to die and when not to but
simply because I know the situation and you do not. You'll
just have to accept my word that it's that important." He
waited for the box to light up but it did not. "No comment?"
he asked, disappointed in a vague way. There had been so
little real contact between him and the reeg; it seemed a bad
omen, somehow.

At last the box, reluctantly, lit.

GOODBYE

"You have nothing else to say?" Eric said, incredulous.

WHAT IS YOUR NAME?

"It's on the forms I gave you," Eric said, and left the hotel
room, shutting the door loudly after him.

Outdoors on the sidewalk he hailed an old-fashioned surface cab and told its human driver to take him to TF&D.

Fifteen minutes later he once more entered the attractive

apteryx-shaped, gray-lit building and made his way down the familiar corridor to his own office. Or what had until recently been his office.

Miss Perth, his secretary, blinked in amazement. "Why, Dr. Sweetscent—I thought you were in Cheyenne!"

"Is Jack Blair around?" He glanced toward the parts bins but did not see his departmental assistant. Bruce Himmel, however, lurked in the dim last row, an inventory chart and clipboard in one hand. "How'd you make out with the San Diego Public Library?" Eric asked him.

Startled, Himmel rose to a standing position. "I'm appealing, doctor. I'll never give up. How come you're back here in Tijuana?"

Til Perth said, "Jack is upstairs conferring with Mr. Virgil Ackerman, doctor. You look tired. It's a lot of work there in Cheyenne, isn't it? Such a big responsibility." Her long-lashed blue eyes showed sympathy and her large breasts seemed to swell a trifle in a motherly, mobile, nourishing way. "Can I fix you a cup of coffee?"

"Sure. Thanks." He seated himself at his desk and rested for a moment, thinking back over the day. Strange that all these things had happened in a sequence which had returned him to this spot, to his own chair at last. Was this in some sense the end? Had he played out his little—or not so little—part in a brawl involving three races of the galaxy? Four, if the rotten-pear-shaped creatures from Betelgeuse were included . . . and out of sentiment he did. Perhaps the load was off him. A vidcall to Cheyenne, to Molinari; that would do it and once more he would be Virgil Ackerman's physician, replacing organ after organ as they gave out. But there was still Kathy. Was she here at TF&D's infirmary? Or in a San Diego hospital? Perhaps she was trying to resume her life, despite the addiction, doing her job for Virgil. She was not a coward; she would keep pushing until the end.

"Is Kathy here in the building?" he asked Til Perth.

"I'll check for you, doctor." She jiggled the button of her desk-com. "There's your coffee, beside your elbow."

"Thanks." He sipped the coffee with gratitude. It was

almost like old times; his office had always been for him an oasis where things were rational, safe from the fury of his botched-up domestic life. Here he could pretend that people were nice to one another, that relationships between people could be merely friendly, merely casual. And yet—that was not enough. There had to be intimacy, too. Even with its threat of becoming a destroying force.

Taking paper and pen, he wrote out from memory the formula for the antidote to JJ-180.

"She's in the infirmary on the fourth floor," Miss Perth informed him. "I didn't know she was sick; is it serious?"

Eric handed her the paper, folded. "Take this to Jonas. He'll know what it is and what to do with it." He wondered if he should go up to Kathy, tell her that the antidote would soon be in existence. Beyond the shadow of a doubt he was obliged to, by the most fundamental structure of decency. "Okay," he said, rising. "I'll go see her."

"Give her my best," Til Perth called after him as he plodded out of the office into the hall.

"Sure," he murmured.

When he reached the fourth floor infirmary he found Kathy, wearing a white cotton gown, seated in a reclining chair, her legs crossed, feet bare. She was reading a magazine. She looked old and shrunken, and obviously under heavy sedation.

"Best wishes," he said to her, "from Til."

Slowly, with conspicuous difficulty, Kathy glanced up, focused her gaze on him. "Any—news for me?"

"The antidote's in town. Or soon will be. All Hazeltine Corp. has to do is whip up a batch and express it here. Another six hours." He made an attempt to smile encouragingly; it failed. "How do you feel?"

"Fine now. Since you brought me the news." She was surprisingly matter-of-fact, even for her with her schizoid ways. The sedation no doubt accounted for it. "You did it, didn't you? Found it for me." Then, at last remembering, she added, "Oh yes. And for yourself, too. But you could have kept it, not told me. Thanks, dear."

" 'Dear.' " It hurt to hear her use such a word to him.

"I can see," Kathy said carefully, "that underneath you really are fond of me still, despite what I've done to you. Otherwise you wouldn't—"

"Sure I would; you think I'm a moral monster? The cure should be a matter of public record, available for anyone who's on the damn stuff. Even 'Starmen. As far as I'm concerned deliberately addictive, toxic drugs are an abomination, a crime against life." He was silent then, thinking to himself, And someone who addicts another is a criminal and ought to be hanged or shot. "I'm leaving," he said. "Going back to Cheyenne. I'll see you. Good luck on your therapy." He added, trying not to make it sound deliberately unkind, "You know, it won't restore the physical damage already done; you understand that, Kathy."

"How old," she asked, "do I look?"

"You look what you are, about thirty-five."

"No." She shook her head. "I've seen in the mirror."

Eric said, "See to it, will you, that everyone who took the drug that night with you, that first time, gets some of the antidote; I'll trust you to do that. Okay?"

"Of course. They're my friends." She toyed with a corner of her magazine. "Eric, I can't expect you to stay with me now, with the way I am physically. All withered and—" She broke off and became silent.

Was this his chance? He said, "You want a divorce, Kathy? If you do I'll give it to you. But personally—" He hesitated. How far could hypocrisy go? What was really required of him now? His future self, his compatriot from 2056, had pleaded with him to break loose from her. Didn't all aspects of reason dictate that he do so and if possible right now?

In a low voice Kathy said, "I still love you. I don't want to separate. I'll try to treat you better; honestly I will. I *promise.*"

"Shall I be honest?"

"Yes," she said. "You should always be honest."

"Let me go."

She looked up at him. Some of the old spirit, the venom

that had etched away the fiber of their relationship, glowed in her eyes. But it was vitiated now. Her addiction, plus the sedation, had weakened her; the power which she had formerly exerted over him, trapping him and hugging him to her, had gone. Shrugging, she murmured, "Well, I asked you to be honest and I got just that. I guess I should be glad."

"Will you agree, then? You'll commence litigation?"

Kathy said carefully, "On one condition. If there's no other woman."

"There isn't." He thought of Phyllis Ackerman; that surely didn't count. Even in Kathy's suspicion-haunted world.

"If I find out there is," she stated, "I'll fight a divorce; I won't co-operate. You'll never get free from me; that's a promise, too."

"Then it's agreed." He felt a great weight slide into the abyss of infinity, leaving him with a merely earthly load, one which an ordinary human being could bear. "Thanks," he said.

Kathy said, "Thank you, Eric, for the antidote. So look what my drug addiction, my years of using drugs, has meant, finally. It's made it possible for you to escape. It did accomplish some good after all."

For the life of him he could not determine if she meant that sardonically. He decided to inquire about something else. "When you feel better are you going to resume your job here at TF&D?"

"Eric, I may have something stirring for me. When I was under the drug's influence, back in the past—" She halted, then painfully continued; talking was difficult for her now. "I mailed an electronic part to Virgil. Back in the mid 1930s. With a note telling him what to do about it and also who I was. So he'd remember me later on. About now, in fact."

Eric said, "But—" He broke off.

"Yes?" She managed to fix her attention on him, what he was saying. "Did I do something wrong? Alter the past and disturb things?"

It was almost impossible, he discovered, to tell her. But she would find out anyhow, as soon as she made inquiries.

Virgil would have received no part, because as soon as she left the past the part left, too; Virgil, as a child, had received an empty envelope or nothing at all. He found this mournfully sad.

"What is it?" she was asking laboriously. "I can tell by your expression—I know you so well—that I did something bad."

Eric said, "I'm just surprised. By your ingenuity. Listen." He crouched down beside her, put his hand on her shoulder. "Don't count on it making much difference; your job here with Virgil can't basically be improved on and anyhow Virgil is hardly the grateful type."

"But it was worth a try, don't you think?"

"Yes," he said, straightening up. He was glad at that point to let it drop.

He said goodbye to her, patted her—futilely—once more, and then he made his way to the elevator and from it to Virgil Ackerman's office.

Virgil, glancing up as he entered, cackled, "I *heard* you were back, Eric. Sit down and tell me how it is; Kathy looks bad, doesn't she? Hazeltine wasn't—"

"Listen," Eric said, shutting the door. The two of them were alone. "Virgil, can you get Molinari here to TF&D?"

"Why?" Birdlike, Virgil regarded him alertly.

Eric told him.

When he had heard, Virgil said, "I'll call Gino. I can hint and because we know each other he'll understand on an intuitive level. He'll come. Probably right away; when he acts he goes fast."

"I'll stay here, then," Eric decided. "I won't return to Cheyenne. In fact maybe I'd better go back to the Caesar Hotel and stay with Deg."

"And take a gun with you," Virgil said. He picked up the vidphone receiver and said, "Get me the White House in Cheyenne." To Eric he said, "If they've got this line tapped it won't help them; they won't be able to tell what we're talking about." Into the receiver he said, "I want to talk to

Secretary Molinari; this is Virgil Ackerman calling personally."

Eric sat back and listened. It was going well now, finally. He could take this moment to rest. Become simply a spectator.

From the vidphone a voice, that of the White House switchboard operator, squalled in frantic hysteria, "Mr. Ackerman, is Dr. Sweetscent there? We can't locate him and Molinari, Mr. Molinari, I mean, is dead, and can't be revived."

Virgil raised his eyes and confronted Eric.

"I'm on my way," Eric said. He felt only numb. Nothing more.

"Too late," Virgil said. "I'll bet you."

The operator shrilled, "Mr. Ackerman, he's been dead two hours now; Dr. Teagarden can't do anything with him, and—"

"Ask what organ gave out," Eric said.

The operator heard him. "His heart. Is that you, Dr. Sweetscent? Dr. Teagarden said the aortic artery ruptured—"

"I'll take an artiforg heart with me," Eric said to Virgil. To the operator at the White House he said, "Tell Teagarden to keep the body temp as low as he can; I'm sure he's doing that anyhow."

"There's one good high-speed ship on the roof field," Virgil said. "It's the ship we flew to Wash-35 in; it's undoubtedly the best anywhere near here."

"I'll pick out the heart myself," Eric decided. "So I'll go back to my office; why don't you get the ship readied for me?" He was calm at this point. It was either too late or it wasn't. He got there in time or he didn't. Haste, right now, had remote value.

Virgil, as he tapped the vidphone switch for TF&D's switchboard, said, "The 2056 you were in is *not* the one connected to our world."

"Evidently not," Eric agreed. And started on the run for the elevator.

13

At the White House roof field Don Festenburg met him, pale and stammering with tension. "W-where were you, doctor? You didn't notify anybody you were leaving Cheyenne; we thought you were somewhere nearby." He strode ahead of Eric, toward the field's nearest in-track.

Carrying the boxed artiforg, Eric followed.

At the door of the Secretary's bedroom Teagarden appeared, his face constricted with fatigue. "Just for the hell of it, where were you, doctor?"

I was trying to end the war, Eric thought. He said merely, "How cool is he?"

"No appreciable metabolism; don't you think I know how to conduct that aspect of restoration? I've got written instructions here which automatically become operative the moment he's unconscious or dead and can't be revived." He handed Eric the sheets.

At a glance Eric saw the vital paragraph. No artiforg. Under any circumstance. Even if it were the only chance for Molinari's survival.

"Is this binding?" Eric asked.

"We've consulted the Attorney General," Dr. Teagarden said. "It is. You ought to know; any artiforg, in anybody, can only be inserted with written permission in advance."

"Why does he want it this way?" Eric asked.

"I don't know," Teagarden said. "Will you make an attempt to revive him without use of the artiforg heart which I see you brought? That's all we're left with." His tone dropped with bitterness and defeat. "With nothing. He complained about his heart before you left; he told you—I heard him—that he thought an artery had ruptured. And you walked out of here." He stared at Eric.

Eric said, "That's the problem with hypochondria. You never know."

"Well," Teagarden said with a ragged sigh, "okay—I didn't realize it either."

Turning to Don Festenburg, Eric said, "What about Freneksy? Does he know?"

With a faint, quivering smirk of nervousness Festenburg said, "Of course."

"Any reaction from him?"

"Concern."

"You're not letting any further 'Star ships in here, I assume."

Festenburg said, "Doctor, your job is to heal the patient, not to dictate policy."

"It would help me heal the patient if I knew that—"

"Cheyenne is sealed off," Festenburg conceded at last. "No ship except yours has been permitted to land since this occurred."

Eric walked to the bed and gazed down at Gino Molinari lost in the tangle of machinery that maintained his temperature and measured a thousand conditions extant deep within his body. The plump, short figure could hardly be seen; the face was completely obscured by a new item, scarcely ever employed up to now, for catching extremely delicate alterations in the brain. It was the brain, at all costs, that had to be protected. Everything could go but that.

Everything could go—except that Molinari had forbidden the use of an artiforg heart. So that was that. Medically speaking the clock had been set back a century by this neurotic, self-destructive injunction.

Already, without examining the now-open chest of the man, Eric knew that he was helpless. Outside of the field of org-trans he was probably no more competent a surgeon than Teagarden. Everything in his own career had hung on the possibility of replacing the failing organ.

"Let's see that document again." He took the paper back from Teagarden, studied it more thoroughly. Surely as wily and resourceful a man as Molinari had imagined some viable alternative to org-trans. It couldn't end here.

"Prindle has been notified, of course," Festenburg said. "He's standing by, ready to speak over TV when and if it's certain we can't revive Molinari." His voice was flat, unnaturally so; Eric glanced at him, wondering how he truly felt about this.

"What about this paragraph?" Eric said, showing the document to Dr. Teagarden. "About the activation of the GRS Enterprises robant simulacrum, the one of Molinari used in the video tape. To be put on TV tonight."

"What about it?" Teagarden said, rereading the paragraph. "The airing of the tape will be scratched, of course. As far as the robant itself goes I know nothing about it. Maybe Festenburg does." He turned questioningly to Don Festenburg.

"That paragraph," Festenburg said, "is senseless. Literally. For instance, what's a robant doing in cold-pak? We can't make out Molinari's reasoning and anyhow we've got our hands full. There're forty-three paragraphs to this damn document; we can't carry them all out simultaneously, can we?"

Eric said, "But you know where—"

"Yes," Festenburg said, "I know where the simulacrum is."

"Get it out of the cold-pak," Eric said. "Activate it as per the instructions in this document. Which you already know to be legally binding."

"Activate it and then what?"

"It'll tell you itself," Eric said, "from then on." And for years to come, he said to himself. Because that's the whole point of the document. There will be no public announcement that Gino Molinari has died because as soon as that so-called robant is activated *it will not be so*.

And, he thought, I think you know it, Festenburg.

They looked at each other silently.

To a Secret Service man Eric said, "I want four of you to accompany him while he does it. Just a suggestion, but I hope you take me up on it."

The man nodded, beckoned to a group of his co-workers; they fell in behind Festenburg, who looked confused and frightened now and in no way self-possessed. He left on his reluctant errand, the group of Secret Service men close behind.

"What about a further attempt to repair the ruptured aortic artery?" Dr. Teagarden demanded. "Aren't you going to try? A plastic section can still be—"

"The Molinari in this time sequence," Eric said, "has been battered enough. Don't you agree? This is the moment to retire it; that's what he wants." We're going to have to face a fact, he realized, that perhaps none of us wants to face because it means we're in for a kind of government—have had a kind of government already—hardly in accord with our theoretical ideas.

Molinari had founded a dynasty consisting of himself.

"That simulacrum can't rule in Gino's place," Teagarden protested. "It's a construct and the law forbids—"

"That's why Gino refused the use of an artificial organ. He can't do what Virgil has done, replace each in turn, because by doing so he'd be open to legal challenge. But that's not important." Not now, anyhow. He thought, Prindle isn't the Mole's heir and neither is Don Festenburg, however much he'd like to be. I doubt if the dynasty is endless but at least it'll survive this blow. And that's quite a lot.

After a pause Teagarden said, "That's why it's in cold-pak. I see."

"And it'll stand up to any test you care to give it." You, Minister Freneksy, anyone, including Don Festenburg who probably figured it out before I did, he realized, but couldn't do anything about it. "That's what distinguishes this solution;

even if you know what's going on you can't stop it." This rather enlarged the concept of political maneuvering. Was he horrified by this? Or impressed? To be honest, as yet he did not know. It was too novel a solution, this collusion of Gino Molinari with himself, behind the scenes. His tinkering with the colossal entity of rebirth in his own inimitable, faster-than-the-eye way.

"But," Teagarden protested, "that leaves another time continuum without a UN Secretary. So what's gained if—"

"The one which Don Festenburg has gone to activate," Eric said, "undoubtedly comes from a world in which the Mole was not elected." In which he went down to political defeat and someone else became UN Secretary. There no doubt were a number of such worlds, considering the closeness of the original vote in this world.

In that other world the absence of the Mole would have no meaning, because he was simply one more defeated political figure, perhaps even in retirement. And—in a position to be thoroughly rested up and fresh. Ready to tackle Minister Freneksy.

"It's admirable," Eric decided. "I think, anyhow." The Mole had known that sooner or later this battered body would die beyond the possibility of reconstruction except by artiforg means. And what good was a political strategist who couldn't look ahead to his own death? Without that he would have been merely another Hitler, who didn't *want* his country to survive him.

Once more Eric glanced over the document which Molinari had presented them. It indeed was airtight. Legally the next Molinari absolutely had to be activated.

And that one, in turn, would see to it that he provided himself with a replacement. Like any good tag-team of wrestlers it could theoretically go on forever.

Could it?

All the Molinaris, in all the time-continua, were aging at the same rate. It could only go on for thirty or forty more years. At the most.

But that would carry Terra through and out of the war.

And that was all the Mole cared about.

He was not trying to be immortal, a god. He was simply interested in serving out his term of office. What had happened to Franklin D. Roosevelt in a previous major war was not going to happen to him. Molinari had learned from the mistakes of the past. And had acted accordingly, in typical Piedmontese style. He had found a bizarre and colorfully idiosyncratic solution to his political problem.

This explained why the UN Secretary's uniform and homeopape shown to Eric a year hence by Don Festenburg were counterfeit.

Without this, they might conceivably have been real.

That alone justified what Molinari had done.

An hour later Gino Molinari summoned him to his private office.

Flushed, glowing with good humor, the Mole in a spanking new uniform leaned back in his chair and expansively, at leisure, surveyed Eric. "So the nurts weren't going to start me up," he boomed out. Then abruptly he laughed. "I knew you'd put pressure on them, Sweetscent; I had it all worked out. Nothing by accident. You believe me? Or you think there was a loophole, they might have gotten away with it, especially that Festenburg—he's plenty smart, you know. I admire the hell out of him." He belched. "Listen to me. Well, so much for Don."

"I think they almost got by," Eric said.

"Yes, they did," Molinari agreed, somber now. "It was very close. But everything in politics is close; that's what makes it worth the effort. Who wants a sure thing? Not me. By the way: those videotapes are going on the air as planned; I sent poor Prindle back to the vault or wherever it is he hangs out." Again Molinari laughed loudly.

"Am I right," Eric said, "that in your world—"

"This is my world," Molinari interrupted; putting his hands behind his head he rocked back and forth, eyeing Eric brightly.

Eric said, "In the parallel world you came from—"

"Garbage!"

"—you were defeated in your attempt to become UN Secretary; is that right? I'm just curious. I don't intend to discuss it with anyone."

"If you do," Molinari said, "I'll have the Secret Service glunk you and sink you in the Atlantic. Or drop you in deep space." He was silent a moment. "I got elected, Sweetscent, but the drats knocked me right out of office in a no-confidence recall thing they cooked up. Having to do with the Pact of Peace. They were right, of course; I shouldn't have gotten involved in it. But who *wants* to make a deal with four-armed shiny bugs who can't even talk, who have to go around carrying a translation box like an indoor potty?"

"You know now," Eric said guardedly, "that you have to. Reach an understanding with the reegs."

"Sure. But it's easy to see that now." The Mole's eyes were dark and intense, fighting this out with vast, native intelligence. "What do you have in mind, doctor? Let's have a look. What did they used to say in the last century? Let's kick it up on the roof and see if it—some damn thing."

"A contact is ready for you in Tijuana."

"Hell, I'm not going to Tijuana; that's a dirty town—that's where you go for a broad, age thirteen. Even younger than Mary."

"You know about Mary, then?" Had she been his mistress in the alternate world?

"*He* introduced us," Molinari said blandly. "My best friend; he fixed me up. The one they're burying or whatever it is they're doing with the corpse. It couldn't interest me less, just so they get rid of it. I've already got one, that bullet-riddled one in the casket. Which you saw. One is enough; they make me nervous."

"What were you going to do with the assassinated one?"

Molinari showed his teeth in a great grin. "You don't get it, do you. *That was the previous one.* That came before the one that just died. I'm not the second; I'm the third." He cupped his ear then. "Okay, let's hear what you've got; I'm waiting."

Eric said, "Um, you'll go to TF&D to visit Virgil Ackerman. That won't arouse suspicion. It's my job to get the contact into the factory so he can confer with you. I think I can do it. Unless—"

"Unless Corning, the top 'Star agent in Tijuana, gets to your reeg first. Listen, I'll give the Secret Service orders to round him up; that'll keep the 'Stars busy for a while, get them off our knabs. We can cite their activity regarding your wife, their getting her addicted; that'll be the covering story. You agree? Yes? No?"

"It'll do." Once more he felt weary, even more so than before. It was a day, he decided, that would never terminate; the huge former burden had returned to weigh him into submission.

"I don't impress you very much," Molinari said.

"On the contrary. I'm just exhausted." And he still had to go back to Tijuana to bring Deg Dal Il into the factory from his room at the Caesar Hotel; it was not over yet.

"Someone else," Molinari said acutely, "can pick up your reeg and bring it to TF&D. Give me the location and I'll see that it's done right. You don't have to do any more; go get drunk or find some fresh new girl. Or take some more JJ-180, visit another time period. Anyhow enjoy yourself. How's your addiction coming? Broken it yet, like I told you to?"

"Yes."

Molinari raised his thick eyebrows. "I'll be darned. Amazing; I didn't think it could be done. Get it from your reeg contact?"

"No. From the future."

"How's the war come out? I don't move ahead, like you do; I move sideways only, into the parallel presents."

"It's going to be tough," Eric said.

"Occupation?"

"For most of Terra."

"How about me?"

"Apparently you manage to get away to Wash-35. After holding out long enough for the reegs to come in with strength."

"I don't care for it," Molinari decided. "But I guess I've got to do it. How's your wife Katherine?"

"The antidote—"

"I mean your relationship."

"We're separating. It's decided."

"Okay." Molinari nodded briskly. "You write out the address you have for me and in exchange I'll write out a name and address for you." He took pen and paper, wrote rapidly. "A relative of Mary's. A cousin. Bit player in TV dramatic series, lives in Pasadena. Nineteen. Too young?"

"Illegal."

"I'll get you off." He tossed Eric the paper. Eric did not pick it up. "What's the matter?" Molinari shouted at him. "Has using that time-travel drug scrambled your wits, you don't know you've got only one tiny life and that lies ahead of you, not sideways or back? Are you waiting for last year to come by again or something?"

Reaching out, Eric took the paper. "That's exactly right. I've been waiting a long time for last year. But I guess it's just not coming again."

"Don't forget to say I sent you," Molinari said, and beamed broadly as Eric put the paper in his wallet.

It was night and Eric walked the dark side street, hands in his pockets, wondering if he was going in the right direction. He had not been in Pasadena, California, for years.

Ahead a major conapt building rose squarely against the sky, more dense than the atmosphere behind it, windows lit like the eyes of some great block-shaped synthetic pumpkin. Eyes, Eric thought, are the window of the soul, but a conapt is a conapt. What lies inside there? A bossy—or perhaps not so bossy—black-haired girl whose ambition it is to appear in one-minute beer and cigarette commercials on TV or whatever it is Molinari said. Someone to goad you to your feet when you're sick, travesty of the marital vows, of mutual help, protection.

He thought about Phyllis Ackerman, their conversation at Wash-35, not so long ago. If I really want to repeat the pattern stamped on the matrix of my life, he thought, I need only look her up; Phyllis is just enough like Kathy to attract me. As both of us understand. And enough different from her so that it would seem—I say seem—like something new in my life. But then all at once he thought, This girl here in Pasadena; I didn't pick her out. Gino Molinari did. So perhaps the matrix breaks here. And can be discarded. And I can go on in something that does not merely seem new but is new.

Locating the front entrance of the conapt building, he got out the slip of paper, again memorized the name, then found the proper button among the host of identical rows in the big brass plate and gave it a vigorous, Gino Molinari inspired push.

A ghostly voice presently issued from the speaker and a microscopic image formed on the monitoring screen set in the wall above the buttons. "Yes? Who is it?" In such absurd miniature the girl's image could not be deciphered; he could not tell a thing about her. The voice, however, sounded rich and throaty and, although nervous with the typical caution of the unattached girl living alone, it had its warmth.

"Gino Molinari asked me to look you up," Eric said, supporting his burden on the rock they all depended on in this, their collective journey.

"Oh!" She sounded flustered. "To look *me* up? Are you sure you have the right person? I only met him once and that was casually."

Eric said, "May I come in for a minute, Miss Garabaldi?"

"Garabaldi is my old name," the girl said. "My name, the name I work under when I do TV shows, is Garry. Patricia Garry."

"Just let me come in," Eric said, and waited. "Please."

The door buzzed; he pushed it open and entered the foyer. A moment later by elevator he had ascended to the fifteenth floor and was at her door, ready to knock but finding it ajar in expectation of him.

Wearing a flowered apron, her long dark hair hanging in

twin braids down her back, Patricia Garry met him, smiling; she had a sharp face, tapered to a flawless chin, and lips so dark as to appear black. Every feature had been cut cleanly and with such delicate precision as to suggest a new order of perfection in human symmetry and balance. He could see why she had gone into TV; features like that, when ignited even by the ersatz enthusiasm of a mock-up beer-bust on a California ocean beach, could impale any viewer. She was not just pretty; she was strikingly, lavishly unique and he had a precognition as he looked at her of a long and vital career ahead, if the war did not catch her up in tragedy.

"Hi," she said gaily. "Who are you?"

"Eric Sweetscent. I'm on the Secretary's medical staff." Or was, he thought. Up to a little earlier today. "Could I have a cup of coffee with you and talk? It would mean a lot to me."

"What a strange come-on," Patricia Garry said. "But why not?" She whirled about, her long Mexican skirt spinning out, and bobbed her way down the hall of her conapt, with him following, to the kitchen. "I have a pot on, in fact. Why did Mr. Molinari tell you to look me up? For any special reason?"

Could a girl look like this and not be conscious of what an overriding special reason she constituted? "Well," he said, "I live out here in California, in San Diego." And, he thought, I guess I work in Tijuana. Again. "I'm an org-trans surgeon. Miss Garry. Or Pat. Okay to call you Pat?" He found a seat at the bench table, clasped his hands before him, resting his elbows against the hard, irregular redwood.

"If you're an org-trans surgeon," Patricia Garry said as she got cups from the cupboard over the sink, "why aren't you at the military satellites or at the front hospitals?"

He felt his world sink from beneath him. "I don't know," he said.

"There is a war on, you realize." Her back to him, she said, "The boy I was going with, he was mangled when a reeg bomb got his cruiser. He's still in a base hospital."

"What can I say," he said, "except that maybe you've put your finger on the great central weak link of my life. Why it hasn't got the meaning it should have."

"Well, who do you blame for that? Everyone else?"

"It seemed to me," he said, "at the time anyhow, that keeping Gino Molinari alive somehow contributed to the war effort." But, after all, he had only done that for a short time and had gotten into it not by his own efforts but by Virgil Ackerman's.

"I'm just curious," Patricia said. "I just would have thought that a good org-tran surgeon would *want* to be at the front where the real work is." She poured coffee into two plastic cups.

"Yes, you'd think so," he said, and felt futile. She was nineteen years old, roughly half his age, and already she had a better grasp on what was right, what one ought to do. With such directness of vision she had certainly patterned her own career out to the last stitch. "Do you want me to leave?" he asked her. "Just say so if you do."

"You just got here; of course I don't want you to go. Mr. Molinari wouldn't have sent you here if there hadn't been a good reason." She eyed him critically as she seated herself across from him. "I'm Mary Reineke's cousin, did you know that?"

"Yes." He nodded. And she's quite tough, too, he thought. "Pat," he said, "take my word for it that I have accomplished something today that affects us all, even if it isn't connected with my medical tasks. Can you accept that? If so then we can go on from there."

"Whatever you say," she said with nineteen-year-old nonchalance.

"Have you been watching Molinari's TV cast tonight?"

"I had it on a little while earlier. It was interesting; he looked so much bigger."

" 'Bigger.' " Yes, he thought; that described it.

"It's good to see him back in his old form. But I have to admit—all that political spouting, you know how he does, sort of lectures in that feverish way, with his eyes flashing;

it's too long-winded for me. I put on the record player instead." She rested her chin in her open palm. "You know what? It bores the hell out of me."

The vidphone in the living room rang.

"Excuse me." Pat Garry rose and skipped from the kitchen. He sat silently, no particular thoughts in his mind, only a little of the old weariness weighing on him, and then suddenly she was back. "For you. Dr. Eric Sweetscent; that's you, isn't it?"

"Who is it?" He labored to get up, his heart strangely leaden.

"The White House in Cheyenne."

He made his way to the vidphone. "Hello. This is Sweetscent."

"Just a moment, please." The screen blanked out. The next image which formed was that of Gino Molinari.

"Well, doctor," Molinari said, "they got your reeg."

"Jesus," he said.

"When we got there all we found was a banged-up big dead bug. Somebody, one of them, must have seen you go in. Too bad you didn't take it directly to TF&D. Instead of that hotel."

"I see that now."

"Listen," Molinari said briskly. "I called to tell you because I knew you would want to know. But don't knock yourself; those 'Starmen are professionals. It could have happened to anyone." He leaned closer to the screen, speaking with emphasis. *"It's not that important;* there're other ways to contact the reegs, three or four—we're looking into how best to exploit it right now."

"Should this be said on the vidphone?"

Molinari said, "Freneksy and his party just now took off for Lilistar, shot out of here as fast as they could. Take my word for it, Sweetscent, *they know.* So our problem is that we have to work fast. We expect to raise a reeg government station within two hours; if necessary we'll do our negotiating on an open broadcast with Lilistar listening in." He glanced at his wrist watch. "I have to ring off; I'll keep you posted."

The screen, then, became dark. Busy, in hectic haste, Molinari had gone on to the next task. He could not sit gossiping. And then, all at once, the screen relit; again Molinari faced him. "Remember, doctor, you did your job; you forced them to honor that will I left, that ten-page document they were passing back and forth when you arrived. I wouldn't be here now except for you; I already told you that and I don't want you to forget it—I haven't got time to keep repeating it again and again." He grinned briefly and then once more the image faded. This time the screen stayed dark.

But to fail is to fail, Eric said to himself. He walked back into Pat Garry's kitchen and reseated himself at his cup of coffee. Neither of them spoke. Because I messed it up, he realized, the 'Starmen will have just that much more time to close in on us, come rushing here to Terra with everything they have. Millions of human lives, perhaps years of occupation—that's the price we'll collectively pay. Because it seemed, earlier today, a good idea to put Deg Dal Il in a room at the Caesar Hotel instead of bringing him directly to TF&D. But then he thought, They have at least one agent at TF&D too; they might even have gotten him there.

Now what? he asked himself.

"Maybe you're right, Pat," he said. "Maybe I ought to become a military surgeon and go to a base hospital near the front."

"Yes, why not?" she said.

"But in a little while," he said, "and you don't know this, the front will be on Terra."

She blanched, tried to smile. "Why is that?"

"Politics. The tides of war. Unreliability of alliances. The ally of today is the enemy of tomorrow. And the other way around." He finished his coffee and rose. "Good luck, Pat, in your television career and in every other aspect of your glowing, just beginning life. I hope the war doesn't touch you too deeply." The war I helped bring here, he said to himself. "So long."

At the kitchen table she remained seated, drinking her coffee and saying nothing, as he walked down the hall to the door, opened it, and then shut it behind him. She did not even nod goodbye; she was too frightened, too stunned by what he had told her.

Thanks anyhow, Gino, he said to himself as he descended to the ground floor. It was a good idea; not our fault nothing came of it. Nothing but a greater awareness on my part of how little good I've done and how much harm—by commission or omission—I'm responsible for in my time.

He walked the dark Pasadena street until he located a cab; he hailed and boarded it, then wondered where he was supposed to go.

"You mean you don't know where you live, sir?" the cab asked.

"Take me to Tijuana," he told it, suddenly.

"Yes sir," the cab said and turned south at great speed.

14

Nightime in Tijuana.

He walked aimlessly, scuffing the pavement, passing one after another the neon signs of the narrow boothlike shops, listening to the clamor of the Mexican hucksters and enjoying as he always did the steady motion and ceaseless, nervous honking of wheels and autonomic cabs and old-time turbine surface cars made in the USA, which somehow, in their last decrepitude, had been brought across the border.

"Girl, mister?" A boy no older than eleven seized Eric by the sleeve and hung on, dragging him to a stop. "My sister, only seven, and never lay with a man in her life; I guarantee before God, you be assuredly first."

"How much?" Eric asked.

"Ten dollars plus the cost of the room; there must be in name of God a room. The sidewalk makes love into something sordid; you cannot do it here and respect yourself after."

"There's wisdom in that," Eric agreed. But he continued on anyhow.

At night the robant peddlers and their enormous, useless, machine-made rugs and baskets, their carts of tamales, customarily vanished; the daytime people of Tijuana disappeared along with the middle-aged American tourists to make way for the night people. Men, hurrying, pushed past him; a girl wearing a crushingly tight skirt and sweater squeezed past him, pressing momentarily against him . . . as if, he thought, we had some durable relationship penetrating our two lives and this sudden heat exchange through body contact expressed the deepest possible understanding between the two of us. The girl went on, disappeared. Small tough Mexicans, youths wearing open-throated fur shirts, strode directly at him, their mouths agape as if they were strangling. He carefully stepped from their path.

In a town where everything is legal, he thought, and nothing achieves worth, you are wrenched back into childhood. Placed among your blocks and toys, with all your universe within grasp. The price for license is high: it consists of a forfeit of adulthood. And yet he loved it here. The noise and stirrings represented authentic life. Some people found all this evil; he did not. People who thought that were wrong. The restless, roving bands of males who sought God knew what—they themselves didn't know: their striving was the genuine primal under-urge of protoplasmic material itself. This irritable ceaseless motion had once carried life right out of the sea and onto land; creatures of the land now, they still roamed on, up one street and down another. And he went along with them.

Ahead, a tattoo parlor, modern and efficient, lit by a wall of glowing energy, the proprietor inside with his electric needle that did not touch the skin, only brushed near it as it wove a cat's cradle of design. How about that? Eric asked himself. What could I have etched on me, what motto or picture which would give me comfort in these unusual times of duress? In times when we wait for the 'Starmen to appear and take over. Helpless and frightened, all of us become essentially unmanly.

Entering the tattoo parlor, he seated himself and said, "Can you write on my chest something like—" He pondered. The proprietor continued with his previous customer, a beefy UN soldier who stared sightlessly ahead. "I want a picture," Eric decided.

"Look through the book." Huge sample-caselike ledger passed to him; he opened at random. Woman with four breasts; each spoke a complete sentence. Not quite it; he turned the page. Rocketship with puffs belching from its tail. No. Reminded him of his 2056 self whom he had failed. *I am for the reegs,* he decided. Tattoo that on me so the 'Star MPs can find it. And I won't have to make further decisions.

Self-pity, he thought. Or is there such a thing as self-compassion? Not much mentioned, anyhow.

"Made up your mind, buddy?" the proprietor asked him, now finished.

Eric said, "I want you to write on my chest, 'Kathy is dead.' Okay? How much will that cost?"

" 'Kathy is dead,' " the proprietor said. "Dead of what?"

"Korsakow's syndrome."

"You want me to put that too? Kathy is dead from—how you spell it?" The proprietor got pen and paper. "I want it to be right."

"Where around here," Eric said, "can I find drugs? You know, real drugs?"

"Across the street at the pharmacy. Their specialty, creaker."

He left the tattoo parlor, crossed against the seething, masslike organism of traffic. The pharmacy looked old-fashioned, with displays of foot-ailment models and hernia belts and bottles of cologne. Eric opened the door, manually operated, and walked to the counter in the back.

"Yes sir." A gray-haired respectable professional-looking man in white smock, waiting on him.

"JJ-180," Eric said. He laid a fifty-dollar US bill on the counter. "Three or four caps."

"One hundred US." This was business. With no sentiment.

He added two twenties and two fives. The pharmacist disappeared. When he returned he had a glass vial which he placed close to Eric; he took the bills and rang them up on his antique register. "Thanks," Eric said. Carrying the vial, he left the pharmacy.

He walked until more or less by chance he located the

Caesar Hotel. Entering, he approached the desk clerk. It appeared to be the same man who had taken care of him and Deg Dal Il earlier in the day. A day, Eric thought, made out of years.

"You remember the reeg I came here with?" he asked the clerk.

The clerk eyed him silently.

"Is he still here?" Eric said. "Was he really cut to bits by Corning, the 'Star hatchet man in this area? Show me the room. I want the same room."

"Pay in advance, sir."

He paid, received the key, took the elevator to the proper floor; he walked down the dark carpeted empty hall to the door of the room, unlocked it, and stepped in, feeling for the light switch.

The room lit up and he saw that there was no sign of anything; the room was simply empty. As if the reeg had gone. Stepped out, perhaps. He was right, Eric decided, when he asked me to take him back to the POW camp; he was on the right track all the time. Knew how it would end.

Standing there, he realized that the room horrified him.

He opened the glass vial, got out one capsule of JJ-180, laid it on the vanity table, and with a dime cut the capsule into three parts. There was water in a pitcher nearby; he swallowed one third of the capsule and then walked to the window to look out and wait.

Night became day. He was still in the room at the Caesar Hotel but it was later; he could not tell how much. Months? Years? The room looked the same but probably it always would; it was eternal and static. He left the room, descended to the lobby, asked for a homeopape at the newsstand next to the reservations desk. The vendor, a plump old Mexican woman, handed him a Los Angeles daily; he examined it and saw that he had gone ahead ten years. The date was June 15, 2065.

So he had been correct as to the amount of JJ-180 needed.

Seating himself in a pay vidphone booth, he inserted a coin

and dialed Tijuana Fur & Dye. The time appeared to be about noon.

"Let me speak to Mr. Virgil Ackerman."

"Who is calling, please?"

"Dr. Eric Sweetscent."

"Yes of course, Dr. Sweetscent. Just a moment." The screen became fused over and then Virgil's face, as dry and weathered as ever, basically unchanged, appeared.

"Well I'll be darned! Eric Sweetscent! How the hell are you, kid? Gosh, it's been—what has it been? Three years? Four? How is it at—"

"Tell me about Kathy," he said.

"Pardon?"

Eric said, *"I want to know about my wife.* What's her medical condition by now? Where is she?"

"Your ex-wife."

"All right," he said reasonably. "My ex-wife."

"How would I know, Eric? I haven't seen her since she quit her job here and that was at least—well, you remember—six years ago. Right after we rebuilt. Right after the war."

"Tell me anything that would help me find out about her."

Virgil pondered. "Well Christ, Eric; you remember how sick she became. Those psychopathic rages."

"I don't remember."

Raising his eyebrows, Virgil said, "You were the one who signed the commitment papers."

"You think she's institutionalized now? Still?"

"As you explained it to me it's irreversible brain damage. From those toxic drugs she was taking. So I presume she is. Possibly in San Diego. I think Simon Ild told me that one day, not long ago; you want me to check with him? He said he met somebody who had a friend in a psychiatric hospital north of San Diego and—"

"Check with him." He waited while the screen showed nothing, while Virgil conferred on the interdepartmental circuit with Simon.

At last the elongated, doleful face of his former inventory

control clerk appeared. "You want to know about Kathy," Simon said. "I'll tell you what this fellow told me. He met her in Edmund G. Brown Neuropsychiatric Hospital; he had a nervous breakdown, as you call it."

"I don't call anything that," Eric said, "but go ahead."

Simon said, "She couldn't control herself; her rages, those destructive binges where she'd break everything, they were coming every day, sometimes four times a day. They kept her on phenothiazine and it had helped—she told him that herself—but finally no matter how much phenothiazine they gave her it didn't help. Damage to the frontal lobe, I guess. And she had difficulty remembering things properly. And ideas of reference; she thought everyone was against her, trying to hurt her . . . not grandiose paranoia, of course, but just the never-ending irritability, accusing people as if they were cheating her, holding out on her—she blamed everyone." He added, "She still talked about you."

"Saying what?"

"Blaming you and that psychiatrist—what was his name?— for making her go into the hospital and then not letting her out."

"Does she have any idea why we did it?" Why we had to do it, he thought.

"She said she loved *you,* but you wanted to get rid of her so you could marry someone else. And you had sworn, at the time of the divorce, that there wasn't anyone else."

"Okay," Eric said. "Thanks, Simon." He cut the connection and then called Edmund G. Brown Neuropsychiatric Hospital in San Diego.

"Edmund G. Brown Neuropsychiatric Hospital." A rapid, overworked middle-aged female at the hospital switchboard.

"I wish to ask about Mrs. Katherine Sweetscent's condition," Eric said.

"Just a moment, sir." The woman consulted her records, then switched his call to one of the wards; he found himself facing a younger woman, not in white uniform but in an ordinary flowered cotton dress.

"This is Dr. Eric Sweetscent. What can you tell me about

Katherine Sweetscent's condition? Is she making any progress?"

"There hasn't been any change since you called last, doctor, two weeks ago. I'll get her file, however." The woman disappeared from the screen.

Good Lord, Eric thought. I'm still watching over her ten years from now; am I caught in this one way or another the rest of my life?"

The ward technician returned. "You know that Dr. Bramelman is trying the new Gloser-Little unit with Mrs. Sweetscent. In order to induce the brain tissue to start repair of itself. But so far—" She leafed through the pages. "Results have been meager. I would suggest you contact us again in another month or possibly two. There won't be any change before that."

"But it could work," he said. "This new unit you spoke about." He had never heard of it; obviously it was a construct of the future. "I mean, there's still hope."

"Oh yes, doctor. There's definitely hope." She said it in such a way as to convey to him that this was merely a philosophical answer; there was hope in every case, as far as she was concerned. So it meant nothing.

"Thank you." And then he said, "Check your files, please, and see what it says as to my place of business. I've changed jobs recently so it may be wrong."

After a pause the ward technician said, "You're listed as Chief Org-trans Surgeon at Kaiser Foundation in Oakland."

"That's correct," Eric said. And rang off.

He obtained the number from information and dialed Kaiser Foundation in Oakland.

"Let me talk to Dr. Sweetscent."

"Who is calling, please?"

That stopped him momentarily. "Tell him it's his younger brother."

"Yes sir. Just a moment, please."

His face, his older, grayer face, appeared on the screen. "Hi."

"Hello," Eric said. He was not sure what to say. "Am I

bothering you when you're busy?" He did not look bad, ten years from now. Dignified.

"No, go ahead. I've been expecting the call; I remember the approximate date. You just called Edmund G. Brown Neuropsychiatric Hospital and learned about the Gloser-Little unit. I'll tell you something the ward technician didn't. The Gloser-Little unit constitutes the only brain artiforg they've managed to come up with. It replaces portions of the frontal lobe; once it's installed it stays as long as the person lives. *If* it helps. To be truthful with you, it should have worked right away."

"So you don't think it's going to."

"No," the older Eric Sweetscent said.

"Do you think if we hadn't divorced her—"

"It would have made no difference. Tests we give now—believe me."

Then even that wouldn't help, Eric realized. Staying with her, even for the rest of my life. "I appreciate your help," he said. "And I find it interesting—I guess that's the word—that you're still keeping tabs on her."

"Conscience is conscience. In some respects the divorce put more of a responsibility on us to see about her welfare. Because she got so much worse immediately after."

"Is there *any* way out?" Eric asked.

The older Eric Sweetscent of the year 2065, shook his head.

"Okay," Eric said. "Thanks for being honest with me."

"Like you yourself say, you should always be honest with yourself." He added, "Good luck on the commitment proceedings; they're going to be rough. But that won't come for a while."

"How about the rest of the war, in particular the takeover of Terra by the 'Starmen?"

The older Eric Sweetscent grinned. "Hell, you're too bogged down in your own personal troubles to notice. War? What war?"

"So long," Eric said, and rang off.

He left the vidphone booth. He's got a point, he admitted to himself. If I were rational—but I'm not. The 'Starmen are probably assembling an emergency plan right now, getting ready for the jump-off; I know this and yet I don't feel it, I feel—

The need for death, he thought.

Why not? Gino Molinari made his death into an instrument of political strategy; he outwitted his opponents through it and he'll probably do so again. Of course, he realized, that's not what I had in mind. I'm outwitting nobody. Many people will die in this invasion; why not one more? Who loses by it? Who am I close to? He thought, Those future Sweetscents are going to be sore as hell about it but that's just too bad. I don't particularly give a damn about them anyhow. And, except that their existences depend on mine, they feel the same about me. Perhaps, he decided, that's the problem. Not my relationship with Kathy but my relationship with myself.

Passing through the lobby of the Caesar Hotel, he emerged on the daytime, busy Tijuana street of ten years hence.

Sunlight blinded him; he stood blinking and adjusting. The surface vehicles, even here, had changed. Sleeker, more attractive. The street, now, was adequately paved. There came the tamale vendors and the rug vendors except that now they were not robants; they were, he saw with a start, reegs. Evidently they had entered Terran society at the bottom rung, would have to work their way to the equality he had witnessed a century from his own time, ninety years from now. It did not seem fair to him, but there it was.

Hands in his pockets, he walked with the surging crowd that inhabited the sidewalks of Tijuana throughout all the ages, until he arrived at the pharmacy at which he had bought the capsules of JJ-180. As always it was open for business. It, too, had not altered in a decade, except that now the hernia belt display had gone. In its place he saw a contrivance unfamiliar to him. Halting, he examined the Spanish sign propped behind it. The thing evidently increased one's sexual potency, he decided. Permitted—as he translated the Spanish—an infinitude of orgasms, one immediately following the other. Amused, he continued on inside the pharmacy, to the counter in the rear.

A different pharmacist, this one a black-haired elderly female, greeted him. *"Sí?"* She leered, showing cheap chromium teeth.

Eric said, "You have a West German product, g-Totex blau?"

"I look. You wait, okay?" The woman trudged off and disappeared among the pharmaceuticals. Eric wandered around the displays sightlessly. "G-Totex blau a terrible poison," the old woman called to him. "You have to sign the book for it; *sí?"*

"Sí," Eric said.

The product, in its black carton, was laid on the counter before him. "Two dollars fifty US," the old woman said. She lugged the control book out, put it where he could reach it with the chained pen. As he signed she wrapped the black carton. "You going to kill yourself, *señor?"* she asked acutely. "Yes, I can tell. This will not hurt with this product; I have seen it. No pain, just no heart all of a sudden."

"Yes," he agreed. "It's a good product."

"From A. G. Chemie, Reliable." She beamed in what seemed approval.

He paid the money—his ten-year-old bills were accepted without comment—and left the pharmacy with his package. Weird, he thought. In Tijuana it's still as it was. Always will be. Nobody even cares if you destroy yourself; it's a wonder they don't have booths at night where it's done for you, at ten pesos. Perhaps there are, by now.

It shook him a little, the woman's evident approval—and she did not know anything about him, even who he was. The war did it, he said to himself. I don't know why I let it surprise me.

When he returned to the Caesar Hotel and started upstairs to his room, the desk clerk—unfamiliar to him—halted him. "Sir, you are not a resident here." The clerk had moved swiftly from behind the counter to bar his way. "Did you want a room?"

"I have one," Eric said, and then remembered it had been ten years in the past; his occupancy had lapsed long ago.

"Nine US dollars each night in advance," the desk clerk said. "Since you do not have luggage."

Eric got out his wallet, passed over a ten-dollar bill. The clerk, however, inspected the bill with professional disavowal and mounting suspicion.

"These were called in," the clerk informed him. "Hard to exchange now because no more legal." He raised his head and scrutinized Eric with defiance. "Twenty. Two tens. And maybe even then I not accept them." He waited, devoid of enthusiasm; he clearly resented being paid in currency of this kind. It probably reminded him of the old days, the bad times of the war.

He had only one more bill in his wallet and that was a five. And, incredibly, through some freakish foul-up, perhaps because he had traded his watch for them, the useless currency from ninety years in the future; he spread them on the counter, their intricate, multi-colored scrollwork shimmering. So perhaps, he thought, Kathy's electronic part had reached Virgil Ackerman back in the mid thirties after all; at least it had a chance. That cheered him.

The clerk picked up one of the 2155 bills. "What is this?"

He held it to the light. "I never see before. You make it yourself?"

"No," Eric said.

"I can't use," the clerk decided. "Go before I call the police; you make it yourself, I know." He tossed the bill back with the others in a gesture of repugnance. "Funny money. Go away."

Leaving the 2155 bills on the counter but retrieving the five, Eric turned and walked out the door of the hotel, his package of g-Totex blau under his arm.

There were many malformed little alleys in Tijuana, even now after the war; he found a narrow, dark passage between brick buildings, littered with debris and the overflow from two immense ashcans that had once been oil drums. In the alley he seated himself on the wooden step by a boarded-up entrance, lit a cigarette, sat smoking and pondering. He could not be seen from the street; the people rushing by on the sidewalk paid no attention to him and he focused his attention by watching them, in particular the girls. This, too, was as he knew it in the previous decade. A girl during daylight hours on the streets of Tijuana dressed with incomprehensible smartness: high heels, angora sweater, shiny purse, gloves, coat over her shoulders, preceded, as she hurried, by high, sharp-as-tacks breasts, the smartness carrying even to the detail of her modern bra. What did these girls do for a living? Where had they learned to dress so well, not to mention the problem of financing such a wardrobe? He had wondered this in his own time and he wondered it now.

The answer, he speculated, would be to stop one of these daytime Tijuana girls in flight, ask her where she lived and if she bought her clothes here or across the border. He wondered if these girls had ever been across to the United States, if they had boy friends in Los Angeles, if they were as good in bed as they looked to be. Something, some force not visible, made their lives possible. He hoped that at the same time it did not make them frigid; what a travesty on life, on the potency of natural creatures, that would be.

The trouble with such girls, he thought, is that they get old so fast. What you hear is true; by thirty they're worn out, fat, the bra and the coat and purse and gloves are gone; all that remains is the black, burning eyes peering out from beneath the shaggy brows, the original slender creature still imprisoned somewhere within but unable to speak any longer, play or make love or run. The click of heels against the pavement, the rushing forward into life; that's gone and only a slopping, dragging sound is left behind. The most horrid sound in the world, that of the *once-was:* alive in the past, perishing in the present, a corpse made of dust in the future. Nothing changes in Tijuana and yet nothing lives out its normal span. Time moves too fast here and also not at all. Look at my situation, for instance, he thought. I'm committing suicide ten years in the future, or rather I'll wipe out a life ten years ago. If I do this, what becomes of the Eric Sweetscent now working for Kaiser in Oakland? And the ten years he's spent watching over Kathy—what does that do to her?

Maybe this is my weak way of hurting her. A further punishment because she's sick.

Underneath my rationality my warped view, he thought. You can't quite manage to punish the sick enough. Is that it? Christ, he thought. No wonder I feel hatred for myself.

Holding the package of g-Totex blau in the palm of his hand, he weighed it, experienced its mass. Felt the Earth's attraction for it. Yes, he thought, the Earth likes even this. She accepts everything.

Something ran across his shoe.

He saw, skittering away into the safety of the shadows and heaps of debris, a small wheeled cart.

The cart was pursued by another of its kind. They met, in the tangle of newspapers and bottles, and then the debris trembled and bits flew everywhere as the carts fought it out, ramming each other head-on, trying for the cephalic unit mounted in each other's center. Trying to knock out the Lazy Brown Dog.

Still alive? he thought in disbelief. Ten years later? But possibly Bruce Himmel still manufactured them. By now Tijuana must be overrun by them, if that was so. It was hard to know how to take such a sight. He continued to watch the two carts as they battled it out to the end; now one had knocked its antagonist's Lazy Brown Dog loose, seemed to be triumphing. It withdrew and, like a goat, maneuvered to locate itself for the coup de grace.

While it was positioning itself the damaged one, in a last burst of native wit, popped into the sanctuary of a discarded galvanized zinc bucket and was out of the fray. Protected, it became inert, prepared to wait things out, forever if necessary.

Getting to his feet, Eric stooped and grabbed up the stronger cart; its wheels spun futilely and then somehow it managed to twist out of his grasp. It bounced clatteringly to the pavement, backed, maneuvered, and then hurled itself against his foot. Surprised, he retreated. The cart made another menacing move toward him and he retreated again. Satisfied, the cart wheeled in a circle and then rattled off, out of sight.

In the bucket the loser could still be seen. Still waiting.

"I won't hurt you," Eric said to it, crouching down in order to get a better glimpse of it. The damaged thing, however, remained where it was. "Okay," he said and straightened up. "I get the idea." It knew what it wanted. There was no point in molesting it.

Even these things, he decided, are determined to live. Bruce was right. They deserve their opportunity, their minuscule place under the sun and sky. That's all they're asking for and it isn't much. He thought, And I can't even do what they do, make my stand, use my wits to survive in a debris-littered alley in Tijuana; that thing that's taken refuge there in that zinc bucket, without a wife, a career, a conapt or money or the possibility of encountering any of these, still persists. For reasons unknown to me its stake in existence is greater than mine.

The g-Totex blau no longer seemed attractive to him.

Even if I'm going to do this, he thought, *why does it have to be now?* Like everything else it can be put off—ought, in this case, to be put off. And anyhow he did not feel well; he felt dizzy and he shut his eyes, although by doing so he was inviting another attack by the fearsome Lazy Brown Dog cart which Bruce Himmel had made.

The slight weight in his hand disappeared entirely. He opened his eyes, saw that the paper bag with its black carton inside, the box of g-Totex blau, had disappeared. And the litter heaped here and there in the alley did not appear quite as extensive. From the long shadows cast by the sun he knew that it had become late in the day and this meant that the JJ-180 had worn off and he had gone back in time to—roughly—his own period. But he had taken the piece of capsule at night, in the dark, and this seemed more like five p.m. So, as before, the return was not exact and he wondered just how far off it was in this instance. After all, the 'Starmen were on their way.

In fact, he saw, they had already arrived.

Overhead a vast, dark, ugly mass hung in the sky, like something that had descended into this world from a lightless land of iron and surprise and frightened, purposeful silence. It was huge enough, he thought, to feed forever; even from the spot where he stood, at the very least a mile from it, he could see that it consisted of a limitless, appetitive self which would begin any time now to gulp down everything in sight. It made no sound. Its engines were off. This ship had come a long way, from the lines deep in intersystem space. It was a seasoned, informed, world-weary apparition, brought out by strange needs from its normal place of residence.

I wonder how easy it's going to be, Eric wondered. For them simply to drop to the surface and enter key buildings and take everything over. Probably easier than I think, than anyone here on Terra thinks.

He walked from the alley to the street, thinking to himself, I wish I had a gun.

Strange, he thought, that in the center of the greatest abomination of our times, this war, I should find something meaningful. A desire animating me equal to that possessed by the Lazy Brown Dog cart hiding in the zinc pail ten years from now. Maybe I'm its compatriot at last. Able to take my place in the world beside it, do as it does, fight as it fights: whenever it's necessary and then some, for the pleasure of it. For the joy. As was intended from the start, anterior to any time or condition I could comprehend or call my own or enter into.

Traffic had slowed to a near stop along the street. Everyone, in the vehicles and on foot, watched the 'Star ship.

"Taxi!" Walking out into the street he hailed an autonomic cab capable of non-surface flight. "Take me to Tijuana Fur & Dye," he ordered it. "Make it as fast as you can and don't pay any attention to that ship up there, including any instructions it might broadcast."

The cab shuddered, rose slightly from the asphalt, and hung stationary. "We've been forbidden to take off, sir. The Lilistar Army Command for this area sent out orders that—"

"I'm in supreme charge of this situation," Eric told the cab. "I outrank the Lilistar Army Command; they're dirt compared with me. I have to be at Tijuana Fur & Dye immediately—the war effort hangs on my being there."

"Yes sir," the cab said, and soared up into the sky. "And it's an honor, sir; believe me, a rare honor to convey you."

"My presence there," Eric said, "is of incomparable strategic importance." At the factory I'll make my stand, he said to himself. With the people I know. And, when Virgil Ackerman escapes to Wash-35, I'll go along with him; it's beginning to unfold as I witnessed it a year from now.

And, at Tijuana Fur & Dye, he realized, I'll undoubtedly run into Kathy.

To the cab he said suddenly, "If your wife were sick—"

"I have no wife, sir," the cab said. "Automatic Mechanisms never marry; everyone knows that."

"All right," Eric agreed. "If you were me, and your wife were sick, desperately so, with no hope of recovery, would you leave her? Or would you stay with her, even if you had traveled ten years into the future and knew for an absolute certainty that the damage to her brain could never be reversed? And staying with her would mean—"

"I can see what you mean, sir," the cab broke in. "It would mean no other life for you beyond caring for her."

"That's right," Eric said.

"I'd stay with her," the cab decided.

"Why?"

"Because," the cab said, "life is composed of reality configurations so constituted. To abandon her would be to say, I can't endure reality as such. I have to have uniquely special easier conditions."

"I think I agree," Eric said after a time. "I think I will stay with her."

"God bless you, sir," the cab said. "I can see that you're a good man."

"Thank you," Eric said.

The cab soared on toward Tijuana Fur & Dye Corporation.